# The Fix 2

# The Fix 2

*K'wan*

**URBAN BOOKS**

*www.urbanbooks.net*

Urban Books, LLC
97 N18th Street
Wyandanch, NY 11798

The Fix 2 Copyright © 2015 K'wan

ISBN 13: 978-1-62286-944-2
ISBN 10: 1-62286-944-3

First Mass Market Printing June 2015
First Trade Paperback Printing January 2015
Printed in the United States of America

10 9 8 7 6 5 4 3 2

Distributed by Kensington Publishing Corp.
Submit Orders to:
Customer Service
400 Hahn Road
Westminster, MD 21157-4627
Phone: 1-800-733-3000
Fax: 1-800-659-2436

# The Fix 2

*K'wan*

# PROLOGUE

Tut stood in the corner of the basement, silently watching the events as they were unfolding. His hand absently went to the end of one of his corn rowed hair, twisting the red and black beads that held the ends in place. It was a nervous tick of his, and he was in a tense situation. The men in the room with him were stone killers, tried and tested, and had been with his boss for years. Tut was the new kid still trying to make his bones, but he was surely on his way to being great, which was more than what he could say for their guest of dishonor, a hustler named Rick. Rick and Tut weren't friends, but got money with the same team so they often found themselves in each other's company. The last time Tut had seen Rick, he was smiling and telling some lame joke, but now he was the joke, naked and tied to a pool table in a random basement. Seeing Rick in his current state made Tut glad that they weren't close, because anyone involved with him or his bullshit was either dead by that point or on their way to being dead.

Standing over Rick, looking at him with judgmental eyes was Tut's boss, Ramses. As usual he was draped in heavy jewels; diamond earrings in each ear, thick bracelets and a gold chain with a ridiculously large medallion hanging from the end. Ramses had a thing for jewels, the bigger the better. At any given time you could catch him with easily near $100,000 in jewels on, even if he was just hanging out. He never worried about anybody robbing him, because with one phone call Ramses could have your whole family wiped from the face of the earth. Ramses was a boss, answering to no one except Pharaoh.

"Wake this nigga up," Ramses said to no one in particular.

Ramses's right hand man, Huck, stepped up. He was a throwback cat, with a salt-and-pepper tapered afro and always wore suits. He had been Ramses's best friend and confidant for more years than almost anyone in the room had been alive. Huck slipped on a pair of gloves before grabbing the cattle prod from the edge of the pool table. Ever so gently, he touched the end of the prod to one of Rick's toes.

"Muthafucka!" Rick awoke with a start. Reflexively, he tried to sit up, but found his wrists were tied down. With confused eyes, he looked around the room at the faces of the men looking back at him. The last thing Rick remembered was drinking with this chick he'd met uptown. At first he had no idea where he was or what he was doing there, but when his eyes landed on Ramses everything became crystal clear. "Ramses," he began, but was cut off by Ramses.

"Rick, if I were you I'd think long and hard about my next words, because they could very well be my last," Ramses told him.

"Ramses, I'm sorry."

"That much I figured out long before you admitted to it. You're a sorry sack of shit, Rick. I just want to know, was it worth it? Was it worth biting the generous hand that's been feeding you since you touched your first dime bag?" Ramses asked.

Rick's eyes watered; the weight of his deeds began to dig into his chest. "You don't understand, Ramses."

Ramses walked over and looked Rick in the eyes. "Then help me to understand."

"They had me by the balls, man," Rick began. "I got stopped with a kilo of pure white. I'm a two-time loser who's already on parole for drugs. They would've finished me if I took it to trial. What was I supposed to do?"

"The same thing Duce did when he got knocked." Ramses nodded toward a young brown-skinned man. "The same thing Bunchy did when she got knocked." He motioned toward the light-skinned girl with the big pink lips. "And the same thing Tut did when he took his pinch, keep your mouth shut, let our lawyers do what we pay them for and live like a king for your whole bid if you gotta lie down for a minute." Ramses slapped Rick across the face hard enough to make his nose bleed. "Stupid muthafucka!"

"I was scared, Ramses. I been around and I seen what y'all do to people who you feel are liabilities. I thought if I brought this to you, Pharaoh would've put the word out to have me killed," Rick said.

"So instead you withheld the information and now it's my word that'll close the curtain on your show, not Pharaoh's." Ramses started back toward his men.

"So this how you gonna do me, huh? I make one mistake and you gonna do me like you did Benny?" Rick called after him. The minute the name left his mouth, he regretted it.

Ramses stopped and turned back to Rick. This time the calm was gone from his eyes and a slow fire began burning behind them. Benny had been Ramses's last protégé. He was a good kid and Ramses loved him like a son, but Benny had made the mistake of letting a snake whisper in his ear, planting big ideas. As a result, Ramses had to have him put down. Ramses had ordered the deaths of many men, but to that day Benny's was one of the only ones that bothered him.

Ramses picked up a pool stick and brought it down across Rick's exposed stomach. "How dare you?" He brought the pool stick down again, snapping it in half when it made contact with Rick's ribs. "Benny might've been overly ambitious, but he ain't never been no cheese-eating fucking rat!" He raised the broken pool stick, and had Huck not grabbed him, Ramses would've driven the jagged edge into Rick's chest.

"Too many eyes for you to get your hands dirty," Huck whispered in his ear. "Let your soldiers do what you keep them around for."

Ramses's eyes stayed glued to Rick with the voice in the back of his head urging him to finish the disrespectful little snitch, but he knew his friend Huck was right. He trusted the men in the room well enough, but not enough to gamble his freedom on. "You're right." Ramses tossed the broken pool stick to the ground. "We'll let a soldier handle this." His eyes drifted to Tut. "What's up, li'l nigga? You ready to represent that name I gave you?"

"Always," Tut said, sounding more confident than he actually was.

"Kill this deal-cutting muthafucka!" Ramses ordered.

Tut knew before Ramses even gave the order what was about to be asked of him. He would've rather Ramses ask someone else, but he hadn't. He had called on Tut; this was his moment.

"Do you have a problem with what I've asked you to do?" Ramses asked, noticing Tut hadn't moved yet.

"No, it's not that. I just don't have a gun on me," Tut said, trying to hide his embarrassment. A few of the other men snickered.

Ramses gave him a disbelieving look. "And why the fuck not? You're a soldier ain't you?"

"Yeah, but you told me not to bring a pistol because I was riding in the car with you on the way over," Tut reminded him.

Ramses was so dumbstruck that all he could do was laugh. "Well, at least one of my young boys does as he's told. I'll tell you what, Tut, let's make this interesting. You kill Rick in under thirty seconds and all that he owns becomes yours. The catch is, nobody is gonna give you a weapon."

"How am I supposed to kill him in less than thirty seconds without a gun or a knife?" Tut asked.

Ramses shrugged. "Be creative about it. So long as he's dead, I don't give a shit."

Tut could feel every eye in the room on him, waiting to see if he would rise to the occasion. Tut was unsure; not afraid, just unsure. He didn't know how he was expected to go about killing Rick, but he had about twenty seconds left to figure it out. Just then Tut spotted the broken end of the pool stick Ramses had discarded and it gave him an idea. He picked up the broken piece of wood, and climbed onto the pool table to straddle Rick's chest. Everyone expected Tut to use the broken stick to stab Rick, but he had something else in mind.

"Don't take this personal," Tut told Rick, before flipping the broken pool stick around, wielding it like a club, and caving Rick's skull in. By the time Tut was done beating Rick, he was a mess of blood and exposed bone. Bloodied and breathing heavy, Tut climbed off the table and tossed the broken pool stick at Ramses's feet. "Was that creative enough for you?"

Ramses burst out into a hearty laughter, clapping his thick hands in applause. "Now that's how you end a nigga." He draped his arm around Tut and hugged him close, ignoring the fact that Tut was getting Rick's blood on his shirt. "Well done, King Tut. You may just live up to that name after all."

***

Ramses stepped out of the basement into the cool night air. At the curb, a black Town Car sat idling. The windows were too heavily tinted to see who was inside, but Ramses didn't need to see to know who the lone passenger was. After giving a cautionary look around, he slipped into the back of the car and it sped off into the night.

"Sorry to keep you waiting," Ramses said.

"Time is nothing to those who plan to live forever," Pharaoh said, lighting his cigar. The flame from the lighter kissed off the blue sapphire on his pinky finger, casting a cluster of light and shadow on the side of his face. "Did you speak to Frankie?"

"Yeah, he's gonna come by tomorrow so we can finalize everything," Ramses informed him.

"Good, the sooner we get it locked up the better. You watch your ass when dealing with him, too. I don't trust the Italians."

Ramses laughed. "You don't trust anybody."

"You better damn well know it, and that's why I'm still in power while my competition withers and dies like untended flowers. The little prince is getting too big for his britches and we're going to eventually have to knock him down a few pegs. His father was a man of reason, but not his heir. If he wants to play war games then I'll entertain him. I will be king of kings or I will be dead," Pharoah vowed.

"So it is said, so it shall be done."

"What about that other thing?" Pharaoh motioned toward the building Ramses had just come out of.

"We got it done," Ramses told him.

"Good," Pharaoh said, exhaling the smoke. "With this new mayor and his crusade we gotta make sure everything is tight. He's throwing football numbers at first-time offenders, and some of these dudes are getting spooked. Nobody wants to grow old in prison, and I respect that, but at the same time we need to ensure that everybody within our inner circle can hold their weight and their water, understand?"

"Yeah, I can dig it," Ramses agreed. "Our shit is gonna be tighter than virgin pussy. I'll see to it personally." •

"Speaking of personal missions, what's up with your boy Tut? Is he ready to take the next step?" Pharaoh asked.

Ramses looked at the blood on his shirt. "Yeah, he's ready."

# PART I

## DRUG RELATED

# CHAPTER 1

*New York City: 2008*

"Tell me why we're doing this again?" Omega asked, adjusting the rubber mask that was sitting cocked on the top of his head. The face of the mask was molded to look like Arsenio Hall. Omega had to cut the back of it open to compensate for his dreads. His lips were half twisted into a disapproving scowl. He obviously didn't want to be there, but his sense of loyalty wouldn't allow him to let his friend go alone.

"Because Pharaoh wants it done," Li'l Monk replied. He wore a wool ski mask, rolled on his head like a sailor's cap. In the recesses of the shadows you could barely make out his face, but his cold eyes glistened faintly when the street lights caught them.

"Pharaoh didn't ask us to do shit. Ramses just happened to mention that Pharaoh wanted someone dead. He never directly came out and asked us to get involved," Omega reminded him.

Li'l Monk spared him a glance. "Ramses said that Pharaoh had a problem and would look favorably on the person who took care of it for him. In my mind, that's just as good as asking. With niggas like Pharaoh and Ramses, you gotta read between the lines. They're never going to come out and ask you to do anything, because they feel they shouldn't have to. If you know the boss has a problem, out of loyalty to your cause, you handle it without being told to. That's how a soldier moves."

"Well, I ain't no soldier. I'm a boss," Omega said.

Li'l Monk laughed. It was a deep, grating sound that always made Omega squeamish when he heard it. "Don't get to thinking that because Ramses gave us that block our opinions really count for shit. We got a little authority, but no real clout yet. Giving us that strip was like a pat on the head for a job well done, nothing more. Moving on this bit of work for Pharaoh, this is the kinda shit that's gonna get us closer to a seat at the big boy table. Let me drop a jewel on you, my nigga, the trick to this shit is anticipating what the boss wants and taking care of it before he asks. Know your allies as intimately as you know your enemies."

"What is that? Some kinda quote from one of those war books you're always reading? The way you keep your nose buried in those things, you'd think you were about to go to war," Omega joked.

Li'l Monk looked at him seriously. "Nigga, we deal in poison and death. Every time we step out of the house we're on the front lines and can get pushed off the planet at any given second. You gotta be mentally and physically ready to kill or die at all times. Tighten up, O." He patted Omega's chest with one of his heavy hands.

"Damn, I was just fucking with you, Li'l Monk," Omega said, rubbing his chest where Li'l Monk had patted him. Sometimes his friend didn't know his own strength. Omega could tell that Li'l Monk was in one of his dark moods. Omega hated when he got like that. Normally, Li'l Monk was a gentle soul with a heart of gold, but when the darkness set in, he became someone else. "So, what's the plan?" Omega asked, letting his partner know he was with him.

Li'l Monk lifted his shirt, showing off several neatly packaged bundles of cocaine. "We orchestrate a drug-related homicide."

Omega shook his head. "You got it all mapped out, huh?"

"Don't I always? You know how we do, Omega. I put them in the holes and you throw dirt over them," Li'l Monk joked.

Omega didn't find it funny. "Anyone have any idea why Ramses wants these dudes gone?"

Li'l Monk contemplated how candid he should be with his partner. When he saw who they had come for, he would no doubt be apprehensive, maybe even to the point of backing out on him. It had been an unexpected surprise to Li'l Monk too, when he volunteered them for the missions and Ramses revealed who the targets were. When Ramses had gone on to reveal the crimes the men had committed to put them out of favor with the Pharaoh, all doubt left his mind as to whether he should take them out. For Li'l Monk, it was personal, but Omega had no such connections, so would he feel Li'l Monk's pain? Would he still be down to commit murder if he knew the true motives behind it?

"They raped a girl, and she killed herself as a result," Li'l Monk said, giving Omega enough to motivate him, but sparing him the details.

"Rapists?" Omega asked, unable to hide the emotion in his voice. He had a special hatred for rapists. "Shit, why didn't you say so? Let's whack these niggas." He drew his 9 mm from his coat.

"Glad you feel that way, because here they come." Li'l Monk nodded toward the building across the street.

Out stepped two huge men, obviously security. Trailing them were three young dudes, wearing heavy jewelry. Clinging to the men like cheap suits were several girls of various shades and shapes. The groupies hung on everything the men said like they were quoting scripture. Every few feet they would stop and pose for pictures for one of the many people who flocked them.

When Omega saw who they had come to murder, his eyes got wide. "Wait, ain't that . . ."

"Sure is," Li'l Monk answered the question before Omega could finish asking it. Seeing his prey made his jaw tighten and the veins in the backs of his hands pop out as he clenched and unclenched his fist. His heart beat so hard in his chest that it threatened to burst in anticipation of the mayhem he was about to wreak on the downtown Manhattan block.

"Wait, I thought we were just coming to clip some regular dudes. We can't get at them, at least not here. There's too many people around and too many cameras!" Omega tried to reason with his best friend. He loved Li'l Monk like a brother, but wasn't quite ready to go to prison for him. What he was planning to do was insane.

"The more cameras, the better," Li'l Monk said over his shoulder while rummaging through a trash can. From it, he produced a black plastic bag. With a flick of his knife, he cut the bag open to reveal the sleek MP5K. "Let their adoring fans watch how ugly I do these thirsty niggas." He pulled the ski mask down over his face and started across the street.

Omega called after him, but Li'l Monk was too far gone to reason with. He had two choices: leave while he still could and hope Li'l Monk didn't land in prison, or watch his partner's back to make sure he got out in one piece. He chose the latter.

Red Dog recording studio was located on the top floor of a loft that doubled as a nightclub on the weekends. For the past twelve hours it had been rented by Big Dawg entertainment so that one of their groups, Bad Blood, could finally finish their album. It had been a long and tedious studio session and all parties involved were happy that it was over.

"Yo, I never thought I'd say this, but I don't even wanna see another recording booth again," Lex huffed. His youthful face looked haggard and his eyes were narrowed to red slits from the weed he'd been smoking during their session.

"Don B. be on some slave master shit," Jay said, stretching his aching muscles.

"If y'all hadn't bullshitted around and got the album done on time, this might not have happened," Tone said. He was the group's manager and handler. They were a mischievous bunch, and he often had to shadow them to make sure they stayed out of trouble.

"Fuck that, I could've spit for at least two more hours. I was born to do this rap shit," Pain boasted. His eyes were glassy and his nostrils were flared. While the rest of the group was tired, the cocaine in his system had him wired.

"I'll bet," Tone said, giving him a suspicious look. He knew Pain snorted; they all indulged from time to time, but lately Pain always seemed to be high off cocaine. He was hard enough to deal with when he was sober, but coked up he became an even bigger asshole. His behavior was starting to affect the public image of the group, and Tone made a mental note to himself to discuss it with Don B.

"Where the fuck is True? Why that nigga ain't in here sweating like the rest of us?" Lex asked.

"Because True laid his vocals for those songs two weeks ago. We were waiting on you slow muthafuckas," Tone told him. True was the other member of the group, and the one with the most potential. He had knucklehead tendencies too, but he was much easier to manage than the rest.

This was the reason why Don B. had picked True to be the first one of the group to drop a solo album. Of course there were some ill feelings among other members of the group because they felt like it was favoritism, and it was, but True had "star" written all over him and Don B. wanted to cash in on it.

"Brownnosing-ass nigga," Pain mumbled.

"The car is outside," Big Sam said, startling them. He was six five and at least 250 pounds, but he walked as light as a cat. Big Sam and his partner Jimmy were handling the security detail for them that night. They were two ex-college football players whose dreams of going pro never came to fruition, so they got into the security business.

"Good, because I'm ready to get out of here. Spending twelve hours with these yahoos is way too many," Tone said, following Big Sam to the exit.

To get outside to their waiting truck, the rappers had to pass the line of people waiting to get into the nightclub. All it took was for one person to recognize them and they were soon mobbed by fans. Big Sam kept the dudes at a safe distance, while letting the women through so that the rappers could take their pick from the groupies. It was protocol when dealing with members of Big Dawg. They would select the ones they wanted and leave the stragglers to the security staff. Big Sam had gotten more pussy working for Big Dawg than he did his whole four years in college.

Tone stood off to the side, shaking his head at the thirst being displayed by the women. It wasn't unheard of for him to take down a groupie or three, but Tone was more reserved and picky when it came to the women he slept with. The rap group had no such reservations and would stick their dicks in anything with a wet hole.

Tone had just instructed them to take their picks and load into the SUV, when his phone rang. The women squealing like school girls over the rappers were making so much noise that he couldn't hear, so Tone stepped back inside the lobby of the loft to take the call. As he talked on the phone, he watched in amusement as Pain took pictures of two white girls, who were kissing on a dare. Tone's eyes wandered to the curb where he saw a young man appear as if out of thin air, on the far side of the idling truck that had been waiting for them. His face was hard as stone and his eyes so cold that Tone felt like the temperature had just dropped in the lobby. Something about the young man tugged at the back of Tone's mind and he realized it was the same kid they'd gotten into it with at the club. At first he thought it might've been a coincidence and the kid Chucky had referred to as Li'l Monk might've just been there to enjoy the nightclub, but when he saw him roll the ski mask down over his face, he knew what time it was. Too bad he was too late to warn the others.

Lex was whispering sweet nothings into the ear of a young lady, when he spotted the man in the ski mask step from behind the SUV. He went to shout a warning to his friends, but his voice was drowned out by the rattle of the MP5K. The powerful slugs tore one of his arms off at the elbow, and obliterated his kidney before any of the others even realized someone was shooting.

Big Sam went into action, reaching for the gun that was in the holster on the back of his pants. He was fast, but not as fast as the bullets that punched lemon-sized holes into his chest. Before Big Sam's body had even hit the floor, Li'l Monk had already turned the gun on Jay, who was trying to flee. He tapped the trigger twice, striking Jay high in his back, flipping him forward.

While Li'l Monk was busy trying to mow down everything in the path of his machine gun, Jim had slid from the SUV and was creeping on him. He raised his gun, level with the back of Li'l Monk's head, intent on taking him out of the game, but he would never have the chance. Omega's 9 mm roared to life, splattering Jim's brains on the side of the SUV. Li'l Monk was about to offer his friend his thanks, when Omega unexpectedly tackled him to the ground. A split second later, a bullet struck the car they had been standing in front of. Pain had drawn his weapon, and was firing at them as he tried to make his escape down the block. In the distance they could hear sirens approaching.

"Let's get out of here!" Omega tugged at Li'l Monk's jacket.

Li'l Monk jerked away. "Not yet," he yelled, knowing this was his best and last chance to do what Ramses required of him. Failure was not an option. Li'l Monk shoved the machine gun and the bundles of cocaine he'd had under his shirt into Omega's unsuspecting hands. "Throw these in their whip. Make sure they got blood on them before you plant them," he ordered.

"You're one crazy son of a bitch," Omega told him.

"Crazy like a fox, now handle your end while I handle mine." Li'l Monk drew a Desert Eagle from his pants. The gun was old and worn, but reliable, and familiar to Li'l Monk's hands. It had been a gift from his father, Monk, when he first decided to take it to the streets. He knew that gun as well as the back of his own hand. Li'l Monk slowed his breathing, like his father had showed him when he was first teaching him how to shoot, and took aim. As he exhaled the last rhythmic breath, he pulled the trigger.

The impact of the bullet lifted Pain off the ground and he flew about six feet, before rolling to a stop against a parked car. Pain wanted desperately to get up and run, but his body wouldn't cooperate. He watched, with terror-filled eyes, as the masked man stalked toward him. It was a wrap, and he knew it. Pain watched in surprise as the man lifted his mask so that he could see the face hidden beneath. "You?" Pain was shocked.

"Yup, me." Li'l Monk reached down and gripped the waist of Pain's jeans. In a display of his brute-like strength, he yanked with so much force that Pain was lifted off the ground as Li'l Monk tore his pants off. It only took one of his massive hands to wrap around both of Pain's ankles and push his knees to his chest. The way Li'l Monk had him positioned, it looked like he was about to sexually violate him, but Li'l Monk had a violation of a different kind in mind. "Since you like to stick your friend in women, uninvited, I'm gonna stick my friend in you uninvited." Li'l Monk jammed the gun roughly in Pain's ass.

The moment Pain saw Li'l Monk he felt the stop clock on his life began to tick. He knew that he was going to die, but he had no idea how horribly.

"Please, don't," Pain begged.

"Did you show Marty mercy when you and your boys raped her?" Li'l Monk asked.

Pain was silent.

"I thought not." Li'l Monk pulled the trigger, covering his hand in blood and shit.

with the NYC public school system. When Persia was allowed to reenroll in St. Mary's after
Michael had made it very clear that he would be
on her ass this go around, if she messed up not
only would he put the punishment back, but
she would no longer get to attend the rest of
her classes. This was her last and first shot.
It had been a wild year for Persia. She had

# CHAPTER 2

It had rained all night and most of the morning, but at long last the sun was finally trying
to peek out, though only in spurts. Considering
how brutal the winter had been, a little rain
wasn't too bad. It signaled farewell to winter, and
hello to the coming spring.

Persia sat, elbows on the table, and chin resting
on her knuckles, watching the leftover raindrops
trickle down the classroom window. She imag-
ined herself outside, splashing in the puddles
left behind by the rain, like she used to as a kid,
but instead she was stuck in fourth period math
class. Had this been a few months ago, when
Persia was still attending Martin Luther King Jr.,
she'd have likely ditched, but this wasn't public
school, it was St. Mary's and her parents were
paying a hefty sum every month for her to attend
the prestigious Catholic school. In addition to the
tuition, they had to pull some serious strings to
get the school to let her in after her brief fling

with the NYC public school system. When Persia was allowed to reenroll in St. Mary's, Father Michael had made it very clear that he would be on her ass this go-around. If she messed up, not only would he give her the permanent boot, but she wouldn't graduate on time with the rest of her classmates. This was her last and final shot.

It had been a wild year for Persia. She had attended private and Catholic schools all her life, so just before senior year she convinced her parents to let her transfer to public school. She had been attending school with the same circles of people for eleven years and desperately wanted a change of scenery. Her parents were against it, but Persia made a very convincing argument. She had always gotten good grades and never had problems in school. She just wanted to spend her final year of high school in a more relaxed environment. Reluctantly, they agreed and that was the beginning of the end.

At the beginning, public school was a dream come true for Persia. The teachers weren't as strict, the work was easier and she got to see her friends from the old neighborhood every day. Up until the time she was five, Persia had lived in Harlem with her mother, Michelle, and her biological father, Face. Face was one of the biggest drug dealers in Harlem, and a man of great respect on the streets. The hood loved Face, but no one loved him more than his little girl. Instead of tricking his money off on cars and jewelry like his friends, Face had made sound investments, one of them being the huge house he had moved them into in Long Island City. Persia was afforded all the things that her parents never had, including a top-dollar education in a new school. She missed her old friends from Harlem, but still got to see them on the weekends. Face busted his ass day and night in the streets to make sure Persia and her mother were taken care of, up until the day he went to prison for killing a man. It was in self-defense, but with Face's rap sheet it was easy for the jury to paint him as a monster. They wanted to give him the long walk, but Face's lawyer was able to plead him out to fifteen to twenty-five years.

When Face went to prison, it left their family incomplete. Persia and her mother, Michelle, weren't hurting for money. Face made sure of that, but him missing from the picture still created a void in their lives. A few years into Face's bid, that void was filled when Michelle married a man named Richard and moved him into their house: the house Persia's father had bought. Richard wasn't a hustler like Face; he was a square dude, who taught history at the local university. He treated them well enough, but it didn't stop Persia from resenting him. She felt like he was trying to take her father's place, and could never bring herself to give him a fair chance.

While Persia's mother Michelle was busy playing homemaker with Richard, Persia was enjoying the newfound freedom of public school. Persia chose Martin Luther King Jr. because that was the school all her old neighborhood friends attended. When she hooked up with Karen, Meeka, and Ty it was just like being back on the block, only they were older now and into "big girl" things. Persia found herself skipping school to run through Harlem with her girls, smoking weed and chasing men. It didn't take long for Persia to get so caught up in their lifestyle that she started losing sight of her own. Her grades were slipping in school, and she became more detached from her family. She was on the fast track and her life, already spiraling out of control, took a nose dive when she met Chucky.

Chucky was one of the older dudes who got money on Karen's block. All the girls wanted to get with him and when he started dating Persia she felt like she had finally arrived. Chucky was fine, had money, a nice ride, and status. He had it all, including an undercover drug habit. Persia,

being as naïve as she was to that lifestyle, didn't
see the signs until it was too late, and Chucky
had pulled her down the rabbit hole with him.
Persia had smoked weed with Karen and them,
and had even taken pills a time or two with
her white friends Marty and Sarah, but it was
Chucky who turned her on to the darker side
of drug abuse. Persia was naïve, but she wasn't
stupid. She understood that drugs were wrong,
but she loved Chucky so much that she was doing
whatever it took to keep him, including dancing
with the devil. The first time Persia wrapped her
lips around a crack pipe, she knew without question that she had hit rock bottom.

In the end, Persia's misguided love for Chucky
had cost her dignity and almost her life when he
left her to die in a crack house. Persia remembered it as vividly as if it had just happened.

From the beginning it had been one of the
worst days of Persia's life. She had just gotten
the news about her best friend Marty's death.
That coupled with the rift between her and her
mother because of her bullshit in the streets
had pushed Persia to an all-time low point. She
tried to reach out for Chucky but he was too busy
running the streets to take her calls, so Persia
was left alone with her grief and it consumed
her. That night, at Chucky's aunt's house, was

the first time she had ever smoked straight-up crack, with no chaser. Persia had been doing hard drugs with Chucky for months, but it was mostly snorting coke and smoking laced blunts, but she promised herself that no matter how far she went, her lips would never touch a crack pipe. In her state of mind her promise had gone out the window and she had her first real dance with the devil.

Smoking crack out of a pipe was the most intense high Persia had ever felt. It was almost like she had stepped out of her body and was watching herself hit the pipe from across the room. She was so out of her head that she had to go into the bathroom and splash water on her face. That's when all hell broke loose.

Persia heard gunshots first. It sounded like someone had just let off a cannon in the middle of the living room. When she gathered up the courage to investigate, she saw men in masks swarming the house. They were gunning down anyone they came across without hesitation or question. Persia locked herself in the upstairs bathroom, listening through the door at the sounds of gunshots and screams, which were getting closer by the second. Persia wasn't sure how long she had been pressed against that door, but it seemed like forever. She listened intently for the sounds of voices or footsteps, but heard none. All was silent. Persia let out a deep sigh of relief, knowing she had once again dodged a bullet. Still leaning on the door, she looked up at the wreck staring back at her from the bathroom mirror. It made her want to cry, but she wasn't sure if she had any tears left. Even if she did, who still cared enough to wipe them? She decided that after that night, she was getting her shit together.

Someone jiggled the bathroom door and her breath got caught in her throat. They had found her! Persia thought maybe if she just explained to them that she didn't have anything to do with what was going on they would let her go. Then she thought of how remorselessly they had been when gunning down Chucky's aunt and her boyfriend and decided that they weren't men who could be reasoned with. There was no way she planned on dying in a crack house.

*Persia looked around the bathroom frantically for something she could use for a weapon, when her eyes landed on the window. If she could climb down the side of the house, she might be able to get away. She was three stories up and it was snowing, but her chances out there were better than her chances in the bathroom.*

*Persia had just managed to work the old window open when the bathroom door came crashing in. The two masked men filed in, guns drawn. When the shorter one saw Persia, he paused and that was all the time she needed to slide out the window.*

*"Bring your li'l ass here," she heard one of the men say. A hand clamped around her leg and was trying to pull her back in.*

*"Let me go, I didn't do anything," Persia began kicking and thrashing.*

*"Stop fighting and come back in here," the shorter one ordered, trying to get a better grip on Persia by grabbing her shirt.*

*Persia could feel herself sliding back through the window. If they got her inside, she was dead. With her last bit of strength, she kicked out as hard as she could. Her feet made contact with the shorter one's face. The force tore her shirt, but she was free from his grip. Persia tried to grab onto the storm drain on the side of the house, but it was slick with snow and she slipped.*

*Persia felt like she was falling forever. The wind felt good, like it was caressing her tenderly. For a few seconds all was right with the world and she was wrapped in her mother's love. That came to a crashing halt when Persia hit the ground and it felt like she broke every bone in her body.*

That was both the scariest and the most enlightening day of her life. Her literal fall from grace had been the best thing to happen to her in months. It was while lying on that cold concrete, in severe pain and thinking she was going to die, that Persia made a promise to God that if she lived, she was going to get her act together. God accepted her wager when He sent the kind soul who found Persia and took her to the hospital. To that day she had no idea who it was who rescued her, but she would be forever in their debt, and one day the opportunity would present itself to thank them.

Persia's road to recovery was a long and difficult one. The physical pains of withdrawal were so bad that she wouldn't wish them on her worst enemy, but they failed in comparison to the mental scars left behind by the whole ordeal. Ironically enough, when things were roughest, it was Richard who was there to help her get through it. He was there to listen when she felt like talking, and to talk when she needed to be encouraged. He even footed the bill for her to be treated in an outpatient program at a private treatment facility to spare her the embarrassment of anyone finding out what she'd been through. After the way she'd treated Richard all those years, most men wouldn't have bothered, but Richard was there to help her put the pieces back together. Persia still didn't accept him as a replacement for her father, but she developed a whole new level of respect for him.

A sharp whacking sound against her desk snapped Persia out of her daydream. She looked up to find Sister Francine standing over her, cold blue eyes glaring at her, and tapping her infamous three foot ruler against her meaty palm. Even before Persia had been a student at St. Mary's the first go-around, she had heard stories about Sister Francine and that ruler. They said she wielded it with the grace and skill of a samurai.

"Ms. Chandler, would you care to share with the class what it is out the window that has you so fixated that you're ignoring today's lesson?" Sister Francine asked in her snooty tone.

"Ah, it's nothing. I guess I was just daydreaming. I'm sorry," Persia said, hoping her apology was enough to send the old crone back to the front of the class and out of her face. It didn't.

"Daydreaming won't get you a passing grade in my class, Ms. Chandler. Knowing the work will."

"Yes, Sister Francine. You're absolutely right. I'll be more attentive," Persia told her, still trying to take the high road.

"Of course I'm right, which is why I'm the teacher and you're the student, a student who is with me for the second time at that. Maybe you feel like you don't have to pay attention like everyone else because you know the work already. Is that it, Ms. Chandler, are you a know-it-all?"

Persia looked up at the nun, feeling her temper swelling. Sister Francine was goading her. For as bad as Persia wanted to slap fire out of the old bag, she knew that would definitely get her booted out of school and possibly brought up on charges. Grudgingly, she swallowed her anger and simply answered, "No, ma'am."

"Oh, but I think you do. So since you know the lesson plan so well, why don't you get up and solve the problem on the board for the class?" Sister Francine challenged.

"I don't think that will be necessary, Sister Francine," Persia said barely above a whisper.

Sister Francine leaned with her pale knuckles on the desk and glared at Persia with her cold blue eyes. "That wasn't a request, Ms. Chandler. You can get up and solve the problem in front of the class, or I'll write you up. We both know what a demerit would do to your delicate record at this point, don't we?" She held a piece of white chalk up in front of Persia.

Persia sighed, before plucking the chalk from Sister Francine's fingers and getting up from her chair. The walk from her seat to the blackboard was like walking the Green Mile, on her way to the electric chair. Persia could feel the eyes of every student in the room locked on her. "Don't fuck up, don't fuck up," she repeated to herself, taking short quick breaths. As she approached the board, her eyes floated across the riddle of numbers, letters, and decimal points, Sister Francine had scribbled on the board. When Persia raised her hand she noticed that it was sweating so bad that the chalk had begun to stick to her fingers. She looked over her shoulder and saw Sister Francine was watching her, smirking smugly. Taking a deep breath, Persia made the first few stokes with the chalk. When she placed it back in the tray, just beneath the blackboard, she turned around and gave Sister Francine a half smile. It took her less than twenty seconds to solve the problem, and embarrass the nun in front of the class.

Sister Francine stalked toward Persia, face flushed red. "You think you're smart don't you?"

"No, but I'm not a dummy either," Persia told her. She had been counting her father's money since she was three, so math came natural to her.

"Are you and I going to have a problem, Ms. Chandler?" Sister Francine asked, with her hand tightening around the ruler.

Persia looked from the ruler to Sister Francine's angry face. "Not unless you create one."

Sister Francine looked like she was thinking about it, but decided against it. "Go downstairs and see Father Michael."

"For what? I got up and solved the problem like you asked."

"Yes, but you disrupted my class in doing so. Now leave, or I'll have you removed," Sister Francine told her.

"This is some bullshit," Persia grumbled, walking back to her desk. She snatched her bag, hastily stuffing her books into it on her way to the door. As she was walking out, she gave Sister Francine the finger.

"It's that attitude of yours that got you into trouble in the first place," Sister Francine called after her. "There are no shortcuts to an education, Ms. Chandler. You can either get it in here or on some random street corner. The choice is yours!"

# CHAPTER 3

Persia sat in the waiting area outside Father Michael's office, waiting her turn to see the school's headmaster. From the shouting coming from the other side of the door, somebody was getting ripped a new asshole. Persia didn't know who it was, but she would've hated to be the recipient of whatever punishment awaited them. There were two other girls in the waiting area, too, sent down for one offense or another to be punished. One of them, a girl she had classes with, tried to engage her in small talk, but Persia wasn't very receptive. She was still fuming over what had happened with Sister Francine.

From her first go at the school, Persia had never been a favorite among the faculty. She was one of the few black girls who attended the prestigious school and the most outspoken. Her mother and Richard contributed to the school, so Persia was given more leeway than most, and she always seemed to be testing her boundaries. When Persia had to come back to St. Mary's, hat in hand, some of the faculty was glad to see her humbled, Sister Francine being one of them. Her mother urged her to be strong and not feed into the bullshit, but at the end of the day she wasn't the one sitting in a classroom getting embarrassed. Thankfully, Persia would be graduating soon, and could put Sister Francine and all the other bullshit that came with being in high school behind her.

There was a break in the screaming. Father Michael's door swung open, and someone shoved a young girl through it before slamming it shut again. She was a thin blonde, with pale skin and pouty lips. Her uniform skirt looked wrinkled, and her tie hung askew around her neck. On her face she wore a bored expression, but her eyes seemed to light up a bit when she saw Persia. The blonde walked over to the row of seats where Persia and the other two girls were sitting. She looked at the girl sitting closest to Persia and motioned for her to move over. The girl didn't utter a word; she just vacated the seat.

"One day someone is going to kick your little pasty ass for being such a bitch all the time, Sarah," Persia told the blonde.

The blonde shrugged. "Probably, but even after the beat down, I'll still be a bitch."

All Persia could do was laugh. "Even when everything else has changed, you're still the same, Sarah." Persia was Sarah's best friend. She and Marty had been the only two white girls to embrace Persia when her family moved into their predominantly white neighborhood years ago. They were like the three *amigas*. When Persia was running the streets with Karen and her crew, she didn't see much of Marty and Sarah, but tragedy brought them back together. While Persia had been on her drug binge, Marty was brutally raped by some rappers they had met at a club. The mental trauma of what had happened was too much for Marty to cope with so she committed suicide, reducing the number of *amigas* to two. Marty's death hit both of them hard, but it rocked Persia. She felt like when her friend needed her most, she wasn't there.

"So, what're you in for, Ms. Goody Two-shoes? I thought you were cleaning up your act," Sarah said.

"I am, but Sister Francine is in rare form today."

Sarah sighed dramatically. "Why doesn't that old bitch just die already?"

"We should be so lucky. So what did you do this time? I hope you didn't stick firecrackers in Brother Lance's cigarettes again. It took a month for his mustache to grow back the last time." Persia laughed. Sarah didn't. From the look on Sarah's face, Persia could tell whatever she did wasn't a simple prank this time. "What happened?"

"Fucking snitch is what happened," Sarah said angrily. "A few days ago I sold those trailer park tramps Vickie and Jean a couple of beans. Them and a few of their nitwit friends popped them and one of the girls tweeked out. Of course when the pressure came down all of them pointed their fingers at me as the supplier. My dad is in there talking to father Michael now, pleading with him not to call the police. I'm in some deep shit, Persia." Sarah broke down and started crying.

Deep shit was an understatement. Sarah's father was a pharmacist and she would regularly tap his inventory, and push pills to the locals. It had been Sarah's side hustle for years and never once had she gotten caught, until now. Not only was Sarah looking at getting expelled, but her father could potentially lose his license and be sent to prison for what she was doing.

Persia hugged Sarah close, and tried to comfort her as best she could. "Everything is going to be okay, Sarah."

Father Michael's door opened again, and out stepped Sarah's father, Herman Thompson. He was wearing a white lab coat, and his glasses sat askew on his nose, as they always did. His thinning white hair sat on top of his head messily, as if he just stuck his fingers in a light socket. Mr. Thompson was a jovial man who was always smiling, but not that day. His thin blue lips were turned down into a frown and anger danced behind his eyes. Persia had never seen him like this and it made her uncomfortable enough to let go of Sarah.

"Are you happy now, Sarah?" Mr. Thompson said in a rough voice that didn't match his nerdish demeanor. On the rare occasions that he got angry you could hear the faint traces of his Polish accent. "I work my fingers to the bone to give you a life better than the one I had growing up. The best clothes, the best school, all the latest electronics. Do you know how many extra hours I have to put in to keep up with the tuition at this place?"

Sarah looked frightened, more frightened than Persia had ever seen her. "No, Papa," Sarah said, barely above a whisper.

"Of course you don't, because you've never done an honest hour's work in your entire life!" Mr. Thompson snapped. "I deny you nothing and in return you piss on my head and tell me it's raining every chance you get."

"Papa, it didn't happen how they said. I was just—" Sarah started explaining, but was cut off when Mr. Thompson slapped her across the face.

"I've had enough of your damn lies!" Mr. Thompson raged. He looked like he was about to slap her again, but Persia stood up and got in between them.

"I think you should calm down, Mr. Thompson," Persia said in her most respectful tone. She hadn't meant to get between the father and daughter, but her legs had already shot her to her feet, before her brain could relay the message that it was a bad idea.

"And who are you to tell me anything, when you're worse than her?" Mr. Thompson looked Persia up and down. "Persia Chandler, you're in no position to give me advice about my daughter with the way you spit on every effort your parents have put forth to give you a good life."

"That's not true," Persia argued.

"Isn't it? Persia, I know all you kids think I'm just the nerdy guy from the pharmacy, who is too caught up in the table of elements to pay attention to what's going on in everyday life, but I know a bit more about the way of the world than you give me credit for. I know your mother and both your fathers, so I know the sacrifices that were made to keep you flying straight. Your father gave his freedom for you to be able to have more than a fighter's chance in the world and you piss your blessings away just like this idiot." He pointed at Sarah. "The problem with the kids of your generation, we give you too much, and never make you earn your keep so you wouldn't know a blessing if it slapped you in the face."

"I know I'm blessed," Persia said, thinking of all that she had gone through and lived to tell about it.

"Then why don't you start acting like it and stop giving your mother and your stepfather your ass to kiss, when they're just trying to make sure you stay straight? If you want to be a statistic, like your little friend Marty, be my guest, but don't bring my kid down with you."

Mr. Thompson's remark cut Persia deep. It had never been a secret that he didn't care for Marty, but to speak ill of the dead was uncalled for. "See, I was trying to keep from disrespecting you, Mr. Thompson, but your ass is out of line. It's easy to point the finger at Sarah, and even me, and talk about how much we're fucking up, but what about the part you play in it as an absentee parent?"

"That's ludicrous! I've been in Sarah's life since the day she was born," Mr. Thompson said proudly.

"Paying the bills and throwing money at her to keep her out of your hair doesn't qualify as 'being there.' Half the time you don't even know where Sarah is because you're either too busy working or entertaining your private clients," Persia spat. A look of shock came across Mr. Thompson's face. "Don't look so surprised, Herman. Just like you know my dirt, I know yours. Don't sling mud if you aren't prepared to have it slung back at you."

Mr. Thompson was so embarrassed that his face turned beet red. "If you were my kid, I'd knock you in the mouth for what you just said."

"Well I ain't your kid and if you even think about raising your hand to me, what's going on with your kid in school will be the least of your concerns," Persia said in a matter-of-fact tone.

Mr. Thompson stood there, glaring at Persia as if he was trying to decide whether he wanted to test her. He was angry, but he was no fool either. For as much as he wanted to slap the taste out of the teenage girl's mouth, he knew there would be repercussions. Mr. Thompson had enough to deal with already and didn't need the kind of problems that would come with getting into it with Persia.

"Mr. Thompson!" Father Michael called from the doorway of his office. He was leaning against the doorframe, thick arms folded across his barrel-like chest. He had seen and heard enough.

Mr. Thompson gave Persia one last look before addressing his kid. "Let's go, Sarah."

Sarah snapped to attention like she had just been struck by lightning. The whole time her father and Persia exchanged words, Sarah stood in the corner, too afraid to move or speak. She knew her father had a bad temper and didn't want her friend getting hurt trying to defend her. Sheepishly she followed her father to the door. Before she left she looked over her shoulder at Persia and mouthed that she would call her later.

Persia took slow deep breaths, trying to calm herself down. She had known Mr. Thompson since she was little, and he had always been kind to her so she felt bad for disrespecting him, but she felt like he forced her hand. When the time was right, she would reach out to apologize, but it wouldn't be any time in the near future.

# CHAPTER 4

"See, that's the problem with you cats. You spend all your time living for the now and don't give much thought to the future. I'm all for enjoying life, but I wanna enjoy it for more than a day. I wanna enjoy it for all my days," Tut was saying to the young men gathered around him. There were about four or five of the young cats and all their eyes were locked on him, hanging on every word that he said. Tut was young, but he had the charisma about him of an old head, which is what put him on Ramses's radar.

Tut was a kid from the rough side of the Bronx, trying to make the best out of a bad situation like everyone else. Unlike the other kids he hung around with on street corners, Tut was from a two-parent household where both mother and father worked and neither of them did drugs. They weren't rich, but they weren't poor either, so Tut getting caught up in the streets was by choice and not circumstances. He watched his parents bust their asses day in and day out at their jobs, just to have to struggle to pay bills and not enjoy their lives and he was determined that wasn't how he was going to go out. Tut could never see himself working for forty years just to put his boss's kid through college. Tut wanted the immediate gratification that came with fast cash, so he set out to make his way.

He started out hustling packs for an older dude in his neighborhood. He was able to make a few coins, nothing major but enough to fill the gaps in his pockets. Tut was trying to stack what he made working for the older dude to one day buy his own work. For as appreciative as he was for the opportunity to feed himself, Tut had never been very good at following the direction of others. He wanted to be the master of his own destiny. His plan was cut short when somebody came through one night and blew his employer's brains out. Tut now found himself back at square one. He needed to find a new plug.

As it happened, Tut went to school with a dude named Omega, who was said to be getting big money uptown. Every time he saw Omega he was dressed in whatever the latest fashions were and kept a bad chick on his arm. Tut knew Omega from having classes with him, and sharing some of the same friends, but he didn't know him well enough to step to him about getting money. One day an opportunity presented itself that would change that.

Some dudes had run down on Omega in the bathroom and tried to rob him for his chain. Tut just happened to walk in on the robbery. He didn't have anything to do with it so he could've easily walked away and left Omega to his fate, but he saw it as his way in. That day in the bathroom, Omega and Tut had stood back to back and fought off the kids. From then on, he and Omega had started hanging out around school, and their relationship eventually spilled over into the streets. Omega started bringing Tut around and introduced him to Benny and Chucky. Tut never really rocked with Chucky, but he had major love for Benny. It had been Benny who gave Tut his first job with their organization, and he always looked out for him when he could.

Tut was a quick learner and a loyal soldier, which helped push him up the ladder of the organization. Between Tut and Omega the future of the organization was looking bright, but Tut's path took a detour when he got locked up. He and Benny had been together when something popped off, which led to Benny pulling a gun on a kid. Nobody got hurt, but someone called the police. When Tut and Benny were heading back to the block their car was pulled over and the police found the gun. Benny was already on parole for a gun, so Tut claimed ownership and took the charge. The whole time Tut was going through his legal troubles the police kept pressing him for information about Pharaoh's organization. They had a hard on for Pharaoh that would make a porn star jealous. They had even offered to let him walk, free of all charges, if he gave them even the smallest bit of information that led to a conviction. Tut never uttered a word. For his silence Tut ended up getting three years' state time for possession of a weapon. It was this display of loyalty to the crew that put him on Ramses's radar. It broke his heart when he was in prison and got the letter, letting him know Benny had been killed, because they had been close, but his sadness wouldn't last long. When Tut came home from prison he was presented with an apartment, $20,000 in cash and a promotion within the organization. He would be elevated from soldier to lieutenant. It was just as Ramses had promised at the beginning of his bid: they took care of their own.

"You still preaching to the choir?" Omega joked as he walked up. His long dreads hung loose around his shoulders making him look like a lion.

"What up, O?" Tut gave him dap. "What brings you up to this end of the world? You know you don't fuck with the Bronx like that."

"I do when its cash involved. You wanna make some extra paper?" Omega asked.

"That's a dumbass question. I'm always looking to come up. What's the lick?" Tut asked greedily. He made decent money on the strips Ramses had given him to look over, but his was one of the smaller and less lucrative locations. To make sure he had Pharaoh's tribute every month, he sometimes had to take on extracurricular work, such as whatever Omega was offering.

"Take a walk with me, right quick." Omega led Tut away from the youngsters so they could speak in private. "Dig, you know me and Li'l Monk got everything sewed up from like 133rd to 145th, right? Ramses doesn't want us dipping any farther south because most of that belongs to them niggas from Harlem Crip. There's more of us than them, but it'd be less messy just to let them have it instead of going to war. There's no doubt we'd win, but fucking with Gutter and Danny Boy, we'd likely lose a lot of soldiers in the process."

"So what does that have to do with me?" Tut asked impatiently. He wanted to get to the part of the story where he got paid.

"If you'll give me a minute, I'll get to that," Omega told him. "Like I was saying, we can't really dip any farther south, but he didn't say we couldn't push north. I wanna lock down everything from across the 145th Street Bridge to the Grand Concourse, and redirect all that money to us, and I'm even willing to make sure you eat off this, too."

"What's the catch?" Tut asked suspiciously.

"These wetback niggas who're set up over there are in my way. It's only a handful of them and they ain't hardly moving enough product to present a problem if we wanted to muscle them, but Ramses won't give me the green light."

"Why not?"

"Well, apparently the kid, Petey, who runs things that way has some kind of history with Pharaoh. I guess his dad and the big boss were cool back in the days. Ramses agrees with my theory about the increase of income if we locked down the border, but doesn't want them squeezed out by none of his people because it would look like disrespect to his late father's memory on Pharaoh's part. You know them old niggas are real big on honor."

"But if something happens randomly to Petey by a third party, it would leave Pharaoh completely blameless and open the block up for you to take fair and square after you topple their leadership." Tut picked up on Omega's thinking.

"Exactly," Omega agreed. "Man, I've tried everything with these dudes from offering profit shares to flat out buying the territory, but they're making this shit way harder than it has to be. I can understand where Ramses and Pharaoh are coming from, but them Spanish niggas are in the way of progress right now."

"I can dig it, but let me ask you something. Why come to me instead of sending your personal attack dog, Li'l Monk?" Tut asked. He had never cared for Li'l Monk, not because of anything he had ever done, but because of where he was in life and where Tut wanted to be. Before he went to prison, he knew Li'l Monk as the dirty little kid who was always fighting. To come home and see Li'l Monk in a position that Tut felt was reserved for him was like a slap in the face. He tolerated Li'l Monk for the sake of keeping the peace in the organization, but he also deeply resented him and every so often the resentment peeked out.

"Knock that shit off, man. Li'l Monk is my partner, not my attack dog. My nigga is a beast out here on the streets when shit needs to get handled, but make no mistake about it, that's my brother. Ya dig?"

"Yeah, I dig," Tut said in a less than convincing tone. "So what's my part in this and my take of the spoils?"

"You help me move dude out and you and your people can run the spots we take. You can add those corners to whatever Ramses has blessed you with so far. In essence, your territory gets bigger and both our borders are guarded. You kick up to me, and I kick up to Ramses and Pharaoh for both of us. It's a simple plan."

"It's always a simple plan to the nigga who ain't putting his ass on the line," Tut capped. "Now, you've already said that Pharaoh and Ramses really don't want these dudes muscled, so what happens when they find out what I did?"

"That's the best part, they ain't gonna know. Petey and his crew been beefing with the Dominicans and the Jamaicans so anyone of them could be just as guilty in punching his clock. Outside of you I haven't spoken to any one else about this plan, so the only way it'll get back to them is if you or your people are talking, because I sure as hell ain't gonna tell them. I could be just as much in the dog house as you for going against Ramses."

Tut weighed his options. It was a risky plan that could potentially put him out of favor with Ramses and Pharaoh, but on the flip side it could increase his profits and his reach. A wise man once told Tut, "Scared money don't make no money," so he had to put his balls on the table every so often to get where he needed to be. "A'ight. I'll take care of this for you, but on one condition."

"Name it," Omega told him.

"I want a piece of Seventh Avenue."

Omega looked surprised. "Nah, I get too much money on Seventh. You bugging."

"Nah, I think you the one that's bugging, Omega. You just came through my hood and asked me to commit treason. I could be killed just for having this conversation with you, or I could be rewarded for exposing your bullshit."

Omega's face twisted into a hard mask. "Damn, I come through here offering you an opportunity to get some bread and you talking about snaking me?"

"Never that, O. We got history. It ain't about snaking you. It's about being the best negotiator in a business deal," Tut said slyly. "Don't take it like that, Omega. I ain't asking for all of Seventh Avenue, I just want one square block, from 142nd to 143rd. The rest of it is yours."

"Why those blocks?" Omega asked curiously.

"Let's just say they have sentimental value to me," Tut told him. Benny had kept an apartment on Seventh Avenue between 142nd and 143rd. He and Tut had some memorable times on that block, living wild and free. It was where Tut had made his very first crack sale in Harlem. He wanted that block to honor Benny's memory.

"Fuck it, you can have it," Omega relented. "But if I give you that block, you gotta split the take with me because technically you'd be cutting into my money."

"You got it, boss," Tut said sarcastically.

"How soon do you think you can have it done?" Omega asked.

Tut looked at his watch. "No time like the present. You got a picture of this dude?"

Omega opened his flip phone, and pulled up Petey's MySpace page. Tut stared at the picture for a while, committing Petey's face to memory.

"A'ight, I got it. Before the sun sets this problem will be a thing of the past," Tut told him.

"I appreciate you doing this, Tut," Omega told him.

"Don't tell me, show me. Make sure my pockets are heavy enough to where I'm more focused on them than this dummy mission I'm signing up for," Tut told him.

"You got that," Omega agreed, "but for what you're asking, I don't just need him gone. I need a message sent."

Tut laughed. "My messages are better than Hallmark cards. Ask ya man Ramses. Don't worry about it, O. I'm gonna make sure your voice is received loud and clear."

Petey came out of his building and stretched like he had just awakened from a long slumber. It was the middle of the day, but to a man who didn't get out of bed until 5:00 p.m. every day, it was early. As usual, he was dressed in a sweat suit, flip-flops and tall white socks with his father's signature straw hat. He was on his way to the local Spanish restaurant where his father had held his meetings every day. Being that their numbers had been decimated over the years since his father's death, it was more out of carrying on tradition than necessity. He strolled down the block waving to the residents of the neighborhood who acknowledged him. Having the love and respect of the people of his neighborhood made Petey's heart swell with pride. His domain only stretched four or five blocks squared, but it was still his. In Petey's little square of the Bronx, he was treated like a mafia don.

Petey had inherited his neighborhood from his father, Peter Suarez Sr. Peter Sr. had been the brother of the notorious Puerto Rican drug lord Poppito, who operated out of Old San Juan, Puerto Rico. Peter Sr. was small time in comparison to his brother, but inherited the notoriety that came with being a part of that family, which garnered him the respect of the larger crews in the area. When he died, the mantel was passed to his son, Petey, but by that time there wasn't much left of Peter Sr.'s kingdom except a few scarce blocks, where he was able to run through a few ounces per day via hand-to-hand sales. It wasn't much to hold on to, but it was all he had so Petey kept things going as best he could.

Along his way to the restaurant he was joined by his constituents, who consisted of some neighborhood knuckleheads and a few older dudes who were still loyal to his father. There were only a handful of them but they held on to what was theirs ferociously. Everyone still in Petey's employ knew that what they had left was only being held on to by a strand.

When Petey stepped inside the restaurant he expected to be greeted by Maria, the owner's wife and his mistress, but she was nowhere to be found. That was unusual because Maria was always around. He looked to the counter and found the happy young girl who always took his orders was at her position, but that day she wasn't smiling. There was a terrified expression on her face.

It suddenly registered to Petey that something was terribly wrong.

Several shots rang out, dropping Petey's entourage around him and leaving him standing there, alone and scared shitless. His nervous eyes drifted toward the direction the shots had come from. Occupying the booth where he usually took his meetings sat a young black man. Next to him was Maria. The black man had his arm draped around her, with a smoking gun in his hand. Sitting on the table in front of him was a large canister of olive oil.

"What the fuck is this?" Petey asked nervously.

"A going-out-of-business sale," Tut told him. "Come sit down and let's rap for a taste." He waved Petey over, but Petey didn't budge. "Petey, whatever you're thinking you might as well unthink. I dropped your boys without getting up from this seat, so you'd be a dead man before you could ever make your move. Now sit your ass down so we can talk."

Slowly Petey approached the booth and took the seat opposite Tut and Maria. "Who are you?"

"The repo man, come to collect," Tut told him. "Let my visit serve as your official notice that shop is closed for you boys."

Petey's face twisted into a mask of anger. "You black bastard, you've got some pretty big balls coming into my fucking territory giving me orders."

Without warning, Tut shot Petey in the arm. "Watch your fucking mouth in the presence of a lady." Tut removed his arm from around Maria and set the gun on the table between him and Petey. He cocked the hammer and looked Petey dead in the eyes. "Let's skip all the fake tough guy shit and get straight to the facts. You are done, over, *finito*."

Petey clutched his bloody arm and winced in pain. "You won't get away with this. My father has run this neighborhood for twenty years. You think we don't have allies who'll retaliate for this shit? My uncle is Poppito Suarez."

The name rang familiar to Tut, but he was too busy showing off to think about where he had heard it before. "Dig this, no disrespect, but I don't give a fuck who your father was or who your uncle is. Any one of your thousand and one Spic-ass relatives are more than welcome to come back acting like they want a problem and they'll all find themselves in a bad way. It's already done, Petey, and me paying you a visit is just a formality. There's progress being made on the streets and you, my friend, are in the way," Tut snatched the gun up and shot Petey twice in the chest.

The women screamed in horror as Petey's life drained away into the booth's bench. He gasped to catch his breath, but couldn't because his lung was punctured. He watched helplessly as Tut got up from the table and picked up the canister of olive oil and began pouring it over his head. Tut pulled a lighter from his pocket and sparked it, holding it in front of Petey's face so that he could get a good look at the flame. When he decided he was done toying with Petey, he dropped the lighter into his lap and stepped back as Petey burst into flames.

"Now that's how you send a fucking message." Tut laughed while watching Petey burn.

# CHAPTER 5

"Ms. Chandler," Father Michael called, reminding Persia that he was still standing there, waiting. His dark eyes stared at her from beneath his bushy eyebrows, urging her to hurry up.

Persia had been in Father Michael's office more than a few times, but it always made her uncomfortable. It was an ode to everything ancient, with its overflowing racks of dusty history books, and shelves littered with knickknacks Father Michael had collected during his travels over the years. His newest addition to his office was what looked like an old airplane propeller, mounted to the wall behind his desk. Persia was staring at the propeller, trying to guess what kind of plane it had come off and how Father Michael had come into possession of it, when the door slammed behind her, causing her to jump.

"Sit down, Ms. Chandler." Father Michael motioned toward the chair Mr. Thompson had just vacated. Persia did as she was told. Father

Michael walked around to the other side of the desk, smoothing his black shirt before he sat down. He took his time, rummaging through his drawer for his hairbrush, and proceeded to tighten up the loose strands of hair on his salt-and-pepper head. Father Michael wore his hair slicked back like the mobsters Persia had seen in the old movies her mother was always watching. In fact, that's what he reminded Persia of: a mobster. The way he talked, the way he walked, it was all street. The only thing that let on to the fact that he was a man of the cloth was the black shirt and collar he wore. After he'd completed his grooming, he addressed Persia. "Why are you here, Ms. Chandler?"

Persia shrugged. "Because Sister Francine sent me."

"I know that, Ms. Chandler, but that's not my question. Why are you"—he jabbed his finger at her—"here? Persia, I have to admit, when you came back to us nobody thought you had it in you to climb back into the fight and get on track with your class work, including myself. Much to everyone's surprise, you seem to be readjusting very well. Even when you found out you were short several credits, and wouldn't be able to march with your class in June, you took it in stride, and kept your nose to the ground to get your diploma in January. You were on course to serving all your detractors a nice helping of crow, and then you went left. Your grades are on point, but you focus has slipped. Has something happened between now and when you came back that's distracting you?"

The question sent Persia's mind back to a dark time in her life and the root of her problem.

The period immediately after Persia completed the rehabilitation program was very dark for Persia. The doctors had suggested that she check into an inpatient program, but Persia didn't want to. She wanted to try to kick on her own. They compromised and Richard paid for her to receive outpatient treatment at a private facility. The physical pains of withdrawal were worse than anything she had ever been through, even falling out of a window. In the first few days she was racked with cramps and fits of vomiting. It was like she had a flu that wouldn't go away. There were times when Persia felt like she was going to die, and a few times she wanted to, but death was not in God's plan for her; suffering was. It got so bad at one point that she couldn't even control her bowels, and would pee and shit the bed. It was utterly embarrassing for her to have her mother clean her up like she was a baby, but there was no way she could do it on her own. It was during her rehab that she saw how strong her mother really was, because Persia doubted if she'd have been able to care for an adult as her mother had cared for her. She loved her mother for that.

Though her family welcomed her back with open arms, she still felt ashamed of what she had put them through. They had been respected members of their community and she's dirtied their name with her antics. They tried to keep it as secret as possible, but thanks to the young man from their neighborhood, who had spotted Persia at a drug house when she was still getting high, word had gotten out. No one ever directly said anything, but she heard the whispers and she felt the looks they gave her whenever she was around. Even stores that she had been going in and out of since she was a kid were now treating her different. They would sometimes follow Persia around as if they expected her to steal something. She felt subhuman, like a crackhead.

As if the mental scars weren't enough, there were her constant cravings. The doctors had warned her that even though her system was clean of the drugs, she would always have the desire to get high, and they were right. It was like a pregnant woman who wanted chocolate ice cream in the middle of the night and no matter what flavor you fed her, it failed in comparison to chocolate. There were times when Persia found herself sneaking into the city, with the intentions on buying drugs, but she couldn't do it. She refused to put herself or her family through that madness again. In order to keep her mind off drugs, Persia needed to find something else to focus on, so she threw herself headfirst into her schoolwork. After a while she was able to restore some semblance of normalcy to her life and then she got the phone call that threatened to undo all her progress.

*One day she and Sarah were in her bedroom doing their homework, when Persia's bedroom phone rang. It was a new number that not many people outside of Sarah had, so she wondered who it could be.*

"Hello?" Persia answered.

"Hey, baby." Chucky's voice came over the other end. *At one point Chucky had been the man of her dreams and the guy whom she thought she would spend the rest of her life with, until he showed his true colors.*

Persia turned her back so that Sarah couldn't see the expression on her face. "How did you get this number?"

"You know you belong to me and I belong to you, so I'll always be able to get a hold of you when I need you, and I need you now," Chucky told her.

"Chucky, you left me for dead in that house. You didn't even come see me while I was in the hospital," Persia said emotionally.

"It wasn't my fault, baby. Look just come meet me and I'll explain everything to you," Chucky said.

"I can't," Persia told him, but she didn't sound sure.

"Oh, so now that you're back on your feet, you're too good for me? That's fucked up," Chucky said, faking hurt.

"It's not like that, Chucky. It's just that I'm trying to get my life in order and I don't need any distractions," Persia explained.

"Damn, I've been reduced to a distraction? That's cold, Persia. When you came to me for help I risked my freedom and took you in, but now you're gonna turn your back on me? Don't do me like this, baby. It's a matter of life and death. I'm begging you, just meet me and hear me out."

Hearing Chucky beg was tearing her apart. She knew he was bad news, but she still loved him so much. "Okay, I'll give you five minutes then I'm gone. Where do you want me to meet you?"

*Chucky gave Persia the address to the place he wanted to meet her and the time. Persia knew that agreeing to meet Chucky was a bad idea, but she just couldn't bring herself to tell him no.*

*After school the following day instead of going straight home like she normally would've, she took the bus to the Long Island Rail Road and rode into the city. Her nerves played havoc on her for the whole ride, causing her to sweat uncontrollably. It was a bad idea, and she wanted to turn around and go back, but she couldn't, not before she looked Chucky in the eyes and confronted him about why he'd done her the way he did. She needed closure.*

*Their meeting spot wasn't far from where the train let her off, so Persia walked the few short blocks. It was a sit-in delicatessen off of Thirty-third Street. When Persia arrived, she saw that Chucky was already there, sitting at a table in front of the window. He'd likely picked that seat so that he could see whoever was coming and going. Chucky had visibly lost some weight since the last time she'd seen him, but for the most part he still looked the same: well dressed, clean cut, and chatting away on his cell phone. He had yet to even notice her, but she could already feel herself getting caught back up in his thrall.*

"*You can do this, Persia,*" she told herself, trying to build the confidence to walk into the delicatessen. She noticed something that gave her pause. Chucky couldn't seem to stop touching his nose. Every so often he would wipe it, like he had a cold. It was a small tell, but enough to make Persia rethink her decision. She couldn't get sucked back in. Wiping the mist from her eyes, Persia turned and headed back to the train station.

Chucky had been calling her consistently since that day, but she never answered his calls. When he became too much of a pest, she would just unplug her phone. One night she'd even thought she'd seen his red BMW riding past her house. She needed to get Chucky out of her system, but he wasn't making it easy.

"No, everything is fine. I just need to focus a little harder," Persia told Father Michael.

"Good, because contrary to what you think, I want to see you succeed, Persia. I have a vested interest in you, so to speak," Father Michael told her.

Persia raised an eyebrow. "And what's that supposed to mean?"

Father Michael spared a glance at the door as if he suspected someone might be on the other side listening. "Persia, St. Mary's is one of the most prestigious schools in the state. To get in, you have to have one of three things, the money, the grades, or the connections. Some kids come from money families, and then you have the ones who test high enough for our scholarship programs. You, my dear, had all three. It wasn't by accident that you landed in St. Mary's. It was a part of your father's plan."

"What does my father have to do with this?" Persia asked, surprised. By the time she was old enough to attend St. Mary's her father was already in prison, so she wondered how he could've had a hand in it.

"Me and Face go way back, back to the days before I wore this collar." He tugged at the white band around his neck. "I used to be a volunteer coach for a summer basketball league in Harlem, back in the eighties. Your dad played on my squad for a couple of years."

This came as a shock to Persia as she had never known her father to have an athletic bone in his body. She found it hard to imagine her father, who she had always remembered being so serious, running up and down the court dribbling a ball. To her knowledge the only balls Face had ever passed were eight balls.

"Don't look so surprised. Your dad was actually a half-decent player, and maybe could've made something of it if he hadn't been so distracted by the streets. Even after your dad gave up basketball, and I took my vows, we kept in contact. Over the years, he would often come to me for advice about this and that. One subject we talked quite a bit about was you."

"Me?"

"Yes, Persia. From the time your father found out your mom was pregnant he immediately started laying the ground work for your future. Knowing he was about to become a father was his awakening of sorts. He came to me seeking advice on legitimate avenues to take with his money. Face was terrified that feeding you with blood money would taint your life, as his father had tainted his," Father Michael informed her.

Persia couldn't hide her surprise at how candidly the priest was speaking about her father's other life. Up until then Persia had thought it was a secret from the people who knew them in Long Island City. She'd been proven wrong twice in under an hour and couldn't help but to wonder who else knew their dark family secrets.

"I gave him a few leads, which thankfully turned out to be fruitful," Father Michael continued. "Gradually, he began to set the wheels in motion to make sure his family was out of harm's way. Around this time I was up for the assistant principal's position here at St. Mary's. That's actually what put the idea in your father's head to buy the house out here. It was far enough from the hood to keep you out of harm's way, but close enough for him to still stay on top of his other affairs. Face wanted to change so that he could be there for his family, and I wanted to do everything I could to help him make that change, including making sure Face's daughter had a top-notch education."

"So, you're saying that I got into St. Mary's because of who my father is?" Persia asked defensively.

"No, you got into St. Mary's because you're an outstanding student, but you were readmitted because of who your father is," Father Michael corrected her. "Persia, I know you've been having a rough time of it, and I sympathize with you, but I also know you're strong enough to overcome it. It's in your genes. Not only that, but you've got a great support system behind you. For whatever gripes you have with your mother's husband, he's a good man."

"I know," Persia said, reflecting on how Richard had been there for her through her whole recovery. "So, if I'm not in any trouble, can I go back to class now?"

Father Michael just stared at her, studying her face and thinking how much she looked like her father. She had that same determined look in her eyes that he did, and he knew so long as she kept it, Persia would be okay. "Yes, Ms. Chandler, you can go." He went back to his formal tone. "I trust we won't have any more incidents that could possibly jeopardize you receiving your diploma in January, correct?"

"No, sir. No more incidents," Persia assured him.

The intercom on Father Michael's desk beeped. The small black box was another one of his odes to everything ancient. "Yes, Sister?" he asked, depressing the talk button.

"Mr. Lansky is here," the mechanical voice announced.

"Great, give me a few minutes and you can send him in," Father Michael told her. "We're done here, Ms. Chandler."

Persia happily got up and started for the door. Her hand touched the knob, and she had an afterthought. "Father Michael, can I ask you a question?"

"Certainly, Ms. Chandler."

She looked from the tattoo on his forearm, which was a tombstone with small tally marks through it, to his dark eyes. "What did you do before you were a priest?"

Father Michael smiled and absently rubbed the tattoo. "Things that I had no business doing. Now get to class, Ms. Chandler."

Persia was so busy rushing to get out of Father's Michael's office that she wasn't watching where she was going and bumped into someone. Strong hands grabbed her arms to keep her from stumbling. The hands were attached to a tall man with chocolate-colored skin; and he wore his hair neatly tapered. He wore a gray V-neck sweater with a white shirt beneath it. He didn't look to be much older than Persia, but he carried himself with an air of a man wise beyond his years. When he flashed his pearly white smile at her, Persia felt her knees threaten to buckle.

"You a'ight, ma?" he asked in a deep voice.

"Yeah, I'm sorry. Should've been watching where I was going," Persia apologized.

"Jesus, kid, I can't take you anywhere without women throwing themselves into your arms," the older man with him joked. His long nose reminded Persia of the old comedian W.C. Fields. He looked to be in his late sixties, with snow white hair and wearing a Mr. Rogers–style sweater. His baby blue eyes twinkled, admiring Persia.

"Cut it out, Sol," the young man said bashfully.

"I'm just giving you shit, Shai." Sol elbowed him good naturedly. "Come on, we don't wanna keep Father Michael waiting." He turned to Persia and dipped his head. "Enjoy the rest of your day, young lady." He walked into Father Michael's office.

"Later, shorty." The young man called Shai winked and followed Sol into the office.

Persia stood there for a few minutes, watching as Father Michael got to his feet and came around the desk to properly receive his visitors. "Mr. Lansky, Mr. Clark," Persia heard Father Michael greet them, before closing the door.

# CHAPTER 6

"Yo, you gonna get the door or keep acting like you don't hear a muthafucka knocking, Maggie?" Chucky asked with an attitude. He was sitting on the couch, shirtless, sucking the life out of a cigarette. On the table in front of him, was a half-full Heineken. It had lost its chill an hour earlier, but it didn't stop him from taking the occasional sip from it, just to complain about how warm the beer was. Chucky was clearly in a sour mood.

After a few seconds, Maggie finally stirred on the loveseat, where she had been curled up, half asleep. At some point during her nod, the blond wig she wore had shifted and now sat askew on her head. Her arm hung over the edge of the couch, lit cigarette pinched between her fingers, and the ash had grown incredibly long. When she moved to sit up, the ash came loose and dropped on the carpet. "Shit," she cursed, but didn't move to clean it up. Maggie was an older woman, with a gorgeous face and a figure to match, but the years of partying were starting to show.

In her day, Maggie had been one of the bad-
dest chicks in West Philadelphia. All the hustlers
wanted her and all the women hated her, and with
good reason. Maggie had come up rough, with no
father and a mother who didn't want to be bothered. At an early age she found herself on the
streets getting it how she lived to take care of her
little sister. When she was younger, she would
boost clothes to sell or steal food from the supermarket to make sure they ate at night, but as she
got older and discovered the power of her natural
gifts, she stepped her game up.

Maggie was a renegade, selling sex to whoever
could afford to feed her for the night until she
hooked up with a pimp who taught her what the
game was really about. He gave Maggie a crash
course in Lost 101, forcing her to read dozens
of books on the subject and watching countless
porno movies. Every night before he put Maggie
on the streets he would quiz her on what she had
learned for the day. Sometimes he would even
make her perform on him, and if she couldn't make
him cum with her mouth or pussy in five minutes
or less, he would beat her. The art of making a
man blow his load quickly would come in very
handy for Maggie in the streets. It would not only
ensure that she could turn more tricks than the
other girls in the course of a night, but her skills

became so notorious that men started seeking her out. Everybody wanted a taste of Maggie's world-famous sex, and she made loads of money for her pimp.

Maggie's run with her pimp came to an end when he was arrested on a parole violation. He had only been given sixty days in county jail, but it was enough time for Maggie to rob him of everything he had, taking her show on the road. Maggie roamed from place to place, keeping time with unsavory men and numbing herself with drugs. Before she knew it, her looks were slipping and she had developed a drug habit. The young girls with less mileage on them began catching all the big-money tricks, and Maggie had to get in where she fit in, finding her sponsors where she could. She had been cursed to a miserable existence and would've probably taken her own life years ago if it hadn't been for the fact that she needed to be there for her sister. They were all each other had left, until Chucky came into the picture.

The knocking on the door continued. "You gonna get that or what?" Chucky repeated his initial question.

"What were you doing that's so important to where you couldn't get it?" Maggie asked with an attitude.

"I'm thinking, that's what I'm doing. Somebody has gotta be the brains of this operation
and you sure ain't in no condition to play the
role, with as high as you be all the time," Chucky
snapped.

"You got some nerve coming for me, like you
ain't got a never-ending oil burner. You do enough
to get you and three other muthafuckas high at
one time." Maggie rolled her neck.

Chucky threw his lighter at her, narrowly missing Maggie's head. "Bitch, don't worry about what
I'm doing. Worry about getting the fucking door!"

Maggie spared him one last roll of her eyes,
before uncoiling her long chocolate legs from the
couch, and oozing to her feet. The tight green
skirt she wore was hiked up, exposing her bare
black ass. On her left ass cheek was a tattoo of
a weed leaf. Maggie took slow steps toward the
door, making sure to throw some extra bounce
in her walk, sending a ripple across her ass. She
knew Chucky liked to see it move. Maggie had
been a dime piece back in her day, and still held
together well, but after a few months of running
with Chucky, she was starting to slip. Still, Maggie was a looker and a stone-cold freak. She did
things to Chucky that he'd be ashamed to admit
out loud and that was part of the reason he

fucked with her, that and she was blindly loyal to him.

Chucky took a brief hiatus from watching Maggie's ass, and addressed the small pile of cocaine on the table in front of him. He took a club flyer and gently scraped what was left of the coke into a line. It wasn't much, barely enough to get his wheels spinning properly, but it would have to do for the moment. Chucky didn't bother looking for a straw or rolling up a dollar, he just dragged his nose across the coffee table, snorting up coke, ashes, and whatever else littered the table. When the coke bobsledded through his nasal cavity, Chucky felt the urge to sneeze, but pinched his nostrils closed to hold it in. He needed everything to go straight to the head. Chucky released his nose and waited in anticipation of the medicine-like drip in the back of his throat, but it never came. It wasn't enough coke to do much more than boost his craving.

Frustrated, Chucky ran his hand over his head and began looking over the table to see if maybe there was some powder residue that might've gone overlooked. When his eyes caught his reflection in the glass tabletop, it gave him pause. His eyes were wide and webbed with red veins from lack of sleep, and if you looked close enough you could see the faint scabs around his nose from constant abuse. The boyish glow that had once been his calling card was now gone, and his skin was beginning to darken, making him look older. Looking at the monster staring back at him, Chucky couldn't help but to wonder how he could've let himself slip so far.

At one time, the streets had great expectations for Chucky. He was a young hustler on the fast track, and a respected lieutenant in one of the most notorious drug crews in the city. He had money, a fly car, and more women than he knew what to do with. In addition to the material things, he had status. Chucky was the right hand to Pharaoh's most trusted captain, Ramses. He was young, sharp, and on his way to being the next big thing in the game, until his ambitions and his demons proved to be his undoing. Ramses had been slow walking Chucky up the food chain, constantly dangling the carrot but never letting him taste it and Chucky got impatient. Though it was Pharaoh and Ramses who were the bosses of their organization, it was Chucky and his soldiers who solidified their positions. The old regime was on their way out, but not moving fast enough for Chucky so he set a plan in motion to speed things along.

Being the manipulative bastard he was, Chucky began gradually spreading the seeds of corruption throughout the soldiers who held the streets, swaying those who were loyal to his cause and making plans to get rid of those who weren't. To stage his coup, he enlisted his partner, Benny, who was another one of Ramses's trusted lieutenants and Chucky's best friend. Collectively, they ran the neighborhood for Ramses with Chucky being the enforcer and Benny was the money man. With their positions it was easy for Chucky to orchestrate a series of bogus robberies, hitting their drug spots. They would chip away a little at a time until they had enough to make the big play. For as long as they kept their capers random and focused on the smaller drug spots, they would be able to fly under the radar and neither Ramses or Pharaoh would wake up to it until it was too late. Things were going smooth, but two things happened: Benny got sloppy and Chucky got knocked.

One of the dudes Chucky had been selling coke to on the side turned out to be an undercover detective they called Lone Wolf. He had bought enough cocaine from Chucky over the course of a few weeks to hang a lifetime sentence on him, but instead of arresting Chucky, Wolf started extorting him. In exchange for Wolf letting him continue to do business, Chucky had to feed Wolf information. Chucky never told on anyone in his crew, but he did feed Wolf a few low-level cats around town. It wasn't until Wolf tried to get Chucky to set Pharaoh up that Chucky put his foot down. He was a lot of things, but he was no fool. If he pointed the finger at Pharaoh there would be no rock he could hide under where Pharoah's people couldn't find him. Chucky might as well have blown his own brains out instead of waiting around for someone else to do it. There was no way Chucky was going to give up Pharaoh, but he had to do something to get Wolf off his back and out of his life, so he played on his larcenous side. Wolf was a cop, but he was also a gambler and Chucky had heard through the grapevine that he had some serious debts. Chucky offered Wolf $100,000 to get out of his life. Just as he'd hoped, Wolf agreed to take a pay off but he wanted a quarter of a million dollars. That was the price for Chucky to purchase his life back. Wolf also made it very clear that if he didn't come up with the money that he was going to drop a bug in Pharaoh's ear about what Chucky had been doing in his spare time.

It was a lose-lose situation for Chucky. There was no way he could come up with the amount of money Wolf was demanding and he sure as hell wasn't going to give Pharaoh up, so he was fucked either way he played it. He thought about going to Ramses and laying out everything that had happened with the dirty cop, hoping his relationship with Ramses would at least get him the benefit of the doubt, but decided against it. He might be able to sway Ramses, but there was no way it would go over well with Pharoah. Even though Chucky had never given up any information on their organization, Pharaoh would have him killed just in case. He wasn't the type of man to take chances. Chucky figured his best bet was to just take whatever money they had made from looting Pharaoh's spots and blow town. He could take what he had and make a fresh start somewhere else, but Benny would make this easier said than done.

For as careful as Chucky had been in laying the plan, Benny was equally careless in ruining it. Benny got lazy and deviated from Chucky's original plan to keep their robberies random, and he hit the same spot twice. Doubling back sent up a red flag and put Ramses on alert, but it was Ramses's new recruits Omega and Li'l Monk who picked up on the trail of breadcrumbs that left a trail leading straight back to Benny.

From the time Chucky had first met the dirty little street rat who called himself Li'l Monk, he knew he was going to be trouble. He had already hated him for the role his father, Monk, was said to have played in the death of his oldest brother

Sonny, but that hate increased tenfold the day Ramses decided to offer him a job opportunity. The day it happened they came across Li'l Monk beating the blood out of one of Chucky's young workers over some offense. Chucky wanted to kill for personal reasons, but he tried to convince Ramses that Li'l Monk should die for putting his hands on one of their workers. Instead of Ramses feeding into what Chucky was saying, he ended up taking a liking to Li'l Monk. So much so that he offered him a job. Li'l Monk was paired with a young up-and-comer who had been a part of Chucky's crew and they were hired as muscle to hold the block down. The two kids were sharp and about their business, and fiercely loyal to Ramses. When Benny sent his people to rob the spot for the second time, Li'l Monk and Omega sent them back in bags. Omega had recognized one of the dead men from seeing him with Benny, and told this to Ramses. That was all it took to unravel Chucky's whole little scheme.

Chucky hadn't even realized that Pharaoh and Ramses were hip to their bullshit until the morning he walked into a recording studio and found Benny tied to a chair and being tortured. The moment Chucky laid eyes on Benny he knew that he was dead. Benny was a mess of bruises, blood, and fresh cuts. From the looks of things they had been putting him through it for hours and there was no telling what information they had pried out of Benny. There was no doubt in Chucky's mind that he would never leave that apartment. Shockingly, Benny had held it down and never confessed to Chucky's involvement, but Ramses was still suspicious. He knew Chucky and Benny were close, and the whole scheme had Chucky's stink on it, but he needed proof of Chucky's guilt or innocence in the plot, so he put Chucky to the ultimate test of loyalty.

The feeling of utter nausea that hit Chucky when Ramses ordered him to kill his best friend was one that would stick with Chucky until the end of his days on earth. It was feeling like you had to vomit, shit, and pee all at once. Chucky was left with a hard decision: murder Benny and walk away or die with him. He looked into Benny's tearful eyes and thought about days when they had to eat at each other's houses when their families didn't have enough food. Benny was his partner, his brother, but he was also careless and had put both of their lives at risk. Chucky pointed the gun, which was trembling in his hand, at Benny, and for a split second he considered it, but couldn't bring himself to do it. Chucky was a snake, but he wasn't a coward, so he turned the gun on Ramses's men and pulled the trigger.

To the surprise of everyone in the room besides Ramses and Huck, it clicked empty. The
gun wasn't even loaded. It had all been a setup
by Ramses. If Chucky had been willing to kill his
best friend it would've proved that he was trying
to bury a secret and hide his involvement, but the
fact that he was willing to ride out for his friend
showed Ramses that his heart was still in the
right place. It was indeed Ramses's ultimate test
of loyalty, and Chucky had almost failed. Chucky
was allowed to keep his life, but he still received
a beat down from Ramses's friend Boo for pulling a gun on them. He got off light considering
what fate awaited Benny.

The last time Chucky had seen Benny it was
in that apartment, still tied to the chair and professing how happy he was that his partner hadn't
turned on him. If he only knew how close Chucky
had been to going the other way with it. Ramses
promised to release Benny and exile him instead
of killing him, but Chucky knew that was a lie.
Chucky wanted to stay behind and advocate further for Benny's life, but there was nothing he
could do, short of putting himself back in harm's
way and dying with him. He couldn't do anything to save Benny's life, but Chucky promised
on his friend's soul that it wouldn't be in vain.
Everyone who had a hand in his friend's death,

and Chucky's humiliation that day, would be held accountable, including Ramses and his minions.

From there things went downhill for Chucky. He was falling out of favor with Ramses, Wolf was still on his back and everything he had stashed from the robberies was returned to the rightful owners. The pressure of everything going on, coupled with Benny's death, pushed Chucky further into his already festering madness and he began relying more heavily on drugs to cope. Ramses never really trusted Chucky after that and began feeding him with a long-handled spoon. Responsibilities that were once delegated to Chucky and Benny were now falling to Li'l Monk and Omega. While the two youngsters were on the come up, Chucky was on his way down the ladder. The pressure was coming from all sides and Chucky knew his days were numbered. It would only be a matter of time before Ramses discovered his involvement in the robberies or Wolf gave him up to Pharaoh. Either way he was fucked with a capital F and needed to bust a move, so he did what any rat on a sinking ship would do: he jumped off.

Chucky had outgrown New York and it was time to head for greener pastures, but not before tying up some loose ends, one of which being Ramses's friend Boo. Chucky had vowed to repay

Boo for putting his hands on him and the part
he played in Benny's murder and embarrassing
him in the apartment that day. He made good
on that promise when he caught Boo slipping
one early morning and blew his brains out. Boo's
death would surely hurt Ramses, as Chucky had
intended it to, and for the final "fuck you" he
robbed one last drug spot, taking enough money
and product to hold him over until he figured out
his next move. By the time Ramses, Pharaoh, or
Wolf realized Chucky had crossed he would've
been long gone, but thanks to that bitch Karen
things had gotten complicated.

Chucky knew that betraying Ramses would've
gotten him killed, but murdering Boo ensured
that he would die very, very slowly, which was
why he had been extra cautious when he did the
deed or so he thought. His shady dealings had
shortened his list of friends so he enlisted a hood
rat named Karen to aid him.

Chucky had been fucking Karen since she was
a young girl and had taught her damn near everything she knew about the hustle. In a sick way
it was almost like he had raised her. Karen was
a rider, and had helped Chucky clean up more
than a few messes. She had gotten rid of a dozen
murder weapons for Chucky so it seemed only
natural that he went to her with the gun he had

used to kill Boo. Chucky had never worried about Karen betraying him. For as long as Chucky kept feeding her dick and dropping the occasional monetary gift on her, she treated him like he walked on water. This all changed when Karen found out Chucky was now seeing her friend Persia.

Persia and Karen had been friends and rivals since they were kids, so when she found out about her and Chucky it crushed her. Had Chucky been a smart man, he'd have done whatever it took to smooth things over with Karen, but he let his ego get in the way. When Karen confronted him and Persia, Chucky played her to the left like a common chickenhead. He was trying to impress Persia, but all he succeeded in doing was infuriating Karen. In the ultimate act of revenge, Karen turned the murder weapon that had killed Boo over to Ramses and officially marked Chucky for death.

Chucky had barely made it out of the city with his life when Ramses's death squad came to his aunt's house looking for him. The hit men slaughtered everyone in the house, and they would've gotten Chucky too had he not been out tying up some loose ends in the city. His one regret was leaving Persia for dead in the house. He had such big plans for her, but when it came down to a choice between her life and his, she got the short end of the stick. To that day he wasn't sure how she made it out of the house alive, but he would make it a point to ask the next time their paths crossed, which would be sooner rather than later. He had been trying to reach Persia since his arrival back in the city, but it was proving easier said than done, which frustrated him to no end.

It was hard to say who ranked highest on his shit list, but Karen was definitely up there near the top. She had seriously jammed him up with her triple cross and he would've killed her had she not disappeared. She was trifling, but she was no dummy. She got out of dodge after pointing the finger at Chucky, hoping that Ramses would kill him before he found her. Fortunately for him, her hopes had been dashed and Chucky escaped execution. Though the smart thing for him to do would've been to put as much distance between himself and the Big Apple, Chucky couldn't just yet. There were more scores to settle and these were of a more personal nature. So instead of leaving New York for good, Chucky bounced from place to place around the tri-state area, plotting and waiting for the right moment to slip back in town and tie up all his loose ends. Now, months later, his time was almost at hand.

"Earth to Chucky." Maggie snapped her fingers in front of his face, bringing him out of his daze.

Chucky blinked as if he was just awaking from a dream. He hadn't even realized that the whole time he had been hunkered over the table staring at his own reflection for the last few minutes. "What?" he snapped.

"See, you wanna be all nasty and shit and all I was trying to look out for was your thirsty-ass. Rissa is back and she scored. She's in the kitchen," Maggie told him.

"About time." Chucky got up and brushed passed Maggie on his way to the kitchen.

"Ungrateful-ass nigga. I shouldn't have told you a damn thing and hogged it all up like you did the last of our stash," Maggie called after him.

Chucky heard her voice, but he was deaf to everything Maggie was saying. The only thing he was concerned about was getting to the kitchen to get first dibs.

When Chucky rounded the corner into the kitchen, he was greeted by a round butt in a pair of tight jeans poking out of the refrigerator. He could hear the clinking of glasses as she rummaged around for whatever she was looking for. Chucky spared a glance over his shoulder to make sure Maggie wasn't behind him before creeping up behind Rissa. He grabbed her by her hips and pumped himself against her ass twice, startling her and causing Rissa to bump her head on the freezer door when she jumped up.

"Damn, why you play so much?" Rissa punched Chucky in the chest with her thin fists. She checked the back of her head to make sure she didn't have a knot. Rissa was a cute girl, with brown skin and a pretty smile. She was on the thick side, but she carried it well, mostly in her hips, ass, and breasts.

"You know I like it when I give it to you from the back." Chucky moved in and invaded her space. He hadn't brushed his teeth yet, so he knew his mouth smelled like cigarettes and warm beer, but he didn't care. Neither did Rissa. Though she tried to act like she wasn't, she was fully in Chucky's thrall just like her sister.

"Chucky, stop playing before Maggie comes in here and tries to kill both of us." Rissa pushed him away.

Rissa was Maggie's younger sister and Chucky's secret lover. Chucky had actually first met Rissa when he left New York and found himself in Pennsylvania. He had a light piece of business to handle down there. Rissa was a rough girl who hailed from the north side of Philly who Chucky had come across when he was trying to establish a cocaine connect in the city. Rissa was hustling dimes and twenties in Germantown before Chucky came into her life. She was young and street just how he liked them so Chucky immediately tried to charm her, but Rissa was into girls and wouldn't be swayed so easily.

It took awhile before Chucky was really able to work his way into her circle of trust. Whenever Chucky came through to buy coke he always made sure to spend at least a couple of hundred dollars with Rissa. It got to the point where Rissa began to look forward to Chucky coming through because those were some of her best days. Eventually Rissa felt comfortable enough with Chucky that she had him with her one day when the dude she was selling drugs for came through to drop off a package. That turned out to be a mistake for Rissa and it would alter the course of her life and career as a drug dealer.

Rissa's supplier was a corny-ass dude from somewhere in Virginia who tried to reinvent himself as something he wasn't when he relocated to Philadelphia. Chucky was able to see right through his façade and immediately started making plans to get him. Maggie was the dude's girl. Chucky took one look at her and knew they were both cut from the same cloth; they were both addicts. Maggie was from the fast track, much too fast for the Virginian, and was just living in the moment. Chucky started fucking Maggie behind the Virginian's back. Within two weeks of getting Maggie on his team, he had convinced her to help him rob the Virginian and was heading to New York, dragging Rissa along for the ride.

Once in New York Chucky changed the rules of the game. Instead of the palace in the sky he'd promised, he had Maggie back on the track selling ass and Rissa in the streets getting it however she could. When he finally got tired of fucking just Maggie, he resumed his pursuit of Rissa's goodies. She was still resistant, but not as much as she had been before being snatched from the only home she'd ever known, and relocating to a foreign city. She was homesick and vulnerable and Chucky used it to his advantage. He had to damn near rape Rissa to get the pussy the first time, but after laying his pipe game down Rissa was with the program. Chucky made sure to keep it a secret since Maggie was currently the breadwinner. He was a marked man in the city and had to be careful where he showed his face, so his movements were limited. Everybody in the house had one hustle or another, but they depended heavily on the money Maggie made from selling pussy to keep them afloat. Maggie finding out that Chucky was fucking her and her baby sister too wouldn't go over well. Maggie had her suspicions about them, but could never prove it and until she could, they could keep sponging off her whore money.

"What you got for me?" Chucky asked, finally ready to get down to business.

Rissa reached down into her bra and pulled out a cigarette box. "It ain't much." She shook it. "But it should do the trick." Rissa was extending the box to Chucky, but Maggie swooped in like a Pro Bowl defensive back and intercepted it. "Thirsty bitch!" Rissa spat.

"Ya mama's a thirsty bitch," Maggie replied, while checking the contents of the cigarette box.

"My mama is your mama, smart-ass," Rissa shot back.

"Whatever." Maggie shook the contents of the box onto the table. Out spilled a small Baggie, containing several grams of cocaine. Maggie frowned in disappointment. "Damn, Rissa, you didn't get no hard?"

"I got what I could get and you should be thankful for that," Rissa told her. "It's hot as a firecracker on the streets, with police on damn near every corner. I don't know how niggas from New York get money on these blocks."

"Because we're born and bred to do it." Chucky snatched the Baggie off the table, and held it up to examine it.

"Let me put some water on so I can cook up," Maggie said, rummaging through the dishes in the sink to find a pot she could fill with boiling water.

"Maggie, you must've lost your mind if you think I'm gonna suck on that glass dick with you. I snort, not smoke and since I went out and got it, it should be my choice," Rissa said.

Maggie snorted. "Bitch, a junkie, is a junkie, is a junkie. It's all cocaine, so no matter how it gets to your brain, you're still a hype. Now come on down from your soapbox so we can get high."

"Stall baby sis out. You know that ain't really her bag. We'll do it her way," Chucky said in a cool voice. He knew Rissa primarily smoked weed and drank, but since she had been riding with Chucky and her sister, she was known to take an occasional bump here and there. The more time she spent around them, the more frequent her bumps came. Chucky was slowly dragging her down the devil's road, but he didn't want to make it seem forced. It had to be of her own volition.

"You awful defensive of her lately, Chucky. Something either of you wanna tell me?" Maggie asked, looking back and forth between them. Rissa couldn't hold her gaze, but Chucky's face was unreadable as usual.

"You gonna start with this shit again?" Chucky asked with an attitude.

"All I'm saying is that every time me and Rissa get into it, you jump on her side," Maggie accused.

"Maybe it only seems that way because you're always on her about dumb shit," Chucky suggested. "Maggie, when you're high you get on some paranoid shit and think I'm fucking every bitch I come in contact with." He sat down at the kitchen table and began shaking the coke out onto a glass plate that they kept in the kitchen for such occasions.

"Not every bitch, just the young and naïve ones," Maggie corrected him.

Chucky knew she was baiting him, but he didn't bite. "Whatever you say, Maggie. I'm about to get high." He began chopping the coke into lines with a razor. The sound of the blade hitting the plate was like a chow bell, as all grievances were temporarily forgotten and both of the women took seats around Chucky, waiting for him to divide up the spoils. He scraped a little over half the cocaine to one side and scooped the remainder onto the back of a magazine, which he extended to Maggie. "You can cook that and we'll fuck with the soft."

A smile spread across Maggie's face. "You ain't such a bastard after all." She flashed him a cigarette-stained smile, before taking the coke and heading over to the stove.

"Fiend-ass broad," Rissa mumbled under her breath.

Chucky leaned in and whispered through clenched teeth. "Why don't you be cool and stop trying to rock the damn boat?"

Rissa chuckled. "Boat? This is more like a sinking ship." Her voice was sharp, but low enough to where Maggie didn't overhear. "On some real shit, Chucky, I didn't come to New York to live like a damn vagabond. You said we were only gonna pass through New York for a minute while you handled your business, but we've been here long enough to need this shithole apartment. I want that trip to Florida and the good life that you promised when I helped you and my sister rip homeboy off in Philly."

"And you're gonna have it, but not before I say so!" Chucky hissed back. "My word is as good as gold, baby sis. Once I handle what I came here to do, we can skate, but until then, stop complaining and stick to the script."

Rissa sucked her teeth. "Okay, Mr. Script. So what's next?"

"We're gonna take a road trip, but first I gotta make a quick stop." Chucky smiled sinisterly.

# PART II

## *GOON RULES*

# CHAPTER 7

Li'l Monk sat on a crate in front of his building, enjoying the warm breeze. It had rained earlier that day, making the air humid and muggy so the breeze was welcomed. Sitting on his lap was a turkey and Swiss sandwich, made especially how he liked: extra mayo, salt, vinegar, onions, and tomatoes. He even had the guy in the store throw the onions and turkey on the grill while making it, adding heat to the sandwich. Li'l Monk took slow, deliberate bites as it was his first meal of the day and he wanted to savor it.

While eating his sandwich, Li'l Monk busied himself watching the world go by. An older lady from the neighborhood was walking down the street, pushing her cart of groceries; she waved and smiled at Li'l Monk. He couldn't recall her name and she had never spoken to him until a few weeks back when he had paid her a kindness. Li'l Monk would always see her struggling back and forth to the supermarket with a push cart that was missing a wheel. One day Li'l Monk had taken it upon himself to buy her a new cart, but instead of giving it to her himself he left it with the supermarket manager to present to her the next time she came in. From the day she received the cart, she would speak to Li'l Monk every time he saw her.

Li'l Monk was always doing things like that in the neighborhood, like when he threw a "back to school" block party for the kids in the neighborhood and had barbers on deck giving the little boys haircuts. Or when people in the neighborhood were blowing out their tires because of all the potholes on the block. The city wasn't in a rush to fix them so Li'l Monk took matters into his own hands. He bought all the supplies and hired a team of crackheads to fill in the potholes. They did a shitty job, but it was the fact that Li'l Monk had even made the attempt that stood out to the people in the neighborhood. Li'l Monk was a criminal, but he was also a man of the people and they loved him for it. People who had once feared and talked about Li'l Monk as if he were some kind of monster now respected him and praised him for the work he did in the neighborhood. There were some who thought that Li'l Monk did the things he did in search of praise, but he did it out of the goodness of his heart.

Li'l Monk was from the mud, so he understood better than most what it was like to go without.

Li'l Monk came up hard, being the kid of one of the most coldblooded killers to ever touch a Harlem street, and a murdered mother. His father, Monk, was both strung out and street poisoned so his son inherited the consequences of that combination. For the most part Li'l Monk was left to fend for himself and make his way in the world as best he could. Big Monk did as best he could with his young son, but because he was out and about in the world living like a savage, the art of survival at all costs was the only thing he could teach his son.

Li'l Monk was an unkempt kid because he didn't have anyone to teach him about personal hygiene or how to wash his clothes. The kids would often tease him, which led to Li'l Monk getting in a fight almost every other day. He had spent many hungry nights in his and his father's apartment. It got so bad sometimes that he would go and steal from the local market. Because he always got away with it, Li'l Monk considered himself a competent thief, but what he didn't know was that the store owner intentionally let him get away with his goods. He knew Li'l Monk's background and figured he would rather let him steal from his store than to have the little boy get caught up in the legacy his father was creating for him. For the most part Li'l Monk was an outcast and a loner. Only a select few kids in the neighborhood would ignore his rank smell and still play with him when he was outside, Persia and Charlie mainly. This made Li'l Monk fiercely protective of them, especially Persia. He had always had a thing for her, but Persia never seemed to pick up on it. Even when they were older, she always seemed to look through him. Li'l Monk held on to hope that one day she would really see him the way he saw her, but the day never came.

Li'l Monk tipped the cold twenty-two ounce Old English to his lips and took long gulps to wash the sandwich down. Omega would've clowned Li'l Monk for drinking the malt beer. He felt that now that Li'l Monk was making a few coins, he should upgrade from the cheap beer to something less harsh. Li'l Monk argued that it had been good enough for him during hard times; it'd be good enough for him during the good times. He wouldn't be switching to Cristal anytime soon.

Li'l Monk and Omega were the best of friends, but were like night and day and it really started to show once they'd started getting a little money. When they went to purchase their first cars,

Omega bought a 2004 BMW, and Li'l Monk bought a 1988 Pontiac Bonneville. When they went jewelry shopping, Li'l Monk bought a modest Cuban link with a gold cross on it, but Omega copped a thick rope chain with a medallion almost the size of his fist. Omega was flashy, and loved to be seen, but Li'l Monk was more reserved, preferring to play the background. They were definitely an odd pair, but their differences balanced out their relationship.

Li'l Monk was about to take another swig of his beer, when he spotted Tasha and Sophie coming across the street. Tasha, as usual, was wearing an outfit that left little to the imagination, a skirt so short you could almost see her ass cheeks, and a shirt that was at least two sizes too small. She strode down the block like she owned it, waving to people she knew on the street and shouting a greeting up to an old woman who was sitting in her window. Everybody in the hood knew Tasha for one reason or another. Tasha was only seventeen, but already quite worldly, for lack of a better word.

Sophie was a different story. She was a cute, light-skinned chick with big doe eyes and a smile you couldn't help but fall in love with when you saw it. Sophie was tall and big boned, but she carried it well, mostly in her hips and breasts.

She was thick, the kind of thick that made something as simple as the tight blue jeans she was wearing look provocative. Sophie was a hood chick, and could get a bit loud at times, but she knew how to turn the hood side of her off and on as necessary. She was cool with a lot of guys from the neighborhood, but hardly any of them could say they'd been with her. Sophie was no virgin, but she wasn't a whore either.

As the two girls approached, Li'l Monk slid the beer behind the crate and stood up to greet them. "Hey, Tash," he greeted her with a nod.

"You speak to her before you speak to your girl?" Sophie said with a fake attitude.

"Only because I had a special greeting waiting on you." Li'l Monk wrapped his arms around Sophie and spun her around. Sophie wasn't a small woman, but she felt petite and fragile, wrapped in Li'l Monk's bulging arms. "I missed you, boo." He kissed her on the cheek.

Sophie frowned. "Oh, we kiss on cheeks now? Let me find out you don't want to kiss me in public because you out here fronting for these hood rats."

"Baby, you know I only got eyes for you," Li'l Monk said sincerely.

"Then act like it and show your lady some proper love." Sophie grabbed Li'l Monk by his squared jaw and planted a kiss on his lips. It was deep and passionate. A few seconds into the kiss, she pulled away and gave him a funny look. "You think your ass is slick, don't you?" She ran her tongue along the roof of her mouth, tasting the alcohol. "Li'l Monk, I know you ain't out here drinking this damn early. Jesus, the sun isn't even down yet!" she scolded.

"It ain't nothing but a beer." Li'l Monk retrieved the bottle from its hiding place and showed it to Sophie.

"Ew, rotgut." Tasha frowned.

Li'l Monk sucked his teeth. "Shut up, Tasha. You don't know shit about rotgut. You ain't even old enough to drink."

"Neither are you, but it doesn't stop you from doing it." Tasha rolled her neck.

Li'l Monk waved her off. "I don't know why everybody is feeling some type of way about what I drink."

"I don't have a problem with what you're drinking, Li'l Monk. I have a problem with where and when you've decided to drink," Sophie told him. "I know you're on the clock, so you've probably got a gun on you somewhere. What if the police roll up on you to harass you about the beer, but find the gun? You'll have turned a simple desk appearance ticket into a felony, just that quick. I'm not riding you about the booze. I just want you to make smarter choices when you're out here on the front lines."

As usual, Sophie was right. She was good at being his voice of reason. Sophie and Li'l Monk had been best friends long before they became lovers. They'd grown up in the same neighborhood, under similar conditions. Their turbulent home lives often drove them into the streets together. The two damaged kids often found in each other what they couldn't get from their parents: comfort. Li'l Monk was able to confide in Sophie about anything and vice versa. Knowing each other so intimately, it seemed only natural that they became boyfriend and girlfriend, but it didn't start out like that. Sophie had always liked Li'l Monk and he had feelings for her too, but his heart was elsewhere at the time. He and Sophie hung out, went to the movies, and did everything couples did, but neither of them would accept the title of a couple. Li'l Monk and Sophie had even lost their virginities. It was a night that they had both tried to put behind them, but also one that neither of them would ever forget.

It had been one of those nights when Big Monk was on a drug trip and felt like using Li'l Monk as a punching bag. He had beaten him something terrible, and Li'l Monk ran away. He didn't have any money or a destination so he went to Sophie's. She lived in a first-floor apartment in the projects, so it was easy to sneak him in through the window.

Sophie tended his wounds with peroxide and bandaged him up with paper towels and tape because they didn't have a real first-aid kit. After patching Li'l Monk up, he and Sophie lay in her small twin-sized bed watching *Poetic Justice* and drinking cheap wine that Sophie had stolen from her mother's stash. Sophie remembered being chilly, so Li'l Monk wrapped his arms around her for warmth. She felt as safe as a child in the womb, snuggled in his embrace. Sophie could lay in Li'l Monk's arms forever. It felt good, natural.

She could feel his manhood stiffening, and poking her in the back. Embarrassed, Li'l Monk tried to scoot back, but Sophie held his arms so that he couldn't. She was teasing him, like they often did to each other. Li'l Monk and Sophie had done some flirting, and shared an occasional kiss, but always stopped before they crossed the line. She stiffened when she felt him plant a gentle kiss on the back of her neck. It sent an electric current through her entire body. She turned so that they were facing each other. Li'l Monk's eyes stared at her lovingly, as if he was feeling the same thing she was feeling at the moment.

Sophie leaned in and kissed Li'l Monk, expecting him to try to pull away, but he didn't. He kissed her back. Neither of them was quite sure how it happened, but they ended up naked under one of her thin sheets.

*Sophie's hands explored Li'l Monk's body, starting with his chest, running her fingers over the thick layer of hair covering him. Mischievously, she moved her hand lower and gripped his manhood. Li'l Monk tensed as she stroked him ever so gently, getting his dick rock hard. Sophie couldn't help but to admire his size and thickness. She rubbed the head of his dick across her vagina and let her mind drift to visions of him buried deep inside her.*

*Li'l Monk felt the head of his dick slip inside Sophie and almost jumped out of his skin. He held her at arm's length. "I don't think we should do this, Sophie. I know you ain't never been with nobody, and you should save yourself for the man you love."*

*"I have." Sophie pulled him closer and kissed him. This time when she guided his manhood toward her love box, he didn't resist. She grunted when the head crossed the threshold. Li'l Monk was very well hung, and it felt like he was tearing her open the deeper he went.*

*When Li'l Monk noticed the tears on Sophie's cheek, he paused. "Am I hurting you? Should I stop?"*

*Sophie wanted to cry out and tell him to stop, but she had been waiting for that moment for so long that she dared not, and motioned for him to continue.*

*Their first bout was awkward and somewhat unpleasant, but not as bad as she thought it would be. Li'l Monk was so brutish that she expected him to tear into her like a savage, but he was surprisingly gentle. He was mindful not to put all his weight on her, and took his time with his strokes, careful not to hurt her. She knew he was about to cum from the ugly face he was making. A small animal-like sound escaped him as his seed filled her and spilled out onto the bed sheet. Li'l Monk looked embarrassed that he had been unable to control himself and that was the moment Sophie realized it was his first time too. Sophie and Li'l Monk had sex twice more that night. Each time was a bit better than the last. The following morning, they went back to their regular lives and playing the role of best friends. Though they tried to act as if it hadn't happened, they both knew that it did.*

After the night they shared, they both expected it to cause some type of awkwardness, but it actually brought them closer together. They still hadn't crossed the line of becoming an actual couple, but it pushed them into the "friends with benefits" zone. Li'l Monk continued to chase something that he couldn't have, while Sophie watched from a distance, suffering in silence. She had tried to move on with her life by having other boyfriends, but always found a reason to break up with them. She was lovesick and only Li'l Monk could cure what ailed her. Eventually Li'l Monk came around, and with great hesitation she let him into her heart. Li'l Monk and Sophie's romance blossomed into something magical, which drew adoration and hate from others.

None of the girls in the neighborhood would give Li'l Monk a second look when he was broke and dusty, but now that he had status it seemed like every time Sophie turned around she had to chase away some skank who was trying to invade his space. A time or two, Sophie even found herself having to lay hands on chicks over Li'l Monk. She had worked long and hard to land her childhood crush, and she had no problems making a women bleed for trying to take what belonged to her.

"You're right, ma." Li'l Monk took one last swig of the beer before pouring the rest out on the curb and placing the bottle down on the side of the crate he had been sitting on.

"Damn, my girl got you pouring your beer out? You must be sprung on her goodies," Tasha teased Li'l Monk.

"Ain't nobody sprung on nothing," Li'l Monk disputed. Times like that he was glad he was dark skinned so that they couldn't tell that he was blushing. "So, where are y'all just coming from?" He changed the subject.

"Had to do a little shopping," Sophie told him.

Li'l Monk looked at her empty hands. "How you shopping and I don't see no bags in your hands?" he asked suspiciously.

"Because I dropped the stuff off at home already," she told him.

"Umm hmm, probably because you didn't want me to see how you fucked up the money I gave you," Li'l Monk said, half jokingly.

Sophie sucked her teeth. "There you go on your bullshit. If you must know, I bought the books I needed for school, not clothes. Furthermore, for as much as I appreciate what you give me, I do have a job, remember?"

"How can I forget when you're always throwing it up in my face?" Li'l Monk asked.

"I don't throw it in your face. I just like to make sure that you don't lose sight of the fact that I ain't no slouch. I'm more than willing to go out and get it instead of waiting around for it to be given. Besides, I'm proud of the fact that I have a job."

"Even if it's just a little supermarket gig," Tasha said slickly.

"Tasha, fuck you with your hating-ass. At least I got a job that don't require me to get checked for STDs every thirty days," Sophie shot back.

"Sophie, you know you don't have to keep working at that supermarket. I can take care of you while you're chasing that college degree," Li'l Monk told her. Nobody had been happier than him when Sophie graduated high school that summer. Li'l Monk suggested that she take some time off to enjoy being out of school for a while, but Sophie wanted to immediately continue her education.

"I know you will, baby." Sophie kissed him on the cheek. "And because I know you're willing is why I don't mind working."

Tasha let out a deep sigh. "It must be nice to have somebody. One day my prince will come along and sweep me off my feet."

"Yup, and deposit you right on your back where you belong," Sophie joked.

"Whatever." Tasha rolled her eyes. "Sophie, if you were really my friend you'd have Li'l Monk talk to Omega and get him to act right."

Li'l Monk blinked. "Nope, I ain't getting in that. Whatever you and O got going is between y'all. I don't do domestics."

"What I can't understand is, why is it that you were able to settle down with Sophie, but Omega is acting like he's allergic to commitment?" Tasha asked.

Li'l Monk wanted to be truthful with her and tell her that Omega had called her pussy overly friendly, but he didn't want to hurt her feelings so he simply shrugged and said, "Wild hearts can't be tamed."

"I hear that hot shit," Tasha said, clearly not happy with Li'l Monk's response. "Omega is gonna keep thinking I'm some little chickenhead bitch he can keep running game on and I'm gonna have to show him what game really is. He talks all that shit about not being comfortable with commitment, but he's comfortable shooting the club up."

"Doing what?" Li'l Monk didn't understand what she meant.

"Shooting the club up. Cuming inside me when we have sex," Tasha explained.

"Wait, you and Omega don't use condoms when y'all have sex?" Sophie asked in total surprise. Tasha was her best friend, but she was also loose and so was Omega. They both had multiple partners and having unprotected sex wasn't exactly the smartest move on either of their parts.

"Yeah, he said condoms take away from the feeling so we don't use them," Tasha revealed. "He say my walls sweet as sugar."

"Your walls are gonna be hot like fire if you don't start taking the proper precautions," Sophie warned her.

"Girl, please, Omega ain't got nothing. I can tell he's healthy by looking at him," Tasha said, not realizing how much of a naïve little girl she sounded like. "I ain't worried about Omega giving me nothing, but he might wanna be worried about me giving him something if he keeps trying to play hard to get. Accidents do happen, feel me?" She rubbed her stomach suggestively. She meant it as a joke, but Li'l Monk wasn't laughing.

"Tash, I fucks with you on the strength of you my girl's best friend, but don't ever let me hear you talking about trying to do no greasy shit to my man," Li'l Monk said seriously.

"Li'l Monk, you know I wouldn't really try to hang no baby on Omega just to keep him. I was only kidding." Tasha tried to clean it up.

"Don't even joke like that, Tasha, because it ain't funny. If Omega had heard you say it, he'd have probably kicked your ass," Li'l Monk told her.

Tasha sucked her teeth. "Ain't nobody scared of Omega."

"Well you should be, Tasha. Don't take that party-boy image he gives off as him being a sucka. Omega isn't someone you want to play those kinds of games with."

"It's cool, baby. Tasha didn't mean anything by it." Sophie draped her arms around him and began planting soft kisses on his face and lips. Gradually she could feel the tension drain from him.

Li'l Monk was enjoying Sophie rubbing his broad back and whispering in his ear about what she had planned for him that evening when he spotted his father on the corner and found his mood suddenly soured. Normally, he would've avoided his father or hoped he didn't see him, but from the looks of things, Monk was about to make a mess that Li'l Monk would no doubt have to clean up.

"I'll be right back." Li'l Monk excused himself from the girls and headed toward his father and the brewing disturbance.

"Shorty, I don't know what you thought but I ain't used to no young snots talking to me sideways. You taking this job too serious and if I were you, I'd tone it down a taste," Li'l Monk heard his father telling the young man he was exchanging words with when he walked up. As usual, Monk was dressed in all black: black jeans, black hoodie, and a black jacket. It was hardly cold enough to have on a hoodie and a jacket, so Li'l Monk already knew what time it was with his father.

The young man Monk was arguing with glared at Monk defiantly. The hockey jersey he was wearing nearly swallowed his small frame, and his jeans were a size too big. He was a small dude, with light skin and puffy cheeks and dark circles under his eyes. People would often tease him saying that he looked like the cartoon character Droopy Dog. "I hear you talking, but that ain't gonna change nothing. Take a walk, old head, before one of the big homies comes and runs you off the block," he spat, adjusting the crotch of his oversized jeans.

Monk's eyes narrowed to slits. "I see you one of them little fuckers who gotta get burned before they realize that the stove is hot, huh?" His hand dropped to his side and eased into the pocket of his hoodie. Before the hand could reappear, Li'l Monk was standing between Monk and the young man.

"What's going on here?" Li'l Monk looked from the young man to Monk.

"Not too much, just about to get acquainted with my new little friend here," Monk said slyly.

Li'l Monk ignored his father and turned to the young man. "Is there a problem, Droopy?"

"Nah, I ain't the one with the problem, he is. I been telling muthafuckas all day that we ain't taking no short, and he is short. Best come back when your money is correct, old timer."

Monk laughed. "I swear, you young boys get bolder and stupider by the day. How about instead of me coming with straight money, I take all your shit and don't give you a dime?"

Droopy produced a box cutter from his pocket, and banged it against his leg to expel the blade. "Crackhead-ass nigga, you put your hands on me and I'm gonna open you the fuck up!"

"Put that away, Droopy, and watch your fucking mouth," Li'l Monk told him. "Now give him what he needs."

"But Omega said—"

"I don't give a fuck what Omega said, I'm telling you to hit him off," Li'l Monk said, this time in a sterner tone.

Droopy mumbled something slick under his breath, while fishing around in his underwear for his stash. He produced two small vials of crack and grudgingly handed them to Monk.

"See, now was that so hard?" Monk taunted him. Droopy didn't reply; he just glared at Monk like he was thinking about doing something. "Whenever you're ready, you know where to find me." Monk read his face.

"Don't antagonize him," Li'l Monk told his father. "Droopy, go wait for me over there." He motioned toward the corner. "After I finish here, I need to holla at you real quick."

"A'ight," Droopy said and diddy bopped toward the corner. His baggy jeans hung so far off his ass, it was a wonder that he could walk without them falling down.

"Y'all putting them on these corners younger and younger," Monk said after Droopy was out of earshot.

"I didn't put Droopy out here," Li'l Monk replied.

"You know I was about to teach that boy a lesson in manners, don't you?" Monk pulled his hand partially from the pocket of his hoodie and showed his son the handle of the gun he was holding. He could've splattered Droopy if the mood struck him to do so and the boy never saw it coming.

"I know you could've and I appreciate you being the bigger person about it," Li'l Monk told him.

"Being the bigger person didn't have shit to do with it. I spotted them," Monk nodded across the street to where a police cruiser was coming out of the McDonald's drive-through. "Next time one of these little bitches you got working under you get lippy, I'm gonna blow their muthafucking faces off."

Li'l Monk knew without a doubt that his father was serious about what he was saying. He had fallen off, but was still a man of respect. Back in the days Big Monk had been the man on the streets, he and Persia's father, Face, were getting major money in Harlem. The hood loved Face, but they were terrified of Monk. He was a cold young man who was quick to violence and had little respect for human life. Things started going downhill for Monk when Face went to prison, and he was barely able to hold on to the empire they had built. Between his love of cocaine and pussy, he just never seemed to get it right. The tipping point in his fall was when he lost the love of his life, Li'l Monk's mother, Charlene. She had been killed in a botched robbery attempt. When she died, she took a piece of Monk with her and he was never the same. To compensate for her love, he turned to drugs to comfort him. Now the once respected hustler was little more than a creature of the night, skulking in the shadows for his next hit and his next victim. Monk was like a vampire, bleeding the streets for what he needed. Even as a crackhead Big Monk was still a feared man. Cats on the streets knew that when you saw him coming, you either gave him what you had or he'd give you what he had, which would likely be bullets.

"What you doing outside before sundown?" Li'l Monk asked his father.

"Trying to get off, E. It was a slow night so I didn't have nothing to wake up on, which is why I was out here asking your little pit bull to do me a solid." Monk nodded to Droopy who was on the corner still grilling him.

"Well the next time you need something, come to me. Don't be out here pressing my workers about no drugs," Li'l Monk said.

"Boy, you know I don't be out here looking for no handouts. I take what I want, like a real nigga," Monk capped.

"I know, you like the Robin Hood of the slums, only you take from the rich and keep all the shit for yourself," Li'l Monk said sarcastically.

"Watch your mouth, li'l nigga. You ain't too big for me to still put these mitts on you." Monk held up his large, callused hands. They bore the many scars of his wars over the years. He had lost a considerable amount of weight since he had been in the streets, but he still had some of the most intimidating-looking hands Li'l Monk had ever seen.

"Whatever, Dad. Just don't be all up on my people like that. It's not a good look," Li'l Monk said.

Monk smiled, showing off his yellowing teeth. "What, you embarrassed to have your new little friends find out your daddy is a fiend?"

Li'l Monk twisted his lips disbelievingly. "You know it ain't even like that with me. What you do is your business. I might not agree with it, but you're still my father."

"Damn right! I'm your daddy and the only blood you got left out here, and don't you go forgetting it," Monk told him.

"Hey, Mr. Monk!" Sophie called from down the street.

"Hey, baby girl." Monk waved. Sophie was one of the few people Li'l Monk kept time with who he actually liked. She was a good girl and good for his son. "You know better than to have your lady out here while you doing business," he told his son.

"She ain't gonna be out here at all. She just slid through for a minute," Li'l Monk told him.

"You be mindful that you don't have her out here like that. When your enemy knows what you love, that'll be the first thing they try to use against you," Monk said passionately.

One look at the moisture dancing in the corners of his father's eyes and Li'l Monk knew where his thoughts were. Rumor had it that the men who had killed his mother had actually come looking for Monk's stash. Though it was never confirmed, Monk went at them anyway. For what they had done to his wife, Monk killed them in the most gruesome ways he could think of, dragging each death out as long as he could. The last one he saved for Li'l Monk. At the time, Li'l Monk was just a young angry kid, trying to figure out how to cope with the death of his mother, but by forcing him to pull the trigger that night, Monk had turned his son into something else. In stealing his innocence, Monk had uncovered the monster that had been hiding inside his son.

"You got it, Dad. We're probably gonna go upstairs and smoke a blunt then I'll put Sophie in a cab," Li'l Monk promised.

Monk smiled. "Good man, way better man than I was at your age. I'm about to go do me, but let me hold a few dollars."

"Didn't I just have Droopy give you some gas for your tank?"

Monk gave him a look. "And what's that got to do with anything? Li'l nigga, I took care of you all of your life so I know you ain't fronting on me over a few funky-ass dollars. As a matter of fact, run that before I go up in your pockets like I do the rest of these sissies." He patted Li'l Monk's pockets playfully.

"A'ight, man. You got it." Li'l Monk laughed, digging in his pocket. He peeled a hundred dollar bill and handed it to his father.

Monk held the bill up to the light, checking its authenticity. "A bill, huh?" He shoved the money into his pocket. "Ramses must be out here feeding y'all niggas real good."

Li'l Monk shrugged. "I'm earning my keep, nothing more and nothing less."

"I'll bet." Monk sucked his teeth as if he had something stuck between them. It's something he always did when he was plotting. "Maybe one of these days me and you will pay a visit to Pharaoh's pad and see what he's hiding in that castle I hear he lives in. What do ya say, son? Me and you like two desperados riding on these pussies and taking everything they lay claim to."

Li'l Monk raised his hands in surrender. "I'm cool on all that mutiny shit, Dad. Pharaoh and Ramses play fair with me so it's only right I play fair with them."

Monk shook his head sadly. "Loyal as a damn dog. That's definitely not a quality you got from my side of the family. Have it your way, but if you should ever change your mind I'm sure you know where to find me." He saluted his boy and left.

# CHAPTER 8

Dealing with his father always took a lot out of Li'l Monk. Li'l Monk's heart struggled to understand how a man who had once been of such high standing could've fallen so far from grace, but his brain understood his father's plight. When Monk had everyone he cared about taken from him, he succumbed to hopelessness. There was nothing left for him to fight for. Looking at his father was like looking into a mirror and seeing how Li'l Monk's life could end up if he didn't play his cards right. One bad decision could derail your whole game plan.

Pushing thoughts of his father from his mind, Li'l Monk turned his attention back to Droopy. He was leaning against the traffic light, smoking a cigarette. For as insane as it was to see a child standing on a street corner smoking a cancer stick, nobody gave Droopy a second look.

"Come here." Li'l Monk waved Droopy over.

Droopy took his time, diddy bopping over to Li'l Monk, taking slow drags of his cigarette. Droopy moved like an adult trapped in a child's body. "Yeah?"

Li'l Monk plucked the cigarette from Droopy's mouth and tossed it on the ground. "That's a disgusting habit."

"Shit, Li'l Monk." Droopy tried to pick the cigarette up to salvage it, but Li'l Monk crushed it under his sneaker. "Man, do you know how much loosies cost?"

"Instead of complaining, you should be thanking me for saving your life. Fuck that cigarette, I got more pressing shit to holla at you about. Walk with me and let's talk," Li'l Monk told him, starting back toward the building where Sophie and Tasha were standing. Li'l Monk gathered his thoughts, thinking of how he wanted to open the conversation. "What you doing out here, Droopy?"

"What you mean?" Droopy played dumb like he didn't know what Li'l Monk was talking about.

Li'l Monk stopped and stood directly in front of Droopy, clasping his hands in front of him. There were no signs of mirth in his eyes. "Droopy, you really wanna play this game with me?"

Droopy looked down at Li'l Monk's scarred and blackened knuckles. The scrapes and bruises told the story of what those hands had been through. "Nah," he conceded. Li'l Monk gave him one last hard look before continuing his walk.

"Droopy, I know you heard me loud and clear the last time I told you that I didn't want your young ass out here pitching stones, so I'm trying to figure out why you back out here like my word ain't no good?" Li'l Monk asked as they approached the building.

"Li'l Monk, you know your word is golden with me, but feel my pain. I'm just out here trying to get a hot meal like everyone else. I don't see what the problem is."

"The problem is that you're thirteen years old trying to play adult games," Li'l Monk shot back. "God forbid if something were to happen to you, we'd all be done off for letting you rock. At your age you should be in school trying to learn some shit instead of being on the block fucking around with us."

"I dig where you're coming from, but let me ask you a question, have you ever tried focusing on school work when you can't hear the teacher over the sound of your own stomach growling? I don't know my daddy and my mama died of the monster. My auntie get a check every month to take care of me, but I don't ever see a dime of that money because she tricks it all off on liquor and niggas. Li'l Monk, I know where you're coming from and I appreciate you trying to look out for me, but to keep it real, I'm tired of not having. If I can't get money out here with y'all, I'm just gonna go find somebody else who'll let me work. Whether I wanna be or not, I'm out here because I ain't got no choice."

Li'l Monk regarded Droopy. Normally he was popping slick and trying to play tough, but at that moment he dropped the façade, Li'l Monk saw him for exactly what he was: a scared kid who was trying to not get swallowed up by the world. Droopy's story hit close to home with Li'l Monk, because he knew exactly how it felt to be hungry and desperate.

"A'ight, Droopy." Li'l Monk sighed. "I'm gonna allow you to get a few dollars out here so you can feed yourself, but I don't want you touching no drugs. You can play lookout or run errands, but keep your little ass away from the work, you understand?"

Droopy smiled. "I got you, man. And thanks."

"Oh, there's one catch."

Droopy looked suspicious. "What?"

"You can only hustle after school. Between the hours of eight a.m. and three p.m., I need you in somebody's classroom at least acting like you're trying to learn something," Li'l Monk told him.

Droopy sucked his teeth. "Come on, Li'l Monk. I ain't—"

"I don't wanna hear it," Li'l Monk cut him off. "You wanna get money, it's my way or no way. You don't like it? Go fuck with them niggas from St. Nick projects and let them work you like a dog for pennies."

"A'ight, you got that," Droopy reluctantly conceded.

"Glad we see eye to eye. Now take whatever drugs you got left on you and pass them off to one of the youngsters," Li'l Monk ordered.

Droopy patted his balls, where he had the drugs stashed. "I'm all out. The two I gave that base head were all I had left."

"Watch your fucking mouth," Li'l Monk snapped.

"Damn, my fault. What is it with you and that old dude? Where you know him from?" Droopy asked. He couldn't understand why Li'l Monk was so defensive over the drug addict.

"I know him from his nut sack. He's my father," Li'l Monk revealed.

The revelation shocked Droopy. "That was Monk? As in Big Monk?" His mouth suddenly became very dry.

"Let that be a lesson to you, Droopy. Watch your mouth when speaking to your elders because you never know who it is you're disrespecting and what the repercussions could be."

"You right, Li'l Monk." He didn't know Monk personally, but had heard enough stories about the old head to know that the confrontation between them could've gone very, very bad.

When Li'l Monk and Droopy got back to the front of the building, Sophie was clearly irritated. "Damn, I thought you were gonna leave me standing over here forever while you were playing with your little friends," Sophie said with an attitude.

"I wasn't playing. I was preventing a homicide." Li'l Monk cut his eyes at Droopy.

"Droopy, you stay in some shit," Tasha said. She had known Droopy since he was a baby and for as long as she could remember he was always involved in some type of mischief.

"So, what y'all about to do?" Li'l Monk changed the subject.

"I don't know. Why, are you trying to get rid of me?" Sophie asked.

"Nah, baby. It ain't like that. I just don't want you on the block like that. It's hot out here," Li'l Monk told her.

"Well, me and Tasha was gonna get some weed from up the block and then probably go back to my house."

"You ain't gotta go in that death trap to get no smoke, ma. I got some weed upstairs. You and

Tasha go to the store and get some White Owls and we can blaze upstairs," Li'l Monk suggested.

"Sounds like a plan to me," Tasha replied for Sophie. "Come on, Soph." She pulled her friend down the block toward the corner bodega.

"Damn," Droopy said watching Sophie and Tasha walk away. "You one lucky-ass nigga, Li'l Monk."

"I be knowing." Li'l Monk cracked a half smile. His attention was drawn from his girlfriend's figure when a livery cab pulled to a stop at the curb a few feet away. Instinctively Li'l Monk positioned himself so that he could spin off and retrieve his pistol, which was inside the mailbox, if necessary. When he saw a familiar face getting out of the back, he relaxed a bit. The tension still lingered, but not because he felt threatened; because he didn't know how to feel about the passenger.

Li'l Monk quietly observed Charlie as he pushed the back door open and looked up and down the block cautiously before daring to step out. He fished in his pocket and came up with some crumbled bills, which he smoothed as best he could and handed them to the taxi driver. There was a brief exchange about the fare versus what the driver was given, which resulted in Charlie flipping him the middle finger and walking off. *Same old Charlie*, Li'l Monk thought, shaking his head.

Charlie was a frail, light-skinned kid with big lips and a slick mouth. He and Li'l Monk had been best friends since they were little, and Li'l Monk was smashing kids in the sandbox on behalf of Charlie. Charlie was what you would call a trouble tree, which meant trouble seemed to follow him.

Over the last few months, Li'l Monk and Charlie's relationship had begun deteriorating over the same thing many friendships crumble over: money. Li'l Monk was on the come up and Charlie was still trying to find his way from ground zero and it bothered him. Li'l Monk had tried to spread love as best he could, but Charlie always found a reason to be bitter, or something to complain about.

His biggest issue seemed to be Li'l Monk's relationship with Omega. For reasons that Li'l Monk still didn't understand, Charlie and Omega were like oil and water. Charlie hated Omega because he felt like he had stolen his spot as Li'l Monk's best friend and Omega claimed he didn't rock with Charlie because he was a leech. When Li'l Monk got to the point where there was nothing else he could do to defuse the tension between the two of them he just stepped back and let the chips fall where they would.

"What's good, family?" Charlie greeted Li'l Monk with dap and a hug.

"Slow motion," Li'l Monk told him.

Charlie looked at Droopy. "What it do, shorty?"

"Whatever Li'l Monk needs it to do," Droopy capped back. He never cared for Charlie. Many thought that it was just because Charlie had been among the older kids in the neighborhood who always gave Droopy a hard time, but it went deeper than that. Several years prior, when Droopy was a child still living with his mother he'd had the misfortune of wandering into her bedroom in the middle of the night while she was turning a trick in exchange for drugs. That trick just happened to be Charlie. It had happened so long ago that Droopy doubted Charlie even remembered the incident or that he was the kid who had come into the room, but it was still fresh in Droopy's mind. No matter how hard he tried, he was never able to bury the vision of Charlie's yellow ass thrusting in and out of his mother.

"Was that Sophie and Tasha I saw going into the store?" Charlie asked, ignoring the piercing glare Droopy was giving him.

"Yeah, they went to get some cigars so we can burn it down right quick," Li'l Monk told him.

"Looks like I came right on time." Charlie rubbed his hands together greedily. "Yo, what's up with Tasha? You think she'll let me fuck?"

Li'l Monk shrugged. "Best I can tell you is to try your hand and see what happens, but you know that girl's nose is wide open for Omega."

Charlie's face darkened. "Damn, it's not bad enough a nonlocal nigga is getting all the local money, but he getting all the local pussy, too?"

"C'mon with that shit, Charlie. You know Omega is fam, so don't start that dirty talk because I ain't really trying to hear it," Li'l Monk told him. He remained neutral in Charlie and Omega's feud, but he never let one talk greasy about the other.

"I feel you." Charlie nodded. "Did you have a chance to give any thought to what I was building with you about?"

When Li'l Monk and Omega started doing their thing heavy in the hood, Charlie ventured out on his own. Li'l Monk never really got into who he was hustling with or where they were doing it, because it wasn't his business, so long as his friend wasn't in the streets destitute, he was cool. They didn't see much of each other on their respective climbs up the criminal ladder, outside of the occasional passing in the hood because Charlie lived on the strip where Li'l Monk and Omega sold drugs. Recently, Charlie had started coming back around and trying to get next to Li'l Monk. Whatever money well he had been tapping was drying up and he was acting like he suddenly remembered where his bread was buttered. Regardless of what Li'l Monk and Charlie had gone through, they still had eighteen years of history and Li'l Monk couldn't turn him away. Li'l Monk wasn't yet comfortable to give him a seat at the table, for he had considered feeding Charlie with a long-handled spoon.

Li'l Monk looked from Droopy to Charlie and gave him a look that said "you should know better." "We'll talk," he said dryly.

Charlie took the hint and wisely changed the subject. "Say, did you see the Yankee game the other day?"

While the three men sat around talking sports, a cat everybody knew as Neighborhood came ambling down the block. Despite the fair weather he was wearing his signature army jacket and a heavy Coogi sweater that had seen better days. It was so tattered that you could see through the gaps of patchwork colorful fabric, straight to the white tank top beneath it. Neighborhood broke his stride briefly to tip his lint-riddled wool skully to an old woman and her child who were passing him, before continuing on his merry way. In his day, Neighborhood had been about his paper. The old timer was responsible for giving some of the most celebrated criminals

in Harlem their very first packages, including
Face and Big Monk. Neighborhood could've been
great, but his love for good times and better
drugs poisoned his destiny. When it was all said
and done Neighborhood was left with nothing
but fond memories and a serious drug habit.

When Neighborhood saw Li'l Monk, he parted
his thick, crusty lips into a wide slave grin showing off what was left of his rotting teeth. "If it
ain't my main man." He walked up on Li'l Monk
and extended a hand that looked like it hadn't
been washed in a few days.

"Chilling." Li'l Monk took the dirty hand without flinching. When Neighborhood leaned in to
embrace him, Li'l Monk's nose was assaulted
with the smell of funk and cigarettes, but he
still gave Neighborhood the respect of a full hug.
"How you be, old timer?"

Neighborhood shrugged. "Been better, been
worse, but I'm still here to complain about it."
He looked to Droopy. "What ya know no good,
Droopy? You got my medicine for the day?"

Droopy patted his pockets. "I'm dry. Li'l Monk
took me off the work."

Neighborhood gave Li'l Monk a look. "You
nursing pups now?"

"Nah, it ain't like that. I'm just trying to stretch
his life expectancy," Li'l Monk told him.

Neighborhood nodded in approval. "Somebody has gotta teach the little ones that there's more to living than dying." He turned to Charlie. "'Sup, junior? How ya mama and them doing?" he asked slyly.

Charlie's face suddenly became very serious. "My nigga, I keep telling you about ya funny shit. Stop playing with me like that, or I'm gonna have to lay hands on you." His tone was sharp. Charlie couldn't stand Neighborhood and had never made a secret of it. Rumor had it that back in the days, Neighborhood had been sleeping with Charlie's mother and there was some speculation about his paternity.

Li'l Monk stood there, watching the exchange between Charlie and Neighborhood, trying his best not to bust out laughing. There exchanges were always epically funny. His eyes drifted up the block, toward the bodega Sophie had gone to for cigars and his smile suddenly melted away. Without saying a word to anyone, Li'l Monk started in the direction of the store.

"Grab me a Pepsi while you're back there," Sophie called from the front of the store. Tasha was in the back rummaging through the freezers while Sophie was at the register.

"Hey, Sophie. Long time no see," the older Hispanic man behind the counter greeted her. "Where you been?"

"School has been kicking my ass, so I haven't really had time for much of anything else, Juan," Sophie told him.

"You're in school? That's great! You always were a smart girl, Sophie, and I'm glad to see you're out here doing something for yourself. More young women need to think like you." He cast his eyes at Tasha, who had just come from the back, when he made the statement.

"Thanks, Juan. I can't wait for it to come, I gotta get out here and get it," Sophie said proudly.

"Nothing sexier than an educated woman," someone behind Sophie said.

She turned around and found herself confronted by a handsome light-skinned man, who rocked a curly fade. Two gold chains dangled from around his neck and he was wearing a gaudy pinky ring. His whole aura screamed "dope boy." Sophie had seen him around before, but didn't know his name nor did she care to learn it. She smiled politely, before paying for her and Tasha's items and leaving the store. She was trying to ditch the young man, but he was persistent and followed her out.

"Damn, it's like that?" He was hot on Sophie's heels. The two gold chains around his neck clanked together as he walked.

"I got a man," Sophie said over her shoulder, without bothering to turn around.

"That's okay with me, because I got a girl. I ain't looking for no commitment, just to be friends," he said slyly.

From a half block away she could feel Li'l Monk's piercing gaze. She didn't have to look up to know that he was staring at her. Sophie knew exactly how things would play out if she didn't get rid of the young man. She stopped and gave him a serious look. "I think it's best that we end this conversation."

"That's fucked up, ma. I'm trying to make you a contender and you out here acting like a chicken dinner." He reached for her hand, but Sophie jerked away. "Relax, baby. I was just trying to shake your hand and introduce myself properly. I wasn't gonna bite you, unless, of course, you asked me to." He smiled.

"Look, dude, I ain't trying to be a bitch about it, but ain't nothing popping. I got a man who I love, so with all due respect I'm not interested in nothing you talking about." Sophie's tone was sharper than she'd meant it to be, but she was nervous.

The young man shook his head. "See, you Harlem broads kill me. Y'all run around screaming how you want a nigga to approach you with respect, but when one does you get to acting all stuck-up and shit!"

From the change in his demeanor he was obviously offended. The look on his face thought Sophie was being rude, but she was actually trying to save him from what was surely coming.

"Oh shit." Tasha's eyes landed on something just behind Sophie.

It was too late.

# CHAPTER 9

The visit with Father Michael had left Persia with some food for thought. Twice already that day she had learned that her family secrets were not so secret and school wasn't even over yet. It was no big surprise that Mr. Thompson had known Face, as his family had been living in the neighborhood already when they first moved there. All of the neighbors had speculated on what Persia's father did for a living, but one person outside of Persia's family knew the truth: Marty's dad, Mr. Rizzo.

Since Persia, Sarah, and Marty were best friends they spent a lot of time together and this led to their fathers developing relationships. Sarah's dad, Mr. Thompson, had always been a bit of an odd nut, so Face kept it casual with him. They would attend barbecues at the Thompsons' or invite them over to their house, but neighborly affection was as far as it went with them. Mr. Rizzo was a different story. From the time they'd met, the two men became as thick as thieves.

Marty's dad was an older Italian man, who had become a father late in life, but only looked half his true age. Whenever you saw Mr. Rizzo he was always immaculately dressed and never had a hair out of place. He prided himself on being well groomed at all times, and it was a trait that rubbed off on his wife and daughter. Marty's mother looked and dressed like a fashion model. She was a socialite who spent more time partying than she did at home, which would often leave Marty to spend nights or days with Persia's family. The Rizzos owned a modest car service, but they lived in one of the biggest houses in the neighborhood. Like Persia's father, not all of Mr. Rizzo's income was legitimate. That's probably why the two of them connected.

Father Michael was the wild card. She had no idea that the priest knew her father, let alone from the streets. Until Persia got to St. Mary's she had never heard either of her parents ever mention Father Michael. Even when she would speak to her father on the phone from prison, and she was telling him about her days in school and stories of the strict Father Michael her father never mentioned knowing him. Why would he keep it a secret? Persia figured that if Father Michael knew her father from the streets, he had his reasons for not mentioning it and it was probably for her own good. She realized that the older she got and thought she had her father figured out, the more she realized she was still clueless of who or what he really was before he went to prison.

Thinking of her father made Persia sad. She hadn't seen him, other than through pictures, in years. He had long ago stopped letting Michelle bring Persia to visit him in prison. Face didn't want to subject his baby girl to the potential scars that could come with a young girl getting used to visiting men in prison. That was a character trait he would not expose her to, no matter who was behind the wall. Their interaction was limited to phone calls, letters, and exchanging pictures. Persia had promised herself that when she turned eighteen she would make the trip on her own to see her father. She had intended to keep that promise until her life got complicated.

Persia had been so busy trying to put the pieces of her life back together that she hadn't had the chance to even write her father back, let alone visit him. Part of her was embarrassed to go and see her father. From the letters he wrote her, she could tell her mother hadn't told him about the things that had happened to her over the past few months. When she asked her why she hadn't told him, Michelle replied, "It's not my story to tell." She would leave that to Persia. Persia knew that he had a right to know, but she couldn't find the words to tell him that the daughter he had sacrificed everything for grew up to be nothing more than a lovesick crackhead. She didn't have the strength, but she knew that she would have to find it. Her visit to see her father in the flesh for the first time in thirteen years was long overdue.

The break in Persia's regularly scheduled school day was both a gift and a curse. It was a gift because by the time she was done with Father Michael, Sister Francine's class was over so she didn't have to see her anymore that day, but it was a curse because her next class was physical education. Persia hated gym, especially in the middle of the day. She always ended up sweating, and left with a choice between showering with the rest of the girls in the stalls, or staying funky until she went home at the end of the day.

When Persia walked into the gymnasium, the first person she saw was Vickie. As usual, she looked a hot mess wearing an oversized T-shirt and a pair of sweatpants that had been washed so many times that you could barely see the school logo anymore. Poorly bleached hair was pulled back into a ponytail, showing off her black roots and the acne marks on the side of her face. Vickie and her sister Jean were two *Jerry Springer* rejects whose mother had been fortunate enough to hit the lotto and move them from a double wide to a two-story house in a middle-class section of Queens. Watching them trying to fit in with the upper-class kids at St. Mary's was like watching a bull try to tiptoe through a china shop. Up to that point, Persia didn't like or dislike Vickie or her sister Jean. The two tramps had never really been on her radar, but that all changed when she found out what they had done to Sarah. She might be getting kicked out of school because of them and they had to answer for it.

When Vickie spotted Persia, she did a double take. The look on her face said that she knew what Persia was thinking. Vickie made hurried steps over to her sister, and began whispering in her ear. Jean was the older sister, but no less trashy. She wore her hair in a shaved blond mullet. She wore a cutoff T-shirt, showing off her meaty biceps. In the proper light, you could've easily mistaken Jean for a man.

Persia also noticed a third girl with her, a black girl named Asia. She had flawless skin that was such a deep shade of black it could've passed for blue. Her hair was done in micro-braids, and pulled into two buns on either side of her head. With high cheekbones and sharp eyes that were the color of Hersey's Kisses, she was a uniquely beautiful girl.

Persia didn't know too much about Asia personally, but she knew what she'd heard around school. Asia's family was from somewhere in Africa. Her mother, Nya, was a popular European model and her father, Mobi, had been a man of great wealth and influence before his untimely death. After her husband's death, Nya took Asia and moved to Germany, where she continued her modeling career until age, and the birth of two more children, had forced her into retirement as a model. She became cofounder of an up-and-coming modeling agency, with Asia as one of its young clients. When the agency decided to open a US location, Nya and her daughter moved to New York and bought a house a few blocks from where Persia's family lived.

Asia's notoriety as an up-and-coming model made her somewhat of a celebrity at St. Mary's. All the girls wanted to be her friend, but Asia was very particular about who she kept around her, handpicking a select few of the girls from the most elite families as her entourage and this is what made her friendship with Vickie and Jean so peculiar. They had nothing in common, expect the fact that they went to the same school, yet the three of them seemed to have forged some type of bond. Persia's beef was with Vickie and Jean, not Asia, but if she felt like she needed to involve herself, she could get it too.

Sister Barbra, the gym teacher, had them line up into teams for volleyball. Persia hated volleyball days. The sport was popular at the school, because they had a pretty good team, but Persia didn't care for it. As a kid, Persia played volleyball every summer at camp, primarily because her mother forced her to. She wanted Persia to fit in with their new class of neighbors, so she made her do whatever the other kids were doing. She actually got pretty good at it, but over time she had lost interest in it. Now that she was older Persia wasn't into it or anything else that involved sweating, unless it was sex. Still, she had to participate because she needed the credit she'd get from the class to receive her diploma.

Vickie and Jean hung close to Asia to make sure they ended up on the same team, while Persia just kind of floated, until Sister Barbara forced her on to a team, which happened to be the one opposite the other girls. Persia played the background, while the first girl on their team took her turn serving. They would each have a turn, and Persia couldn't wait for hers. She grilled Vickie from the other side of the fence. She was trying to get into her head and it was working. Vickie missed two easy balls that had come her way, drawing flack from Asia and her other teammates.

Finally, it was Persia's turn to serve the ball. She ignored the girl who was lined up directly opposite and kept her eyes on Vickie, while she took her spot, rolling the ball over in her hand. Vickie tried to return her stare, but her heart wasn't in it. When Sister Barbara signaled for them to begin, Persia tossed the ball into the air. When she leapt to meet it, she was as graceful as a gazelle, but the force of her serve was like a gorilla. Persia's fist struck the ball and sent it streaking directly toward Vickie. It happened so quickly that she didn't even have a chance to cover her face as the ball made impact with her nose. Vickie went down in a heap, crying and bleeding all over the gymnasium floor. Persia smirked, thinking about how all those summers of being forced to play volleyball had finally come in handy.

"My nose, she broke my nose," Vickie sobbed, holding her hand over her nose, trying to stop the bleeding.

"Are you okay?" Sister Barbara knelt beside Vickie. "Somebody get some towels!" Two girls ran off to get some towels while Sister Barbara attended to Vickie.

"Oh my God, I'm so sorry," Persia said, sounding less than sincere.

"You did that on purpose, bitch!" Vickie snapped.

"Nonsense, it was an accident. I always tell you girls to stay alert when we're on the court, and things like this are the reason why." Sister Barbara helped Vickie to her feet. "Go down to the nurse and get some ice on that nose before it swells."

Sister Barbara had one of the girls who had gone to get the towels help Vickie to the nurse's office.

Persia stood there, watching Vickie drip a trail of blood in her wake as she was escorted out of the gymnasium. "That's for Sarah, bitch," Persia mumbled. She looked to the other side of the volleyball net, where Asia and Jean were standing. Jean was furious to the point where she took a step toward Persia, but Asia held her back. She whispered something in Jean's ear that seemed to calm her down, but the girl still looked furious.

The accident put an end to the volleyball game and Sister Barbara had the girls run laps for the rest of the period. Persia didn't mind. It was a small price to pay for being able to pay Vickie back for what she had done to Sarah. As they did their laps, Persia noticed Asia speaking in hushed tones to a girl named Claire, who was a notorious gossip. Every so often they would look back at her then return to their whispering. Persia knew there would be retaliation for what she had done to Vickie, but she was more than ready for it. She had been having a rough day and needed to relieve some stress. Whipping a bitch's ass seemed like the perfect way to do it.

# CHAPTER 10

"What's popping?" Li'l Monk rolled up on the group. His tone was even, but his face was hard.

"Nothing, babe. We were just on our way back with the cigars." Sophie held the blunts up for proof, but Li'l Monk didn't give them a second look. He was staring daggers at the young man who had been trying to get with Sophie.

"Looks like y'all brought back more than cigars," Li'l Monk said. "Who this nigga?" He nodded at the young man.

The young man matched Li'l Monk's glare. He knew the brute was trying to intimidate him, but he didn't scare so easily. "The name is Chief, maybe you've heard of me?"

Li'l Monk looked Chief up and down. "Nah, I ain't never heard of you."

Chief laughed. "You're a funny guy, but I like that. Judging by the way you're looking at me, I take it this is your chick?"

Li'l Monk didn't answer, he just kept glaring at Chief.

"Oh, the strong, silent type, huh? I feel you, big man." Chief's voice was dripping with sarcasm. "Look, player, I didn't mean no disrespect. I was just trying to get to know the lady, but she explained to me that she had a little situation. I know how to take a hint."

"I sure can't tell, because if you did, you'd be walking the other way instead of trying to get cute with me," Li'l Monk grumbled.

Sophie could see the storm raging in his eyes so she stepped between her man and Chief. "He didn't mean no harm, baby. Let's just go upstairs and smoke, Li'l Monk."

"Oh, you're the infamous Li'l Monk?" Chief recognized the name. "I heard a lot about you, man."

"Is that so?" Li'l Monk asked, trying to keep himself from slapping the smug grin off Chief's face.

"Yeah, you work for Omega, right?"

"Nah, I don't work for nobody, but that's my partner," Li'l Monk corrected him.

Chief gave him a comical look. "Tomato, tomato, same shit right? We got some friends in common, so I expect we'll be seeing more of each other. No need to get off on the wrong foot, right, big man?" He patted Li'l Monk on the shoulder harder than he needed to.

Li'l Monk looked at Chief's hand like it was covered in shit and flared his nostrils. "My nigga, I think you best be going."

"You got it, tough guy. I don't want no static, B. I was just taking a walk through the garden, checking to see how ripe the fruit was, but sadly even the most delicious-looking apples always seem to have worms in them." He cut his eyes at Sophie.

That was the last straw.

Sophie saw it coming first, but there was little she could do to stop it. "Li'l Monk, don't!"

Li'l Monk gripped Chief by the front of his shirt with one of his massive hands. "You just couldn't leave well enough alone, could you?" He slapped Chief viciously across the face. The force of the openhanded slap sent blood flying from Chief's mouth. "Bitch niggas like you always think it's fun to rattle cages until you wake the animals sleeping in them."

"Nigga, get your fucking hands off me! I'm with King Tut!" Chief yelled.

King Tut was a name Li'l Monk did recognize. He was one of the new young dudes Ramses had recruited. If Chief was truly under King Tut, then by extension that made him family as being a part of their organization; but family or not, he had violated and needed to be disciplined. "Well, then Tut should've taught you better. Blame him for this ass whipping your disrespectful ass is about to take." Li'l Monk slapped him twice more. Every time Li'l Monk's hand made contact with Chief's face it sounded like thunder.

"Baby, please stop." Sophie tugged at Li'l Monk's arm, distracting him.

Chief took the opportunity to fish the small Gemstar razor from his pocket. In desperation, he swung the blade for Li'l Monk's face, but Li'l Monk moved out of the way at the last second so instead the blade came down across his chest.

Li'l Monk winced in pain when the razor opened his skin. It was a small cut, but it burned like hell and he could already feel the blood trickling down his chest. He turned his dark eyes to Chief and cracked a smile. "At first I was just going to rough you up, but now I'm going to maim you." He cracked his knuckles. "I hope you got insurance."

"Come get it, nigga." Chief swung the razor again, but this time Li'l Monk was expecting it. He grabbed Chief by the wrist and twisted it until he heard his bones snap and the razor fell harmlessly to the floor.

"I don't give a fuck about you"—Li'l Monk slammed his fist into the side of Chief's head—

"King Tut"—he slugged him in the ribs, breaking two of them—"or nobody else your bitch-ass name drops." He punched him in the stomach. When Chief doubled over, Li'l Monk grabbed him by the front of his pants and his neck, lifting him over his head like a wrestler. With a grunt, Li'l Monk slammed Chief to the floor with bone-jarring force. "It don't matter who you wit', li'l nigga, this is my fucking strip. You and everybody else will either respect it, or become a victim of my wrath." He raised his size twelve boot, ready to deliver the finishing blow to Chief's exposed face, but Charlie and Neighborhood grabbed him.

"Chill before you kill him!" Charlie tried to reason with Li'l Monk.

"That's the general idea. Now get the fuck off me," Li'l Monk growled and tossed Charlie to the side like a rag doll, and started back toward the unconscious Chief. Neighborhood jumped on his back, while Charlie latched onto one of Li'l Monk's legs, while Tasha pushed at his chest. They managed to slow him down, but they couldn't stop the juggernaut. In the end it was the beauty who soothed the savage beast.

"Li'l Monk!" Sophie's voice cracked like a whip. She stood between Li'l Monk and his victim with her arms folded.

"Move, Sophie," Li'l Monk ordered.

"No," Sophie said defiantly. "I'm not going to let you do something stupid to get yourself in trouble. It wasn't that big of a deal."

"Anytime a nigga come through my hood acting like he don't know what time it is, he gotta learn." He was so angry that his body trembled with rage.

"And you've taught him." Sophie pointed to the unconscious man. Sophie placed her hands on either side of Li'l Monk's face and made him look at her. "A true leader knows when to take a man's life and when to spare it. You've made your point, Li'l Monk. Let this bullshit go."

Li'l Monk's body relaxed. He was still angry, but no longer trying to get to Chief. Sophie was one of the only people who could have that type of calming effect on him. Still, he was still angry as hell and needed to expel the built-up energy before it consumed him. Li'l Monk growled like a bear before putting his fist through the window of a parked car. The glass cut his knuckles up, but didn't do any real damage.

Sophie looked at Li'l Monk's bleeding hand and shook her head. "Are you happy now? Let me see it, you might need stitches." She reached for his hand, but he pulled away.

"I'm good." Li'l Monk turned and started walking down the block.

"Li'l Monk!" Sophie called after him, but Li'l Monk didn't turn around, he just kept going. Sophie made a move to follow him, but Neighborhood stopped her.

"Best to let him go his way and cool off. Them Monks can be a sour and unpredictable pair when they're angry," Neighborhood told her.

"I know how to deal with my man," Sophie said with an attitude. She hadn't meant to be short with Neighborhood, but she was in her feelings about everything that had happened.

"Just like a lion tamer knows how to deal with lions, but it don't change the fact that they get bit every so often. Take an old man's advice and give him some space," Neighborhood told her and walked off.

After a few minutes Tasha was able to calm Sophie down and they went their way. Charlie had vanished not long before, leaving only Droopy and what was left of Chief. It had been a full five minutes and the young man was still on the ground, sleeping soundly. Droopy gave a brief look around before kneeling beside Chief and going through his pockets. He relieved him of his cash and the two gold chains he was wearing.

"Bitch-ass nigga." Droopy stomped Chief once more for good measure before running off to enjoy his spoils.

# CHAPTER 11

Persia spent the rest of the school day on high alert. Since Marty was dead and Sarah had gotten suspended, she would be on her own if something went down. There were a few other girls in the school who she was cool with, but not cool enough to depend on them in a fight. This was a situation Persia would have to deal with alone, which was fine by her. Her father had raised her to never show fear or back down, no matter what the odds, but just to be on the safe side she put a lock inside of one of her gym socks and carried it around in her pocket for the rest of the day. She saw all three of the girls in the halls throughout the course of the day, but outside of a few dirty looks exchanged nothing happened. They were trying to rock Persia to sleep, but she was no dummy. She knew they were just looking for the right time to pounce.

Thankfully, Persia managed to make it through the rest of the day without incident, but this

changed as she was preparing to leave school.
While she was in her locker, loading books and
taking out her purse and Discman, she accidentally dropped one of her CDs, cracking it. The
worst part was that it had been one of her favorite
CDs, Mary J. Blige's *My Life*. Persia would always
listen to that CD when she was going through
something. It was like soul therapy for her. Persia
decided that before she got on the bus to go home,
she would walk the few blocks to Best Buy to re-
place her CD.

Persia had intended on getting in and out of
Best Buy and back to the bus station quickly,
but Best Buy happened to be crowded that afternoon. They were having some type of meet
and greet event, and it had brought out scores of
young people, and media outlets. At first Persia
thought it was for a rapper, or singer, but when
she found out that it had something to do with
an upcoming sporting event, she lost interest
and focused on the task of tracking down her
CD. As Persia was browsing the R&B section,
she couldn't help but to notice there was a young
man in the rap section who kept looking over at
her. He stood about six foot four, with rich chocolate skin and innocent eyes.

When Persia finally caught him looking at
her, there was an energy that passed between

them that she couldn't explain. She could tell he felt it too. The hairs on her arm stood up, as they silently communicated, using nothing but their eyes. Persia felt like she knew him, as if the chocolate young man had been the figment of some long-forgotten dream, made real. It was only when Persia felt the subtle warmth building at the center of her that she managed to tear her eyes away. It had been ages since she had slept with anyone and the last man she let touch her had defiled her in ways that she cared not to remember.

Persia kept scrolling through the CDs. She found the Mary J. Blige CD she had been looking for, and stood there for a few minutes, reading the track list. Persia knew the album forward and backward, but it was a stall tactic to keep from making eye contact with the young man again. She wondered if he was still looking her way, but dared not peek. Eventually her curiosity got the best of her and she looked over her shoulder to where the young man had been standing. Part of her was disappointed when she'd noticed that he had gone and part of her was relieved. If he had still been standing there staring, she didn't trust herself not to say anything to him and with those gorgeous lips of his, there was no telling where a simple exchange of words would've taken her.

"I think *Share My World* was a better album," someone said over Persia's shoulder, scaring her damn near half to death. She turned and saw it was the chocolate young man.

"Damn, didn't anybody ever tell you that it's rude to just be walking up on people like that?" Persia asked, with an attitude to mask the fact that he had rattled her.

"I'm sorry. I didn't mean to scare you," the young man said.

"I didn't say you scared me. I'm just not used to people invading my space," Persia shot back.

"I see your mouth is still as slick as ever, Persia." The young man smirked.

Persia was taken aback. "I'm sorry, do we know each other?"

The young man shook his head. "I don't know why I'd expect you to remember. You were smashed out of your mind the night we met."

Persia suddenly felt ill. She knew that during the period of her life when she was into drugs and partying she had done some things that she would've liked to have forgotten and some things that she just flat out didn't remember. She hoped to God that she had never done anything embarrassing in front of that fine specimen of a man.

The young man picked up on the conflicted look on Persia's face and knew exactly what she was trying to figure out, which made him laugh. "Nah, it wasn't like that. I met you and your two white friends at a club. I'm Vaughn." He extended his hand.

Suddenly it all came back to Persia and she realized why she felt like she knew him when she saw him. She and Vaughn had met for the first time on the night everything had happened at the club. He was with the entourage of rappers they had met in the VIP area. Vaughn wasn't a part of the rap group, but the cousin of the group's manager, Tone. If she recalled correctly, he was a college student at the time. She remembered Tone saying he played football at some school in Virginia. Unlike the loud and brash rappers, Vaughn was soft-spoken and polite. In fact, it had been Vaughn who tried to stop Persia from going overboard when she was drug bingeing with everyone else. He seemed like a nice enough guy and to her knowledge hadn't had anything to do with what had happened to Marty, but in Persia's mind he was guilty by association.

"Now I know where I remember you from," Persia spat and stomped off toward the register.

"Wait a second, Persia." Vaughn caught up with her and grabbed her by the arm, but Persia jerked away angrily. He held his hands up in surrender, letting her know he meant no harm.

"Listen, I'm sorry to hear about what happened to your friend, but on my life I didn't have anything to do with it."

"Did you try and stop it?" she asked.

"No," Vaughn said shamefully, "but had I known what would happen, I would've. When your friends left with my cousin and the guys, I went home to get some sleep and headed back to Virginia the next day. I didn't hear what happened until a few days later. I haven't spoken to my cousin since then."

"Why, because you didn't want to be marked as an accomplice?" Persia asked sarcastically.

"No, because I'm no fucking rapist and don't want to be associated with one, even if it is my family," Vaughn said seriously.

"So why are you telling me this? Are you trying to assuage yourself of the guilt?" Persia asked.

"To be honest, I don't know why I'm telling you all this, except for the fact that I feel like I needed to say it. I'm no angel, but I'm no monster either," Vaughn said sincerely. "There hasn't been a day that has gone by where I don't ask myself if I had stayed, could I have prevented what happened to that girl."

Persia wanted to spit in Vaughn's face and tell him to get away from her. She wanted to claw his eyes out and scream, "This is for Marty!" but she couldn't. What happened to Marty was no more his fault than it was hers. Marty was dead and so were her attackers, so there was no sense to holding on to old grudges. One of the things she had learned in recovery was how to let go of the past and hold on to the future.

"Vaughn," someone called from the end of the music aisle. Persia looked up and saw an attractive white girl, dressed in a formfitting skirt and expensive shoes. Her pale green eyes stared at Persia accusingly. *Typical country nigga,* Persia thought about their interracial relationship. Vaughn held up his finger, signaling to the girl that he needed a minute.

"You better get going. I don't want your girlfriend thinking I'm trying to steal her man's heart," Persia said sarcastically.

Vaughn laughed. "You can't steal something that's given willingly. Anyway, I'm not gonna take up too much of your time, Persia. I just wanted to offer you my condolences for your friend and to tell you that I'm sorry."

"You said you didn't have anything to do with what happened to Marty, so what're you sorry for?"

"I'm not apologizing for what happened to Marty, I'm apologizing for allowing you to leave with that clown-ass dude you were with instead of making you mine that night."

His statement made Persia blush. "You really think you've got game, don't you?"

"Whether I've got game or not is a matter of public opinion, but that's another story all together. Maybe one day I'll tell it to you."

Persia twisted her lips in disbelief. "I hear you talking."

"No, you don't, but you will. See you around, Persia," Vaughn told her and started toward the white girl.

Persia stood there for a few minutes, watching Vaughn and the white girl. From her body language and the way she kept cutting her eyes at Persia, she could tell the white girl was agitated. This made Persia smile, knowing that she still had it in her to make other women insecure. She spent so much time being down on herself after her bout with addiction that she sometimes forgot that she was a beautiful girl. Her conversation with Vaughn reminded her of that. She promised herself that if she saw him again, she would thank him for the wakeup call.

# CHAPTER 12

Persia got off the bus at her stop, feeling pretty good about herself. There was nothing like Mary J. and the affections of a handsome man to make a girl feel like all was right with the world. She was floating on a cloud, but little did she know, there was a storm on the horizon.

She spotted them as she was walking home. Asia, Jean, and Vickie were posted up in front of the hamburger joint where all the kids in that neighborhood congregated. There were about seven or eight of them all together and they were all glaring across the street at Persia. Persia wasn't a coward, but she wasn't a fool either. There were too many of them to take all at once so she started walking like she didn't even see them.

The gang of girls fell in step behind Persia and followed her down the block. She could hear them behind her, calling her bitches and other nasty names, but she didn't turn around. Persia quickened her steps and the girls matched her pace. The insults got louder and the mob more unruly. It was obvious they weren't going to leave it alone. Persia slipped her hand into her purse, and kept walking. She heard the heavy footfalls of someone running up behind her, and that's when she finally made her move. Persia spun, pulling the lock in a sock from her purse and swung it. The weapon connected with the cheek of the girl who had been rushing up behind her. The impact from the lock in a sock knocked the girl completely senseless and put her to sleep on the curb. She was some random chick Persia had never seen before, but it didn't matter. The battle was on and anybody who wanted it was going to get it.

Persia took a defensive stance, twirling the lock in a sock like a helicopter blade. "Okay, bitches, who's next?"

Another one of the girls foolishly tried to penetrate Persia's defenses and it cost her. Persia tried to cave her skull in, but when she raised her arm to protect her face, it took the brunt of the strike. From the cracking sound and the way the girl shrieked it was a good bet that her arm was broken. When the rest of the girls saw that Persia meant business, they wisely kept their distance.

"Punk bitch, why do you need a weapon?" Vickie shouted. Her tone was nasally because of her broken nose.

"Same you need a bunch of chicks with you to fight!" Persia shot back. She was whirling the lock back and forth, keeping it in motion so she wouldn't have to wind up if she had to swing again.

"You broke my sister's nose and you think I'm just gonna let that go?" Jean spoke up.

"It ain't for you to hold on to or let go, Jean. You and your sister know why she got her nose broke and if it wasn't for the little lynch mob I'd be over there breaking the rest of her," Persia spat. "Sarah didn't deserve that and under different odds, I'd be showing the both of you how I feel about people shitting on my friends."

"Fuck you, Persia." Vickie acted like she wanted to charge at Persia but two of her friends stopped her. Her struggle to get free of them was a less than convincing one. "I don't need any backup to kick a crackhead whore's ass! I swear to God I wish they would let me go so I could break your nose like you did mine," Vickie boasted.

"Then show me right," Persia challenged. "Just me and you, Vickie. No crews and no weapons."

"Forget all this, let's just rush her. She can't take us all down," Vickie suggested. The mob of

girls moved to surround Persia, but a look from
Asia stopped them. Vickie looked from her crew
to Asia, clearly confused. "What are you doing,
Asia? Let's kick her ass and be done with it."

Asia's looked from Persia to Vickie. "Like you
said, you don't need any help with a crackhead
whore." When she spoke her words were clear
and sharp, still carrying the faintest traces of
a German accent. "Break her nose like she did
yours. We won't deny you your glory."

The move had caught Vickie totally off guard.
She had expected them to rat pack Persia and
beat her down, but having a one on one fight
wasn't something she had planned for.

"Y'all gonna get it in or not?" Asia instigated.

Vickie stood there like a deer caught in head-
lights. It was obvious that she really didn't want
to fight and she was trying to think of a way to
worm out of it. Jean picked up on her sister's fear
and knew that she had to save face for both of
them.

"Damn all this. I'll fight you." Jean stepped
into the center of the crowd, and put her guard
up.

Persia was hesitant. Jean was a big girl, but
Persia was sure she could take her. If play fights
on the playground with dudes like Li'l Monk and
Charlie had done anything they taught her how
to defend herself.

"No need to worry, Persia. You're good and you have my word on that," Asia assured her from the sidelines where she stood with an amused look on her face.

Persia didn't know Asia very well, but there was something about the way she carried herself that made Persia feel like she was an honorable chick and would keep her word if she gave it. As Persia leaned down to put her lock on the ground and prepared to square off with Jean, she only hoped her instincts had been right about Asia.

"This is for my sister, bitch," Persia heard Jean shout, before her meaty fist made contact with Persia's jaw. She had launched a sneak attack while Persia was laying her weapon down.

Persia stumbled and almost went down, but pressed her hand against the ground to steady herself. Jean tried to rush her while she was down, but was met by Persia's foot to her chest. The big girl staggered back, gasping and trying to recover the wind Persia had just knocked out of her. In an instant, Persia was back on her feet, pressing her attack. Persia hit Jean with a mean two piece to the face, and followed up with a punch to one of her big-ass breasts. It was dirty pool, but there were no rules in street fighting.

Jean came back, throwing vicious but unco-ordinated hooks trying to knock Persia's head

off, but the smaller girl danced out of her reach.
Persia faked high, but went low and landed two
solid punches to Jean's stomach. Jean retaliated
with a right cross, that Persia slipped under
and clocked her on the chin. For every punch
Jean threw, Persia hit her with two. Jean was as
strong as a bull, but she was unskilled and slow
while Persia was swift and knew how to box.
Persia danced around Jean, destroying her with
hooks to the head and body. Jean tried to dip her
head and rushed Persia in an attempt to over-
power her, but that proved to be her undoing.
Persia fired her knee up, connecting with Jean's
chin and knocking her down.

Persia was straddling Jean, about to finish her,
when she caught a flicker of movement from the
corner of her eye. She tried to move out of the
way, but wasn't fast enough to avoid the book-
filled knapsack that Vickie was swinging at her.
Persia was able to raise her arms to keep it from
hitting her in the face, but the force still knocked
her over. Persia was down and vulnerable, leaving her at the mercy of the next attack Vickie was
about to launch. Persia braced for impact then
the most unexpected thing happened. Asia came
seemingly out of nowhere, and socked Vickie in
the mouth and knocked her to the ground.

Vickie lay on the ground, clutching her blood-ied lip, looking up at Asia in disbelief. "What the fuck, Asia? We're supposed to be on the same side!"

Asia moved to stand over Vickie and when she did the remaining girls moved with her like a shadow. "Yes, we were supposed to be, but that was poor judgment on my part. A snitch can never stand on the same side as me," she spat. "Claire told me what you and your sister did to Sarah."

Vickie's already pale face turned a sickly shade of green at hearing she was exposed. "Asia, I can explain."

Asia held her hand up for silence. "No expla-nation needed. You're foul and deserve whatever you get. But, just because you and your sister are foul doesn't mean that I am. I'll give y'all a sixty-second head start before I let these bitches loose on you." She motioned to the girls around her.

"But, Asia—"

"Sixty, fifty-nine, fifty-eight," Asia began count-ing.

Embarrassed, and terrified of Asia's wrath, Vickie helped her sister to her feet and they both took off down the block. Before they made it very far, Asia unleashed her mob and they proceeded to give Vickie and Jean the ass whipping that had been reserved for Persia.

"I thought you were gonna give them a sixty-second head start," Persia said.

Asia shrugged her shoulders. "I lied, same as they did when they got me to organize this little lynch mob."

For a long while the two girls just stood there staring at each other in awkward silence. Asia seemed to be studying Persia, but her stone face betrayed none of what she was thinking. It was Persia who finally broke the silence.

"So what now?" Persia asked, not sure if the battle would continue once Asia's girls had finished with Vickie and Jean.

"Nothing," Asia said flatly. "The only reason I even involved myself in this foolishness is because Vickie made it seem like you were bullying her for no reason. It wasn't until I spoke to Claire and she told me what they had done to your friend that I knew she was full of shit. I ain't got no beef with you, Persia." She extended her hand.

Persia was suspicious at first, but so far Asia seemed genuine enough. Cautiously, Persia shook her hand.

"You live in the Gardens, right?" Asia asked. It was what they called Persia's neighborhood because of the impressive lawns of the houses on that street.

"Yeah," Persia confirmed.

"I live a few blocks away on Randall," Asia told her. She dug in her purse and produced a pen and piece of paper, which she quickly scribbled something on. "Take my number." She handed her the piece of paper. "I don't know you very well, but you seem like a stand-up chick. Maybe we can hang out sometime."

"Cool." Persia nodded.

"See you around, Chandler." Asia winked and started back across the street toward the hamburger joint. A few seconds later the mob of girls rejoined her.

Persia stood there for a while, trying to figure out what to make of what had just happened. She'd initially thought that Asia was just another wannabe tough chick like the other few black girls in the school, but from what she could tell she was the genuine article. Everybody painted a picture of Asia as being this prim and proper young model, but Persia was seasoned enough to see what hid beneath the surface of what Asia showed everyone else. Much like Persia, Asia definitely had some gangster in her blood.

With these thoughts in mind, Persia started back down the street to continue her walk home.

Just as she was about to cross the street, a red
BMW ran the red light and almost hit her. As the
car passed she got a glimpse of the driver and her
heart skipped a beat. It couldn't be . . . could it?

# CHAPTER 13

"Damn, Chucky, you almost hit that girl!" Maggie said from the passenger seat.

"But I didn't, so mind your damn business and let me worry about the way I'm driving, unless you wanna take the wheel," Chucky snapped. Seeing Persia after all that time had put him in his feelings.

Chucky thought that by popping up in Persia's neighborhood he could force her to talk to him and potentially put her back under his spell, but the fight derailed that plan. He started to get out with his gun and chase the girls away from Persia, but instead decided to watch and see how it would play out. Chucky sat a half block away in his car, watching as Persia destroyed the girls who had rolled up on her. The way she handled herself made him proud. She was no longer the fragile young girl from the suburbs he had first met. Persia now had a hard edge to her, no doubt from all that Chucky had put her through.

At one time Persia had been Chucky's girl, or so he led her to believe. Persia tried to play the role of a street chick, but in reality she was young, naïve, and easily influenced, which was perfect for what Chucky had planned. To her credit, Persia was one of the finest young chicks Chucky had ever had the pleasure of having on his arm; he was more interested in her genes than her looks. When Chucky was a kid he watched his older brother Tim get gunned down right in front of him. They had come seeking revenge for the murder of their oldest brother, Sonny, but instead Chucky ended up losing another sibling. The common thread in both murders was a man named Face, Persia's father. Since Chucky couldn't get to Face, he would take his revenge against his daughter, Persia.

Roping Persia in was easy. All Chucky had to do was snatch off the blinders that her mother and stepfather had strapped her with, and show her what she was missing in the world. Chucky introduced her to his life of fast cars and money and Persia was instantly turned out. She was seventeen years old, riding in foreign vehicles, hanging out among all the hood stars, and being treated like royalty, and dating an important man. Nobody could tell her anything that would make her think that Chucky was anything less than a God. Chucky had so viciously twisted her mind that Persia left her big house in Long Island City to live from pillar to post with Chucky, because she thought she was in love and her parents' rules were standing in the way of that. Chucky would show her that love came with a very heavy price tag.

It didn't take long for Chucky to start dragging Persia down his rabbit hole. Persia had already been experimenting with weed and popping the occasional pills here and there, but it was Chucky who introduced her to the harder drugs. It started with him lacing their blunts with cocaine. Initially Persia protested. She feared she'd become one of the *Walking Dead*–looking addicts she passed in the streets, but Chucky explained to her that those were the effects of smoking crack and that cocaine was the drug of choice for the rich. Persia was naïve, but she still knew better than to dabble in cocaine. She didn't really want to do it, but the fear of disappointing Chucky if she didn't do it overrode her common sense. Once she hit the laced blunt, and Chucky saw her jaw lock up, followed by the euphoric look that crossed her face, he knew he had her feet firmly planted on the road to damnation.

Chucky had successfully alienated Persia from everyone who cared about her and made her dependent on him. He whittled away at her confidence and self-respect until there was nothing there but a fresh slab of clay for him to mold as he pleased. Persia had stopped going to school and had taken to running the streets with Chucky. He kept her so busy running, only feeding her drugs to keep her going, that before Persia knew it she had a habit, and not the faintest idea of how to deal with it. Chucky had wanted to drag her to rock bottom before viciously shattering the loving image she'd had of him, before revealing to Persia what his real intentions were. He wanted her to know that he had fucked her life up on purpose and why he did it. His revenge against the man who had been responsible for the deaths of both his brothers would be to slowly destroy the thing he loved most: his daughter.

Unfortunately for Chucky the plan didn't go off as he expected, thanks to Karen. The night Ramses sent his men to the house where Chucky and Persia had been holed up was to be the night they left New York. Chucky was going to drive Persia somewhere down South and bring their little game to an end in most horrible fashion. He'd left Persia in the house with his aunt and her boyfriend while he went to handle a quick piece of business before they made the mad dash, but when he came back he found Ramses's death squad descending upon the house. Long before the story would air on the news later that night, Chucky already knew that everyone in the house would be dead, including Persia. There was nothing he could do without putting himself at risk, so he left her to die. To his surprise, Persia had survived the attack and was on the mend. Chucky had been trying to worm his way into Persia's life and bring his sick plan full circle since he slithered back into New York, but she wasn't making it easy.

"So, what now? I know you didn't bring us all the way out here just to watch them little bitches scrap," Rissa said in an irritated tone from the back seat. It had been a few hours since the last time she'd gotten high and she was getting irritable. Rissa might not have realized it yet, but Chucky and Maggie saw that she was developing a habit.

Chucky looked at Rissa through the rearview mirror. "You worse than your sister with all the damn complaining y'all do. It's obvious you two share the same genes."

"That ain't all we share," Rissa mumbled.

Maggie turned around in her seat and looked at her little sister. "What did you say?"

"Nothing, I'm just ready to get on the road already if we're still going, that's all." Rissa tried to clean it up.

"Don't worry, baby sis. I just gotta make a quick stop in Manhattan to see somebody and we can get on our way," Chucky assured her.

"You sure you wanna play it that close, considering everything?" Maggie asked him. Chucky had confided with her about his troubles in New York. Though he had never told Maggie the entire story, he told her enough to where she knew that going anywhere near Harlem could be risky.

"It's all good, baby. We'll be in and out before anybody even catches wind that I'm in town. I just gotta see my friend right quick and we gonna go handle that other thing," Chucky told her.

"I thought you were all out of friends," Rissa said sarcastically.

Chucky laughed. "Let me tell you something, shorty. No matter what I do in the world they'll always be niggas who got love for me, because I've given them reason to. I make it so my presence adds value to their lives, so that no matter what their eyes tell them, their hearts will dispute the information."

Rissa shook her head. "I would sure love to meet the pour soul who, other than us, is dumb enough to put their faith in your sneaky-ass."

Charlie sat in the back of City Diner on Nine-tieth and Broadway, tapping his finger on the table nervously. In front of him sat an untouched burger and fries that had sat long enough to get soggy. Every time the front door opened, his eyes shot up expectantly, only to be disappointed to find that it wasn't the person he was waiting for.

While he waited, he replayed his conversation with Li'l Monk in his head and wondered what he should take from it. Had it been the old days, Li'l Monk wouldn't have given a second thought to fulfilling Charlie's request to get put on, but these weren't the old days; they were the new.

Since kids, he and Li'l Monk had come up like brothers and always had each other's backs, no matter what the circumstances. When money came into play, everything changed. Though Charlie would never admit it, it was his fault that there was a rift between him and the young man who had once been his best friend. It had always been him and Li'l Monk out in the streets, pulling capers and doing what they had to do to survive. Charlie would always come up with the schemes and Li'l Monk was the muscle. They made the perfect team, so when Li'l Monk was called up to the big leagues and Omega became his partner instead of Charlie, it bothered him. He always felt like Li'l Monk had chosen the new guy over him and it planted the seeds of resentment in his heart. Charlie had a love and hate relationship with Li'l Monk. That was still his friend, but he couldn't accept Li'l Monk doing better than him, so it always pushed Charlie to feel like he had to go the extra mile to catch up with him, even if it meant breaking bread with snakes.

Charlie felt wrong for being there, and in his heart he knew that he was, but he felt obligated. Where he was from, when people looked out for you during hard times you did the same if the opportunity presented itself, even if you didn't agree with what was being asked of you. This was where Charlie found himself: trapped in a battle between his good sense and his loyalties.

Finally, the man Charlie had been waiting for showed up. Chuck looked different from the last time Charlie had seen him. He was thinner than Charlie remembered and he had huge bags under his eyes. It was like he had aged several years in only a few months. The clothes he wore were high end, but looked like they had been slept in, which was unlike Chucky. When he had been running the block, Chucky would never be caught dead looking anything other than dapper. The man standing before Charlie bore the signs of hard living.

Chucky looked around the diner suspiciously, as if he was expecting someone to jump out and ambush him. Charlie couldn't say that he blamed him. Chucky had done a lot of people dirty the last time he was in New York and according to the streets there was still an open bounty on his head. Charlie knew that for Chucky to risk coming back to New York he was either crazy or desperate, and before it was all said and done Charlie would find a way to use it to his advantage. Chucky wasn't the only one who had come to the meeting with an agenda.

"My main man," Chucky greeted Charlie with dap and a hug.

"What up, Chucky." Charlie embraced him. Chucky's clothes reeked of cigarettes and something else Charlie couldn't quite place.

"I'd like to introduce you to some friends of mine." Chucky waved the girls over. "This is Maggie and her sister Rissa," he introduced them respectively. "Now, let's get down to business." He motioned for Maggie to slide into the booth on his side. When Rissa tried to squeeze in too, he stopped her. "Baby girl, why don't you sit over there next to Charlie so he ain't all alone?"

Rissa's face said she didn't like it, but she knew better than to argue with Chucky in public, especially in front of one of his Harlem friends. Rissa and Maggie talked shit to him behind closed doors, but they knew better than to do it out in the open. The last time Rissa tried him, Chucky slapped her so hard that her ear rang for the rest of the day. Mumbling under her breath, she slid in next to Charlie.

"So, how you been, Charlie?" Chucky asked as if he really cared.

"I can't complain, I'm living," Charlie said modestly.

Chucky gave him the once-over. "Looks like you're doing a little more than living. You look good, Charlie," he lied. Charlie still looked like the exact same larcenous little bastard Chucky remembered, but he needed to stroke his ego.

"I'm trying to get like you." Charlie glanced over at Maggie, who was sitting next to Chucky with a zoned-out look in her eyes. The older woman was clearly on something, but Charlie didn't care. All he saw were tits and ass.

"Yeah, Maggie here is a real rider. She does anything daddy needs her to do." Chucky draped his arm around her. "Ain't that right, baby?"

"Sure thing, Chucky," Maggie said dryly. She was only half paying attention. Her nerves were playing havoc on her. They'd had to split the rest of the drugs three ways on the ride over and it wasn't quite enough to put her in her zone.

"We can talk about pleasure in a while, Charlie. For now let's stick to business. Did you cut into him yet?" Chucky asked.

"I been working on it, but it's slow motion. Li'l Monk has been on some real paranoid shit lately and is real careful about who he lets into his circle, even me," Charlie said.

"Man, you and that dude go back to the sandbox and you mean to say he ain't letting you eat with him? What kind of friend is that?" Chucky asked.

"It ain't like that with me and Li'l Monk. Things are just tense within the organization because of everything that's going on."

This caught Chucky by surprise. "What do you mean by that?"

Charlie looked around to make sure nobody was eavesdropping before explaining. "Well, the way I hear it Pharaoh's authority is being challenged by some new nigga by the name of Clark or something."

Chucky raised his eyebrow at the mention of the name. He was familiar with the Clarks and knew they were a formidable family. He also knew that the father had been murdered a few years prior and his son, Shai was now running his family. Chucky didn't know much about the youngest Clark, Shai, except everyone who had been sent at him so far was never heard from again. Rumor had it that he had been making the rounds, wiping out all the independent crews who wouldn't fall in line under the Clark flag. Though Shai was barely out of his teens, he had inherited an army and commanded them like a born general. Shai Clark was smooth as silk and as deadly as a razor blade. If he and Pharaoh were at each other, it was something Chucky might've been able to use to his advantage.

"So, Pharaoh and the Clarks are at war, huh?" Chucky asked.

"Not officially, but I'm hearing the tensions are getting high and it'll only be a matter of time before something pops off. They say dudes are choosing sides and it isn't looking too good for Pharaoh," Charlie told him.

"See, and that's all the more reason I need you to speed things up with Li'l Monk, Charlie. When the shit hits the fan, and it will hit the fan, I want us there to get the big pieces and not the scraps." Chucky told him.

Long ago Chucky had sold Charlie on the idea of the two of them taking over Pharaoh's territory and becoming the next bosses of Harlem. At the time it was a loosely slapped together idea to get Charlie to do what he wanted, but in light of recent developments it might've been something that could've actually worked. If Chucky successfully got Pharaoh and Ramses out of the way, there would be nobody to stop him from coming back to New York permanently and recapturing his former glory.

Chucky had respect in the streets before he went rogue, and there was a chance that if he got the power players out of the way he could rally enough support to establish his own organization. If he played his cards right he might even be able to do it with the blessings of the Clarks. But before he made a move on Ramses he needed to get Li'l Monk out of the way. Omega would be given the option to get down or lie down, and Chucky was fifty/fifty as to which way Omega would go if the price was right, but the fiercely loyal Li'l Monk would present a problem.

"I don't see why we gotta do it all sneak, Chucky. Li'l Monk and me been tight since the cradle and I'm sure if I just talked to him—"

"If you just talk to him he'll run back and tell it, ruining our plans," Chucky cut him off. "Look, kid, I know Li'l Monk is your friend, but that boy is like a pit bull, loyal to whoever is holding his leash at the time and right now that ain't us. Ramses has got him all fucked up in the head, so even though you're trying to look out for him, he isn't gonna see it that way. We can't wake him up to what's going on until we've made our move then you can explain everything to him and see if he'll get on board. You have my word that no harm will come to him unless it's absolutely necessary."

In all truthfulness, Chucky had no intentions on allowing Li'l Monk or anyone else to eat from his plate, especially Li'l Monk. Not only had he helped usurp Chucky and cost him his position, but his father had also been responsible for the death of his eldest brother, Sonny. He was firmly etched onto his shit list right along with Persia and they would both pay for the sins of their fathers.

"If you say so, Chucky," Charlie said with uncertainty in his voice.

"Trust me, kid. It's better this way. Now what about that other thing I had you look into for me?"

"Oh yeah." Charlie reached in his pocket and produced a piece of paper, which he slid across the table to Chucky. "I got the address off of a letter that she sent my moms."

Chucky studied the piece of paper and couldn't help but to laugh when he saw that it was an address in Scranton, PA. The person he was looking for had been hiding damn near next door to him the whole time he was in Philadelphia. If he jumped on the road immediately, he could get to Scranton, handle his business, and get back all in a few hours.

"Good work, Charlie. You have no idea how helpful you've been," Chucky told him.

"No doubt. I just want my sister to do the right thing. I know how I would feel if a bitch was having a baby by me then ran off so I could never see my kid," Charlie said emotionally.

Chucky had to stop himself from laughing in Charlie's face over how stupid he was. The story he'd fed him was that he was looking for Charlie's sister Karen because she was pregnant by him and ran away so that Chucky couldn't force her to have an abortion. He was totally clueless as to the real reason Chucky was looking for her and what he planned to do to Karen when he finally caught up with her.

"Don't worry about it. By the time it's all said and done I'm gonna settle up with everybody I owe something to." Chucky smiled knowingly.

# CHAPTER 14

When Persia walked in her house the first thing she noticed was the smell of chicken frying. This made her smile, because she loved her mother's fried chicken more than anything. If she was frying chicken that meant she was in a good mood.

Persia dropped her knapsack by the front door, and headed into the kitchen. Her mother, Michelle, was standing over the stove dropping a fresh batch of chicken into the grease. Michelle looked like a light-skinned version of Persia, except she had more hips and ass. The hair around her temples had started to sprout the first strands of gray, partially due to age and partially due to the stress Persia had put her through. Michelle had been Persia's best friend and the one person she could depend on no matter what. When Face went away, before Michelle met her future husband, she had played both mother and father to Persia. She went out of her way to provide Persia with the best of everything a little girl could want, and Persia paid her back by taking Michelle to hell and back with her bullshit. There was not a day that went by that Persia didn't regret the grief she had heaped upon her mother and since she'd gotten clean she had been working super hard to regain her trust and repair their relationship.

Michelle had her headphones on so she didn't notice Persia walk in. This gave Persia the idea to play a little joke on her mother. She crept up behind Michelle, and kissed her on the cheek. Startled, Michelle jumped, dropping the chicken into the hot grease, splashing some of it on her bare foot.

"Son of a bitch, damn it to hell, shit!" Michelle launched a barrage of curses, while wiping the grease off her foot with a dish towel.

Persia covered her mouth in embarrassment. "Oh my God, I'm so sorry, Mom."

"Persia, you know better than to be sneaking up on me like that. Hand me some butter out of the fridge so I can put it on this burn. I don't want my feet all scarred up to where I can't wear sandals when the weather breaks."

Persia went to the stainless steel refrigerator and got a stick of butter out of the tray. "You want me to do it for you?" she asked, holding up butter.

"No, you've done enough." Michelle snatched the butter and began applying it to her foot. "How was school?"

Persia thought about the hectic day she'd had. "Boring as usual," she lied.

"I was never a big fan of school either, but unfortunately an education is one of the most important tools to have in life. The good thing is that you only have to deal with it a little while longer until you get your diploma in January."

"Yeah, but then it's off to college," Persia said.

"Yes, but that's in the fall and fall is still quite a ways away. You trying to skip out on me early?" Michelle joked.

"Of course not, Mom. In fact I'll even enroll in a city college so that way I don't even have to leave the nest," Persia said playfully.

"Oh no, you won't. You're going to go away to college so you can get the full experience. That's the one thing I regretted, going to school in New York instead of going away. I think it'll do you some good to go out and see different places. The world is bigger than New York, Persia."

"I know. I just hope I'll be ready for it when the time comes," Persia said, sounding less than confident.

Michelle stopped her home remedy, and gave her daughter her undivided attention. "Let me tell you something, baby girl. God will never heap more on you than He feels you can handle. Before you even turned eighteen you had been through more in those short years than people twice that age, and are still here to tell your story. The fact that you were able to get yourself back on track and stay focused shows how strong you are, Persia. You don't think you're ready for the world, but in all actuality the world may not be ready for you."

Persia smiled. "I can always depend on you to pick me up when I'm feeling down." She hugged Michelle.

Michelle rubbed her daughter's back soothingly. "That's what mommies are for. Your parents are both fighters and you will be too." She stroked Persia's face. When Michelle felt the raised bruise on her cheek, she abruptly stopped. "What happened to your face?"

Persia pulled away. "Nothing, I accidentally got clocked with a volleyball," she lied.

Michelle gave her a disbelieving look. "Are you sure? If one of them white girls in that school put their hands on you, I'll throw my sneakers on and come get in somebody's ass." She threw a few phantom punches.

Persia rolled her eyes at her mother's display. "No, Mom, you don't have to kick anybody's ass. It was an accident. Where's Richard?" She changed the subject.

"Out in the back yard. He told me to have you come see him when you came in," Michelle told her.

"For what?" Persia asked.

"How should I know? Why don't you go out there and find out for yourself."

"Okay," Persia said with a sigh. She dragged her feet across the kitchen floor toward the glass door that lead to the back yard, dreading the impending chat with Richard. Ever since she had got out of rehab he always seemed to want to have these deep, philosophical conversations with her. Sometimes they were uplifting and others were just annoying. Persia knew that Richard was concerned about her, but he had never been in the streets like that so he couldn't totally identify with her.

She found Richard at the far end of the back yard, near the high fence that separated their property from the neighbor's. Strapped to his face was a pair of protective goggles and in his hand he had a motorized saw. He was shirtless, wearing only a pair of khaki pants. Persia watched in amusement as Richard began to hack the branches off the neighbor's peach tree that were hanging over onto their side of the fence.

The peaches would fall off the tree into their yard and when they rotted they attracted rodents. Richard had warned them more than once that if they didn't do something about the tree, he would and he was making good on his threat.

There was a pile of braches and a film of sweat was covering his chocolate arms. Richard was a gym rat so he was in very good physical shape. Richard was so conservative Persia couldn't ever remember seeing him without a shirt. On the back of his left shoulder she noticed for the first time that Richard had a tattoo. It appeared to be a pyramid with an eye hovering over it, like on the dollar bill. This surprised Persia because he didn't seem like the type to have tattoos. It was just then that it occurred to her that she had spent so many years giving Richard a hard time that she never really had a chance to learn much about him.

Richard must've felt Persia watching him, because he suddenly turned around. "Oh, hey Persia. How long have you been standing there?" he asked, shutting off the motorized saw.

"Just a few minutes," she said trying to hide her embarrassment. She hoped he didn't catch her staring at him and get the wrong idea. "Mom said you wanted to see me."

"Yes, I did. First, how was school?" Richard asked.

Persia shrugged. "It was okay, I guess."

"I spoke with Father Michael today," Richard told her.

Persia was hoping that he hadn't called and told Richard or her mother about her trip to his office. "What did he say?"

"He said you were doing great in school, and that your grades were turning around. I'm proud of you," Richard told her.

"Thanks," Persia said.

"Now, would you care to talk about the fight you had near the burger joint today?" Richard asked.

The question came as a total shock. It had only just happened, and he already knew. Richard always had a way of finding things out. It was like he had his own personal network of spies. "Who blew the whistle on me?"

"I have my sources."

"Are you going to tell my mom?"

Richard folded his arms across his chest and studied her for a few seconds as if he was weighing it. "Not if you can give me a good reason why you were involved in a street brawl."

Persia tried to think of a good lie, but reasoned that since she was already busted she might as well tell the truth. She went on to give Richard the short version of the events that lead up to the fight. When she was done telling her tale, he simply shook his head in disappointment.

"Persia, you've got too many good things going for you to risk blowing them over some bullshit street code that doesn't apply to you anyway because you're a civilian," Richard told her.

"You wouldn't understand, Richard."

"Why wouldn't I? Is it because I'm not a 'street nigga'?" Richard made air quotations with his fingers. "Let me let you in on a secret, little girl. You don't have to be a street nigga to have common sense, and common sense is what you need to exercise before you end up undoing all the work you put in. You've come too far to start back sliding."

"I hear you, Richard," Persia said in an irritated tone.

"Don't just hear me, Persia, listen to me."

"I will. So, are you going to tell my mother or what?" Persia asked, clearly ready to take her leave of Richard.

"No, not this time, but any more talk of you in the streets fighting and I'm going to have to let the cat out of the bag."

"Thank you." Persia turned on her heels and walked back to the house.

Richard stood there shaking his head. "This must just be my week for young people to test my patience," he mumbled and went back to hacking down branches.

Persia welcomed the peace and quiet of her bedroom. She'd been having a rough day and all she wanted to do was get in her bed and watch television or curl up with a good book. She had picked up a novel called *Eve* that she'd been hearing good things about, and figured that night was as good as any to crack it open.

Persia took off her school uniform and slipped on a pair of sweat pants and a T-shirt, with a pair of fluffy socks. She flopped on her bed, and played the messages on her answering machine. There were fourteen messages and ten of them were from Chucky. You would think that by then he would've gotten the hint that she didn't want to be bothered, but he just kept harassing her. She thought about changing her phone number again, but if she did she'd have to explain to her mother why she wanted it changed. The last thing she wanted to do was make Michelle worry more than she already did. Still, if Chucky didn't back off, she would have to do something about it.

Times like those, Persia missed Li'l Monk. Whenever she had a problem she could always

count on him to beat it to death. Ever since they
were kids, Li'l Monk had always been her knight
in dusty armor. Li'l Monk's days of being dusty
and her savior were long gone. Li'l Monk was
in the streets handling his business, and Persia
was an afterthought. She couldn't say that she
blamed him after the way she treated him. Persia
knew that Li'l Monk was sweet on her, but she
was on a hunt for a baller. Li'l Monk had called
to check on her a few times during her rehabilitation, but he never visited. The last time Persia
had actually laid eyes on him was the night of
Marty's rape.

Persia had been in the club with Chucky,
Marty, and Sarah, whacked out of her skull on
pills, weed, and liquor. It was her first time ever
in a real club and it showed by the way she was
acting. She really got out of control when she
ended up in the VIP with the rap group Bad
Blood. Liquor and drugs seemed to come in
endless supply, and Persia indulged in a little
bit of everything they had. Somehow she ended
up dancing on a table with Marty, while strange
men groped her and tossed money.

As it happened, Li'l Monk was in the club that
night too. When he saw the condition Persia
was in, he tried to come to her aid, but she had
played him in front of the rappers. When Persia

wouldn't come with him willingly, Li'l Monk tried to force her and that's when he got into it with the rappers. Things got real ugly real quick and the party ended up getting shut down.

That night, Persia left with Chucky while Marty and Sarah left with the rappers and everything fell apart. Persia had replayed that night over in her head dozens of times and wondered what would've happened if she played it differently. If she had allowed Li'l Monk to get her and her friends out of harm's way that night, Marty might still be alive and she might not have become a crackhead.

Persia sat on the edge of her bed, running her fingers through her hair. Dwelling on the past was driving her nuts, and she was spending so much time in her bedroom that it was starting to feel like the walls were closing in on her. It was Friday night and she was sitting in her bedroom staring at the walls. Maybe her mother was right and she needed to get out and do some things, anything, just as long as she was doing something that kept her mind off the past. Normally she would've called Sarah and Marty, but Marty was dead and Sarah was probably grounded until she was old enough to collect social security. She wanted to hang out, but didn't have anybody to call. Then she remembered!

Persia grabbed her purse and fished around until she found the piece of paper she was looking for. She grabbed her phone and punched in the number and waited while it rang. She didn't know if what she was doing was a good idea, but if it wasn't, it wouldn't be the first or the last bad idea Persia had acted on. Just as she was about to hang up, someone answered the phone.

"Hi, is Asia at home?"

# PART III

## *OLD FRIENDS, NEW ENEMIES*

# CHAPTER 15

"You think she's home?" Rissa asked from the back seat.

"How am I supposed to know when I got here at the same time as you and have been sitting in the car right along with you?" Chucky asked as if it was the dumbest question ever.

"You ain't gotta get smart, Chucky. I was just asking a question," Rissa said with an attitude.

They had been sitting outside the apartment complex the address had brought them to, watching and waiting for signs of Karen. It had been an hour already and there was still no sign of her. Rissa was getting irritated and, truthfully, so was he. Chucky still had other business to handle and didn't have time to waste waiting around for Karen. The more he stuck around the greater the risk of him being discovered.

"I wish the both of you would shut up with that arguing because you're blowing my high," Maggie spoke up from the passenger seat. She was sitting there with her eyes closed, taking slow drags off a cigarette and enjoying the effects of the crack they'd scored before jumping on the road.

As soon as Charlie had given him the address, Chucky stated making his way to Scranton, PA, but not before stopping off and getting some supplies for their road trip. He was a marked man in Harlem, and couldn't go there to score anything, so he had to scrape the bottom of the barrel to get what he needed. Chucky knew some low-level kids who hustled downtown on Amsterdam Avenue. Their drugs weren't very potent and always seemed to be in short supply, but he didn't have a choice. There was no way he was going to ride two hours in a car with Rissa and Maggie while their monkeys were clawing at their backs.

Chucky cased the group of young men who were standing around on the block, and picked out the one who appeared to be the least sharp. He was a doe-eyed light-skinned dude, who smiled a bit too much for Chucky's liking. It made him look soft and that was the reason Chucky had singled him out. Chucky approached the kid and told him what he wanted to buy. From the excited expression on his face, Chucky knew that it had been a slow day and the kid was thirsty to make the sale. Because of the amount of drugs Chucky wanted to buy, the kid had to go to his stash to get more in order to fill Chucky's order. Chucky convinced him that he should go in the building with him so that he wasn't standing outside looking suspicious while waiting for the kid to come back. As soon as he revealed the location of his package, Chucky robbed him of his drugs and his money. The comical part of it was that Chucky never had to pull his gun. He punched the kid in the face and promised him another one if he didn't come up off his goods. He turned over everything he had without as much as a struggle. It just went to show that no matter what you pretended to be, when the pressure was on the real you would always come out.

Securing the drugs helped make the trip an easier one, but of course Rissa still found a reason to complain. All the kid had on him was crack and no cocaine, which presented a problem for her because all Rissa did was smoke laced blunts and sniff coke. It was all relatively the same thing, but she felt like because she didn't smoke rocks it made her less of a fiend. The child was delusional, but Chucky didn't have time to argue chemistry with her. He grounded some of the rocks up into fine crystals for Rissa to put in her blunt just to shut her up. Rissa was the worse kind of addict, one who was still so far in the

closet that she probably didn't even realize she
was an addict yet. She reminded Chucky very
much of Persia.

Thinking of her made Chucky pull out his
phone and try to call Persia again. As usual, it
rang out and went to the answering machine.
He started to leave her a message, but figured
there was no point. He had been trying to reach
her since he'd gotten back to the city, but she was
giving him her ass to kiss, which made Chucky
mad. At one time she had been so madly in love
with Chucky that it was almost like having a
personal slave. She would lie around with him,
snorting, smoking, and praising Chucky. Now
that she had gotten clean she thought she was
better than him. After he finished with Karen, he
was going to hatch a plan that would knock Ms.
Persia Chandler down a few pegs. He had been
saving his trump card as a last resort, but Persia
was leaving him no choice other than to pull it.
She would bend to his will again whether she
wanted to or not.

"Is that her?" Melissa asked, pointing out the
window to a young girl coming down the street,
with a young dude. She was a thick dark-skinned
chick, who had a booty so big that it looked like
it was going to burst the seam of her tight skirt.
An expensive-looking purse dangled from her

arm. They were both carrying bags from different clothing stores like they had just come from shopping.

Chucky peered through the window. She had gained a bit of weight and now wore her hair cut short, but it was definitely Karen. "Yeah, that's the bitch," he said in a low growl. Karen passed so close by him that Chucky could smell her perfume through the partially cracked window. If she had but turned her head even the slightest bit, she would've seen him in the car, lying in wait, but Karen was more focused on her boy toy and her gifts. Same old Karen. Seeing her again brought back the old hatred and it was hard for Chucky to keep himself from jumping out and blasting her on the spot. He had reacted based on emotions once when it came to Karen, which is what put him on the shit list in the first place, and he wouldn't make the same mistake gain.

"So what do you wanna do?" Rissa asked nervously. She was all for giving Karen a good beating, but the rage in Chucky's eyes said he wanted to take things a step further.

"Just hold tight for a minute. I got a plan," Chucky said, leaning back in his seat.

When Karen walked into Mike's apartment the first thing she did was kick off the heels she was wearing. Her feet were killing her. The stiletto heels were cute, but hardly made for spending hours walking through the mall. The only reason she wore them was because she knew they turned Mike on. When she was wearing the right heels, she could get him to do just about anything she wanted.

Mike was a dude Karen had met not long after she relocated to Scranton after double-crossing Chucky. Karen had mixed feelings about what she had done. She was a street chick, tried and tested so snitching was never an option, but Chucky had hurt her and she needed to hurt him back. At first she thought about turning the gun over to the police, but that would've raised too many questions and could've possibly led to her incriminating herself in the process. She couldn't turn Chucky over to the judge, so instead she gave him to the executioner, Ramses.

The minute she gave the gun over to Ramses and told him what Chucky had done, she regretted it. She knew that he would have Chucky killed for what he had done, but what she hadn't thought about at the time was her role in it and the fact that her knowing what was about to go down would make her a liability. Ramses wasn't a man who left witnesses to his evil and Karen knew that as soon as they were done with

Chucky they'd likely want to get rid of her too, just to be on the safe side. Ramses had given her several thousand dollars for her trouble and told her that he would send a private car to her house to pick her up and get her out of town, but Karen knew that was bullshit. If she got in any car Ramses sent she would never get out again. She thanked him, took his money, and hopped the first bus out of town.

Coming to Scranton was the result of fleeing New York without a solid plan. Karen hadn't done much traveling outside of New York in her life so she had no idea where to go. That's when she remembered her family in Scranton. She knew if she kicked her aunt a few dollars, she would let Karen stick around for a while until she figured out her next move.

Karen also had cousins down there who were about her age. It had been one of her cousins who introduced her to Mike. At the time it had been the cousin who Mike was seeing, but it didn't take long for Karen to seduce him and steal Mike from the cousin. It was a grimy move, but Karen didn't care. In her world it was survival of the fittest and she needed what Mike had to offer more than her cousin did.

Karen stealing her cousin's man didn't go over well with the family and they put Karen out on the streets. Her homelessness didn't last long, because Mike happily moved her in with him. It was a small one-bedroom apartment in a rough section of town, but it beat sleeping in the streets or at a homeless shelter.

Outside of meeting Mike, Karen's time in Scranton hadn't had many high points. The town was slow, and the men were slower. She was used to the hustle and bustle of Harlem, and though Scranton had a few hot spots they all failed in comparison to what she was used to in New York. Still, she was stuck down there so she had to make the best of it, which is where Mike came in. He was a local dope boy who had dreams of being Scarface. Mike was hardly moving any major weight, in comparison to some of the guys she had dated in New York, but he was a big deal in the town. Mike wasn't very attractive, and was about as interesting as tenth grade algebra, but he provided her with a source of income and a roof over her head, so he would do; at least until something better came along.

"Damn, looks like you bought the whole fucking mall out." Mike set the bags down on the living room floor.

"You mean you bought the mall out," Karen said slyly. "That's why I fuck with you, Mike. You really know how to treat a girl."

"Anything I wear on my arm has got to look good, from my women to my watches." Mike hiked his sleeve to show off the diamond watch he was wearing. It was the one thing he had bought for himself on their little shopping trip. He didn't particularly like the watch and thought that the price was too steep, but Karen seemed to like it. Sucking it up, he dropped the bread on the timepiece. He would likely be on the block hustling around the clock for a week to make the money back he'd spent on it.

"I'm going to jump in the shower right quick and when I come out I'm going to show you how much I appreciate your generosity, Mike." Karen went into the bathroom.

"Don't be in there all day," Mike called after her. No sooner than Karen had closed the bathroom door, Mike started coming out of his clothes. Karen was a stone-cold freak and every time he took her shopping she showed him some new sexual trick. After what he had dropped at the mall that day, she better pull out all the stops.

Mike was just wiggling out of his pants, when he heard someone knock on the door. "Fuck," he cursed, sliding his pants back on. He didn't know who it was, but unless it was the white dude from Publishers Clearing House with a check, he was going to get rid of them with the quickness.

Angrily, Mike snatched the door open, ready to bark on whoever was on the other side. He found himself staring at an attractive older woman wearing a tight skirt and sheer top, and no bra. Her brown nipples stared at Mike from beneath the thin fabric.

"I'm sorry to bother you, sugar, but my car ran out of gas down the street. I need to call Triple A, but I don't have a cell phone. Do you have a phone I can use?" Maggie asked.

"Sure, come on in and I'll grab my cell phone." Mike stepped back to let her in. When Maggie passed he took a long, hard look at her ass. Mike instructed Maggie to have a seat while he retrieved his cell from the kitchen counter and handed it to her.

Mike stepped off to the side to give her some privacy while she used the phone. This also allowed him the opportunity to size her up. While she talked on the phone, she crossed one leg over the other, causing her skirt to rise up on her hips. She wasn't wearing any underwear. Mike's brain screamed, *working girl.* He knew all the prostitutes in that area, but she was a new face. He and Karen had talked about having threesomes before, and she promised him they could have one soon and it looked like soon had finally arrived.

"Shit," Maggie cursed as she ended the call.

"Everything good, sweetie?" Mike asked.

"No, not really. My Triple A is expired. I forgot to renew it last month. I don't know what I'm going to do now," Maggie said in a defeated tone.

"Is there anyone you can call to come and get you?" Mike asked.

"No, I'm from Maryland. All my family is down there. I'm going to see if I can maybe call my baby daddy to Western Union me a few dollars, but I hate asking that asshole for anything," Maggie said.

"Maybe I can help out," Mike suggested.

"Thanks, but I don't do handouts," Maggie said, faking offense.

"I can respect that," Mike told her. A few seconds passed, with them just staring at each other trying to figure out what the next move was. "I have a suggestion, and if I'm out of line, I apologize. I was thinking maybe we can work out some type of arrangement." Mike looked at her suggestively.

Maggie's eyes widened as if she was just realizing what he was implying. "Baby, you cute and all, but I'm not giving up my pussy for a few dollars in gas money."

"Even for five hundred dollars?" Mike asked. At the mention of money he saw the thirsty look in Maggie's eyes. "Look, ma, it's my girl's birthday," he lied. "I've been promising her a three-some for the longest and I think it'll make a great present."

"Wait, I thought you meant just fucking you, but if you want me to do some girl-on-girl shit it's gonna cost you extra," Maggie told him.

"How much?" Mike asked excitedly.

"A thousand."

Mike frowned. "That's a lot of money for some pussy."

"You presented the idea, not me. Tell you what, give me eight hundred and I'll even bring my sister into it, but you gotta cum quick. We can't be here all day."

"Say no more." Mike rubbed his hands greedily. "Where's your sister?"

As if in answer to his question there was a second knock on the door. "That's probably her right there, wondering what's taking me so long. I'd better let her in." She prepared to get up, but Mike motioned for her to stay put.

"I got it, baby. Just sit tight." Mike walked to the door, thinking about all the fun he was about to have. If the woman's sister looked anything like her they were about to have one hell of a party. He didn't know how Karen would feel about him springing it on her, but he didn't care. Whether she was with it or not, Mike planned on fucking the woman. Karen could get with the program or get gone, but nobody was going to deny him his glory.

When Mike undid the lock the door came crashing open. Before he could figure out what was going on, something heavy crashed into the side of his head, sending him spilling to the floor. Clutching his bloody head, Mike looked up and found himself staring down the barrel of a gun held by a man he didn't know.

"What the fuck is this?" Mike barked.

"For now, a simple home invasion, but if you decide to get cute"—Chucky cocked his pistol—"it can very easily turn into a homicide. Now where's your bitch?"

Karen stepped out of the shower smelling good and feeling better. After running in and out of stores all day, she was fatigued and feeling a bit sticky. The hot shower was just what she needed to give her a second wind. Beyond the bathroom door, she thought she heard Mike talking to someone, so she pressed her ear to the door and listened. All was silent. Figuring he was probably talking on the phone, she went back to the business of drying herself.

From one of the bags she had brought into the bathroom with her, she pulled out the outfit she planned on wearing for Mike. It was a pink corset, complete with garters and crotchless panties. She'd owned something similar when she was living in New York and Chucky used to go wild when she put it on. She was hoping that it had the same effect on Mike.

After putting on the outfit, she slipped her feet into a pair of furry, high-heeled slippers. After giving herself the once-over in the mirror to make sure she was presentable, Karen prepared to make her presence felt. She had just touched the bathroom doorknob, preparing to turn it when she felt a cold chill in her bones. Her grandmother used to say that it was a sign that someone had just walked over your grave. Shrugging off silly superstitions, Karen opened the door and stepped out of the bathroom.

The first thing that caught her attention was the smell of cigarette smoke. Karen smoked, but Mike didn't and always made her go outside if she was smoking anything other than weed, so it was odd that the smell would be in the house. Karen continued down the hall toward the living room. As she neared the living room, she noticed that some of the outfits she had just bought were no longer in the bag. Some were on the floor while other pieces were strewn over the arm off the couch. "What the fuck?" Karen mumbled under her breath. She didn't know what Mike was snooping for in her bags, but she was about to check his ass.

When she rounded the corner, her jaw dropped. Standing in the middle of the living room were two women who she didn't know, trying on her brand new clothes. Mike sat on the couch nearby with a terrified expression on his face. Karen didn't understand what was going on, but when she saw Chucky standing by the door, holding a gun, everything became abundantly clear.

"Hey, baby girl," Chucky greeted her with an evil grin.

Karen felt a bit of pee squirt from her and run down her leg at the sight of Chucky. It only took a few seconds for her legs to receive the signal her brain was sending and she bolted for the bedroom. From the sound of heavy footfalls behind her she knew that Chucky was on her ass. She glided in the furry heels as if they were sneakers, trying desperately to make it to the bedroom and the gun she knew Mike kept stashed in there. If she could get to it, she would level the playing field. She had made it within mere feet of the door, when she felt a sharp pain in her head.

"Not so fast, bitch," Chucky told her, dragging her back down the hall by her hair. Karen kicked, scratched, and spat at Chucky, but he would not release his grip. She found her opening and tried to kick him in the nuts, but he moved at the last second and the kick ended up landing on his thigh. This seemed to only infuriate Chucky. He lifted her to her feet by her hair and punched her in the face. After that everything went black.

Karen wasn't sure how long she had been out, but it had to have been awhile because it was afternoon when she came in from shopping and now the sun was starting to set. Her jaw throbbed from where Chucky had punched her and she could feel that her lip was swollen. A bruised jaw and swollen lip were the least of her concerns though.

Sitting on the couch next to Karen was Mike. He was looking at the floor, too ashamed to meet her gaze. She couldn't really see his face, but from the way his body heaved up and down she knew he was silently sobbing. For all the tough shit he talked, she couldn't believe that he was now crying like a bitch in the face of danger. It was pathetic. Sitting on the arm of the chair was the younger of the two girls Karen had seen trying on her clothes. She was wearing Karen's BCBG dress, and smoking a cigarette. Karen trembled when the ashes fell onto the dress, and the girl wiped them away, leaving a nasty-looking smudge. Her eyes went to the middle of the living room and landed on the man of the hour: their uninvited guest, Chucky.

She didn't know if she was more shocked at the fact that he was still alive or that he had found her. No one knew where she was except her mother, and Karen was sure that she hadn't told it. That only left her brother Charlie. He was the only one she could think of who had their head shoved so far up Chucky's ass that they would betray a family member. She promised herself that if she survived the encounter, she was going to kill him, sibling or not.

"Do you know how long I've been trying to track you down?" Chucky asked. Karen didn't answer. "Oh, you're quiet now, but you had plenty to say when you were telling Ramses my business. Of all the people in the world, I'd have never expected you to betray me, Karen. I guess that's what I get for putting my trust in a scurvy bitch such as yourself."

"You've got some nerve coming in here trying to chastise me about loyalty after what you did, Chucky. Of all the girls in the world you could've thought to sleep with, did it have to be my friend?" Karen asked emotionally.

Chucky laughed. "Friend? Girl, you throw that word around far too loosely. Persia wasn't no more your friend than I am. You talked about Persia like a dog every chance you got. Everybody knew you hated her and so did she, which is probably why she gave me the pussy so freely." Chucky was speculating about the last part, but he did it to rub salt in the wound.

"So, what are you going to do now, kill me?" Karen asked.

"After a time, I guess I will, but not before I've had my fun. Yo," Chucky called to the bedroom. A few seconds later, out walked the older of the two girls Karen had seen trying her clothes on. She was as naked as the day she was born and carrying a rolling pin. Karen wasn't sure what she was going to do with it, but she doubted if she planned on using it to make cookies.

"Chucky, don't do this, please," Karen pleaded.

"Save your pleas, because I got no mercy for a rank skank like you, Karen. You tried to fuck me, so I'm gonna have my bitch fuck you. Now come up out all that cute shit and show me some skin," Chucky ordered.

"Chucky, please—" Karen began, but was cut off when he slapped her viciously in the face.

"Whore, don't make me tell you again," Chucky hissed.

With tears in her eyes, Karen did as she was told and took off her outfit. There was a time when her being naked in front of Chucky felt natural, but not anymore. It was like him even seeing her naked made her feel dirty and violated.

"Yeah, that's what I'm talking about," Chucky said, tugging at his dick through his jeans. "Now lie back on the couch and spread them fucking legs." Karen did as she was told, but her hands shook so bad she was having trouble holding her legs up on her own. "Help her out," Chucky told Mike.

"I can't," Mike said just above a whisper.

Chucky closed the distance between him and Mike, placing his gun to the frightened man's head. "You gonna hold them legs up or when I'm done with her, I'm gonna give you a taste too."

Reluctantly Mike moved toward Karen to do as Chucky had ordered him. The look she gave him was one of pure hate. "I'm sorry, baby," he told her, pushing her legs back so that her knees touched her chest.

"Okay, Maggie, get to it," Chucky ordered.

Maggie moved to kneel in front of Karen with the rolling pin. She could tell that Karen was terrified, and she really felt bad about what was going to happen, but she dared not advocate for her. She knew better than most how cruel Chucky could be and wanted no part of his wrath. She reasoned it was better Karen than her.

"If you try to relax yourself a bit and don't fight, it won't hurt too bad," Maggie told Karen before sliding the tip of the rolling pin inside her.

Karen cried out in pain as the rough wood entered her. She tried to close her mind off and mentally check out, but every time she felt the tip of the pin enter her she was brought back to her living hell.

"Deeper," Chucky barked.

Maggie slowly slid the rolling pin farther into Karen until the thick edge was lingering just outside her pussy.

"Deeper," Chucky repeated.

Maggie stopped and looked at him. "But this is as far as it'll go."

"Either she gonna take that rolling pin or you gonna take a bullet."

With no other choice, Maggie forced the pin deeper inside Karen. The pin met with some resistance before slipping in to the point where the thick roll was just inside Karen's walls. She worked it slowly in and out, while Karen cried and Chucky laughed. When she pulled the pin out to reposition it, she saw that it was bloody.

She wanted to stop, but if she did there was no telling what Chucky would do to her.

"Okay, that's enough," Chucky called from behind her. Maggie thought that he had finally come to his senses, but when she looked back she saw that his pants were around his ankles and his throbbing, hard cock was in his hand.

"Chucky, I know you ain't about to run up in this girl. Her walls ain't no more good," Maggie told him, hoping he would change his mind.

"Karen's walls ain't never been no good," Chucky joked. "Don't worry, where I'm going is uncharted territory." Chuck grabbed Karen by her neck and forced her onto her stomach, while positioning himself behind her. When he leaned in to whisper in her ear, she could smell his foul breath. "Since you tried to fuck me with no Vaseline, I'm going to do you the same courtesy," he told her before shoving his cock in her ass.

Rissa had to turn her eyes away and covered her ears against Karen's screams while Chucky violated her. He was slamming himself roughly in and out of her, while occasionally taking a minute to punch her in the back of her head. The more she screamed the more excited Chucky seemed to become. Rissa was disgusted by the whole ordeal. She knew that Chucky was a warped son of a bitch, but she had no idea how far he would be willing to go once he had been crossed. He was showing her just what kind of monster he really was. She regretted the day she had ever gotten into the car with Chucky and her sister.

It was almost twenty-four hours later when the police got the anonymous call that directed them to Mike's apartment. Rissa knew she was taking a chance, but the things she watched Chucky do haunted her. She knew she would surely be on a first class trip to hell for the part she played, but calling the police so the girl wasn't left their to rot gave her a small measure of peace.

The crime scene was like something out of a movie. They found a girl, beaten, raped, sodomized, and shot twice in the head. A few feet away they also found her boyfriend shot in the head. The kicker was the fact that whoever had killed them had also cut the boyfriend's dick off. The crime scene investigators searched high and low for his manhood, but could find no sign of it. It wasn't until the autopsy of the girl was performed that the mystery of the missing penis had been solved. Whoever had killed them took the time to stuff the boyfriend's penis down the girl's throat.

# CHAPTER 16

Li'l Monk was awakened by the sound of banging on his apartment door. He rolled out of bed and planted his bare feet on the floor. His brain was still heavy with the fog of sleep. He reached for his gun on the nightstand and winced in pain when he tried to close his hand around it. His knuckles were bruised and his fist had swollen. That was the price he paid for putting it through a car windshield.

The banging took Li'l Monk's attention away from the examination of his hand and brought it back to the door. Using his off hand, Li'l Monk scooped the gun up and made his way down the hall. It seemed like the closer he got to the front door the more intense the banging became. When Li'l Monk got to the end of the hall, he raised his gun to eye level with the door before carefully looking through the peephole. When he saw who was standing on the other side of the door, he lowered his gun.

"Took you long enough." Omega invited himself inside the apartment once Li'l Monk had finally opened the door. He wore a green Adidas hoodie, pulled partially over his head, with his dreads spilling out around his face.

"Come right in and make yourself at home," Li'l Monk said sarcastically, closing the door and re-locking it behind Omega.

"Yo, what's going on with you, B. I been trying to reach you for the past few hours," Omega said.

Li'l Monk shrugged his broad shoulders. "I didn't much feel like being reached. I got a lot going on right now."

"So I've heard. You know you put that kid in the hospital, right?" Omega was referring to Chief.

"He's lucky I didn't put him in a bag," Li'l Monk spat. "That sucka-ass nigga came through the block like him and his people got some claim to our strip. Fuck was that about?"

Omega shrugged. "Beats me," he lied. He hadn't yet had a chance to tell Li'l Monk about the deal he had cut with King Tut. He wanted to break it to him in his own time, and Chief's big-ass mouth almost ruined it. "You know, there are a lot of people in their feelings about what you did to Chief, Li'l Monk, including King Tut." Omega changed the subject.

"Fuck King Tut and anybody else who might feel some type of way about how I handle my business in the streets. If a nigga come through the strip on some disrespectful shit, I'm putting them in the hurt locker, straight like that. And since when did how Tut felt about anything become so damn important?"

"Since Ramses promoted him," Omega revealed. "Word is, he's pulling Tut in out of the cold and giving him a management position. Tut will be given domain over a small crew that operates just across the bridge in the Bronx. Chief was supposed to be a part of that crew until you took him off the active duty roster. Ramses wants the two of you to squash this shit before it goes any further."

"No problem, you tell Ramses that as long as no more of Tut's boys wander into our territory talking reckless I won't put any more of them in the emergency room." Li'l Monk chuckled.

"Ain't good enough. Ramses wants the two of you to sit down for a face-to-face meeting. He just wants to make sure that this business between you and Tut isn't going to spill over and start fucking up the money. I'm supposed to drive you to the meeting spot."

Li'l Monk gave Omega a disbelieving look. "Are you kidding me? I got better things to do than get sent for like some little-ass boy, and you of all people should know better."

"Oh, I do know better, which is why I'm here instead of Huck. Ramses was going to send him to fetch you, but I volunteered to come. I figured you'd take the request better coming from me than him," Omega said.

"I don't take kindly to being fetched by nobody."

"If I was you I wouldn't repeat that in front of Ramses, or it might go bad for you," Omega joked.

Li'l Monk turned his murderous glare on him. "You think I won't? I ain't afraid to speak my mind to no man, including Ramses."

"I was only joking, Li'l Monk. Why don't you calm down?"

"I don't know, O. Sometimes it's hard to tell when you're joking and when you're serious. You know I don't take kindly to nobody playing on my intelligence," Li'l Monk said angrily.

Omega knew that Li'l Monk was in his feelings. Li'l Monk was a good dude and a loyal soldier, but he had never been the sharpest knife in the drawer. Ever since he was a kid he had always been the strong and silent type, never speaking much, which led to people sometimes referring to him as Big Dummy behind his back. His violent temper landed him in special education classes when he was in school, which only added to his ridicule. As a kid he suffered in silence but as a young man he addressed mockery with violence which eventually stopped the teasing. Li'l Monk always acted like the teasing didn't bother him, but those closest to him knew otherwise. At times Li'l Monk could be a coldblooded monster; then there were other times when he was almost as sensitive as a child. Omega almost always had to deal with Li'l Monk wearing kid gloves.

"You know I didn't mean it like that, Li'l Monk. You're my brother so I'd never get at you on some funny shit. We're bound for life, remember?" Omega reminded him.

"Yeah, I remember," Li'l Monk said, thinking back to the incident that would forever intertwine their destinies.

*Li'l Monk was still new to the organization and had just started working with Omega. Things were tense in the hood because of a rash of robberies of Pharaoh's drug spots, so Ramses brought Li'l Monk in as extra muscle. It was his job to watch Omega's back and help him maintain order on their drug strip.*

*Omega had just gotten into it with Neighborhood, so Li'l Monk took him for a walk to try and calm him down. They were on their way to the*

*Chicken Shack when they passed by a building and noticed something suspicious going on in the lobby. Upon closer inspection they noticed that they had just stumbled upon a robbery. Some dudes wearing masks were inside robbing a kid named Burger, who sold drugs on the strip for them. Their first instincts were to call Chucky or Ramses for reinforcements, but they reasoned that by the time help arrived the robbers and the drugs would be long gone, so Li'l Monk and Omega decided to handle the problem on their own.*

*Li'l Monk and Omega were too late to save Burger, but they took their revenge on the men who had been trying to rob their spot and had killed the young man. They gunned them down in the lobby like the common dogs they were. At the time Li'l Monk and Omega hadn't known each other very long, but the acts committed in that lobby would be the tie that bound them. They would burn together or prosper together.*

"That night changed everything," Li'l Monk said solemnly.

"Yes, but it changed things for the better. Had we not dropped those bodies we'd probably still be hustling corners under Chucky," Omega said.

The mention of Chucky's name put Li'l Monk in a foul mood. From the first night Li'l Monk had come to work for Ramses, Chucky had made it clear that he didn't like him. Some said it was because during their first meeting, Li'l Monk had been whipping out one of Chucky's workers, but Li'l Monk suspected that Chucky's dislike for him stemmed from something deeper.

Li'l Monk and Chucky had always had a strained relationship, but it became even more frayed when he found out that Chucky had started seeing Persia. Li'l Monk's and Persia's fathers had been best friends so they'd known each other all their lives. Li'l Monk had loved Persia since he was old enough to understand the difference between boys and girls. He often fantasized about her one day being his girlfriend, but a fantasy was about as close as he would get to the object of his affection. No matter how much Li'l Monk tried to show Persia how he felt about her, she never saw him as anything more than a friend. It hurt Li'l Monk, but he had to accept it.

Every time he saw Persia with Chucky it was like someone sticking a knife in his heart. He knew that Chucky was no good for her and tried to convey it to Persia, but she was a girl so head over heels in love that she couldn't see the forest for the trees. Li'l Monk watched helplessly as Chucky dragged Persia down with him, and the girl he loved was transformed into someone he didn't even recognize anymore. Persia had become fast and loose, getting caught up with Chucky's bullshit. The final straw came when he found out that Chucky had gotten Persia strung out on drugs. Li'l Monk wanted to kill Chucky on the spot, but to touch him would've been a death sentence. Chucky was a piece of shit, but he was still Ramses's second in command and therefore untouchable. For as long as Chucky was under Ramses protection, there wasn't anything Li'l Monk could do about it but sit and stew. Then when Ramses's protection was lifted and Chucky's head was put on the chopping block, Li'l Monk was handed the cleaver. Chucky had fucked up when he decided to kill Ramses's right-hand man, Boo.

Boo's murder had been both unexpected and suspicious. Boo was not only a made man, but extremely cautious. He was shot at close range, so it had to be someone he knew if he let them get that close. It didn't help matters that he and Chucky had had a physical confrontation not long before his murder. When Ramses approached Chucky about it, he professed his innocence. He even had a chick vouch for his whereabouts at the time of the murder. Ramses didn't press it, but his suspicions remained. The whole thing never sat right with him. The missing piece of the puzzle came further down the line when a source, whom

Ramses refused to name, tipped him off to what really happened the morning of Boo's murder. To validate their story, they even provided Ramses with the murder weapon. It was Chucky's gun. The rabid dog finally had to be put down, and Ramses called on Li'l Monk to assist with the task of collecting Chucky's head.

Li'l Monk, and Ramses' right-hand man Huck, tracked Chucky to his aunt Letti's house in Mount Vernon. Their instructions were to kill Chucky and leave no witnesses to the crime. This meant everybody in the house had to die.

Armed with heavy firepower, and wearing masks, Li'l Monk and Huck went from room to room, gunning down everyone they found. Li'l Monk felt sick, covered in blood and damn near choking on gun smoke, but Huck seemed to be getting a kick out of the mass killing. He laughed like a school kid every time he dropped a body.

They searched almost the entire house, but still found no signs of Chucky. They moved their killing spree to the top floor where they found a locked bathroom door in one of the bedrooms. Huck got excited, thinking they had Chucky cornered, but when they finally kicked the door open all they found was a strung-out female. They were about to finish her off too when Li'l Monk realized he knew her.

She looked like death warmed over, but it was definitely Persia. It crushed him to see her in that condition. He'd heard stories about how far she had slipped, but seeing it first hand was almost too much to bear. There was no way Li'l Monk was going to kill Persia and he was prepared to turn his gun on Huck if he tried to. He was torn between his love and his loyalty. Persia saved Li'l Monk the trouble of having to decide when she made a break for the window. She was scared to death, and desperate to get away from the masked men. Li'l Monk was trying to pull her back inside to save her, but thinking he was out to hurt her, Persia fought him. During the struggle she slipped and fell two stories to the cold ground below.

Li'l Monk's breath caught in his throat thinking Persia was dead. Ignoring Huck yelling for him to stick to the script, Li'l Monk rushed outside to Persia. Thankfully, she was still alive, but there was no telling how extensive the damage was. Mission be damned, Li'l Monk was going to get Persia to the hospital. Huck argued with him about it, saying that they should let her die, but when Li'l Monk told him who Persia was and their connection, he surprisingly agreed to help Li'l Monk get her medical attention. Li'l Monk wasn't sure why Huck agreed so easily to let her live; and to his knowledge he had never told Ramses about the girl they had let live. For whatever reasons he had for keeping Li'l Monk's secret, Huck had earned his respect.

"You okay?" Omega asked, noticing the far-off look in Li'l Monk's eyes.

"Yeah, I'm cool. Was just thinking about something," Li'l Monk told him.

"From the way your mouth was hanging open, you must've been daydreaming about some pussy. Don't make Sophie fuck you up for cheating on her in your head," Omega joked.

"Fuck you, O." Li'l Monk tossed a cigar at him. "Roll something up while I jump in the shower real quick before we dip."

While Li'l Monk went off to shower and dress, Omega made himself comfortable in the living room and started rolling the weed. Looking around, he had to admit that Li'l Monk had done a complete 180 with the place, compared to how it had looked a few months prior. He'd bought new furniture and a big-screen television. Li'l Monk had made it a cozy little place for him and his dad.

As if he'd sensed Omega thinking about him, Big Monk appeared seemingly out of thin air. He was standing near the front door, wearing a black hoodie and gloves. He looked like every bit the Grim Reaper. "'Sup, li'l nigga?"

"Ain't nothing, Monk." Omega nodded in greeting. The way Li'l Monk's dad was looking at him made Omega's skin crawl, which was no surprise. Omega always felt uncomfortable when he was around Big Monk alone. He was dangerous, unpredictable, and sneaky.

Keeping his eyes on Omega, Monk walked over and sat on the coffee table directly in front of Omega. For a few long moments he didn't say anything; he just watched Omega roll the weed. "What's that, some of that hydro y'all kids be smoking?" He finally broke the silence.

"Nah, this is Purple Haze. You trying to get blazed?" Omega extended the expertly rolled blunt to Monk.

"Nah, you know that ain't my drug of choice. If it don't go snap, crackle, pop when you light it, I ain't fucking with it," Monk told him. "While I got your attention, let me ask you something, li'l nigga."

"What's up?"

Monk spared a glance over his shoulder to make sure Li'l Monk wasn't within earshot, before speaking. "Word on the streets is that your boss has run afoul of some real nasty folks."

"Really? That's news to me." Omega faked ignorance.

"Somehow I doubt that. If it had been Junior back there playing dumb, I might believe it, but not you, O. You keep your ear pressed so far to the ground I'll bet you can hear the devil when he passes gas."

Omega laughed. "You got jokes."

"I'm glad that I amuse you, but let me tell you what ain't so funny." Monk leaned in so that he and Omega were eye to eye. "Your boss has finally come across somebody who ain't gonna lie down and be bullied. Poppa Clark might've been willing to play diplomatically with Pharaoh, but his kid won't. Shai Clark is too young and too wet behind the ears to even know what diplomacy is, so at the first signs of trouble his first reaction is going to be to wipe you muthafuckas out, and he's got the guns and the muscle to do it."

Omega didn't take kindly to Monk kicking dirt on his team. "I hear you talking, old timer, but even if there was a beef brewing, which there isn't, I think Pharaoh is more than capable of holding his own."

Monk gave a throaty laugh. "Simple minded-ass nigga, this ain't the nineties no more and your boss ain't as strong as you think. Ghost stories about the great and powerful Pharaoh ain't enough to keep these wolves at bay anymore. Why do you think Pharaoh keeps himself hidden away and uses dumb little niggas like you and my son for his dirty work? All of you are expendable and just don't know it. But fuck all that, let me get to the point I'm trying to make. There's a shit storm coming and no doubt you and Li'l Monk are gonna end up caught in the middle of it. I need to know that while he's out there, my son has solid niggas watching his back. Are you a solid nigga?"

"Of course. My gun go off," Omega said proudly.

"Yeah, your gun go off, but can you hit anything?" Monk fired back.

"I got my homie's back, you have my word on that," Omega pledged.

"You damn well better. I know how snake-ass niggas like Pharaoh and Ramses do. When things get too hectic for them to handle they send a bunch of you young cats out to give your lives for their weak-ass cause, so you best be expecting it and move accordingly. Because if something happens to my son out there because one of you knuckleheads wasn't on point, it's gonna go bad for all of you."

Omega respected Monk on the strength that he was an O.G. as well as his best friend's father, but he didn't know how he felt about how Monk was coming at him. "Is that supposed to be some kind of threat?"

"Not at all, O." Monk pulled a gun from the pocket of his hoodie and pointed it at Omega's face. "This is a threat. If by some strange twist of fate my son ends up being one of the sacrificial lambs in this foolishness, I'm gonna pay a call on all you bitches' mamas and girlfriends before I pick you off one by one, even Mr. High and Mighty Pharaoh. Your new purpose in life is to keep my son alive, ya dig?"

"You got it, Monk. You got it," Omega said nervously.

"Good." Monk slipped the gun back in his pocket.

"What the fuck are y'all sitting so close together for?" Li'l Monk asked, coming out of the bedroom. Like his father, he was wearing a black hooide and black jeans.

"Nothing, Junior. Just having a little chitchat with ya man." Monk got up off the coffee table.

There was something about the look on Big Monk's face that he didn't like. He always knew when his father was up to no good. "You headed back out?"

"Nah, I'm in for a while. I got a freak bitch coming by who's down to fuck for a buck. Let me hold something so I can get my Friday night popping."

Li'l Monk gave his father a disbelieving look. "What happened to the money I gave you earlier?"

"What the fuck do you think happened to it? I smoked it," Monk said as if it should've been obvious.

Li'l Monk sucked his teeth and dug in his pocket for his bankroll. "This shit here is gonna have to stop."

"I know you ain't acting funny over a few funky-ass dollars." Monk sounded offended. "Boy, don't you know—"

"I know, I know, you've been taking care of me all my life," Li'l Monk cut him off and shoved a few bills in his hand. "Take this money and go about ya business, man."

Monk took a second to count through the bills. "Appreciate you, son." He disappeared into his bedroom.

"Whatever, nigga." Li'l Monk waved him off. He was getting tired of his father's antics and knew it would only be a matter of time before he would have to get his own place. He turned his attention to Omega, who was sitting there looking like he had seen a ghost. "Fuck you sitting there looking crazy for? Light the weed."

Omega handed him the blunt. "Do your thing. I don't feel much like getting high right now."

After Li'l Monk took the blunt to the face, he and Omega hit the streets. He wanted to go and have his meeting with Ramses and get it over with so he could have the rest of his night free. He and Sophie hadn't parted on the best terms and he wanted to make it up to her. He remembered her saying something about a movie she wanted to see and planned to take her. It was a chick movie, and not really Li'l Monk's style, but he'd sit through it for her.

Li'l Monk and Omega were walking down the street talking among themselves when Li'l Monk spotted a car with tinted windows slow coasting beside them. He peeked at the plates and saw that they were from Virginia. As the passenger window rolled down, Li'l Monk's hand dipped near his waist, where he had his gun stashed. He was about to draw until he saw that there were two pretty Spanish chicks in the front seat. The driver was a brunette wearing fire engine red lipstick and the passenger was a green-eyed blonde. From the skimpy tops they had on they appeared to be looking for a good time.

"What's good, fellas? Where can we get some weed?" the blonde asked.

"We don't sell drugs, ma," Li'l Monk told her and kept walking.

"Stop acting like that, baby. We ain't cops, we're just trying to get high," the blonde explained, but her explanation fell on deaf ears with Li'l Monk. Seeing she wasn't getting anywhere with him she set her sights on Omega. "What about you, handsome? You scared of girls too?"

"More like they're scared of me," Omega boasted. The minute he had seen that there were females in the car he slowed his stroll and started plotting.

"Really, now why is that?" the brunette asked from behind the wheel.

"If you have to ask then you don't need to know," Omega shot back.

"Spoken like an important man," the blonde flirted.

"Baby girl, you didn't know? I run these streets," Omega bragged.

"O, let's bust a move so we can handle business," Li'l Monk called. He was getting irritated. They had shit to do and Omega was chasing pussy, as usual. They had things to do and Omega was slowing them down.

Omega gave him a look that said to be cool and went back to talking to the women. "Like I was saying, baby, this is my hood."

"Yeah, right," the blonde dismissed him. "The way we hear it, a guy named King Tut is in charge over here."

Omega frowned. "Baby, you've been misinformed. King Tut works for me. He don't move unless I say so." He threw his friend under the bus.

The smile that had been plastered across the blonde's face suddenly melted away. "That's good to know." She made a hand gesture. The back window of the car rolled down and out sprang a young Spanish girl holding a shotgun.

"Down!" Li'l Monk screamed, before tackling Omega. They both hit the floor a split second before a blast from the shotgun knocked out the side windows of the car they had been standing on the other side of.

Li'l Monk sat with his back pressed against the parked car, while the shotgun fired over and over. When the shotgun clicked empty, he heard the sounds of tires screeching. They were trying to escape, but it wouldn't happen on Li'l Monk's watch. He popped up from behind the parked car in time to see the shooters peeling down the block. The girl with the shotgun was still hanging out the window, reloading her weapon. Li'l Monk jumped out into the middle of the street and opened fired on the fleeing car with his cannon. The Desert Eagle slugs punched silver dollar-sized holes in the body of the car and shattered the back window. The brunette lost control of the car and went speeding across the Avenue, crashing through the gate and front window of the Dollar Store.

"Got you bitches now." Li'l Monk jogged across the street to finish what he had started. When he arrived at the crash scene, he found the girl who had shot at them staggering to her feet, still holding the shotgun. Without breaking his stride, he put a bullet in her brain as he passed her on the way to the car. Li'l Monk didn't even turn around to see the body drop. About that time, Omega had joined him and Li'l Monk noticed that he was walking with a limp. "You hit?"

"Nah, I banged my damn knee on the sidewalk when your heavy-ass tackled me," Omega told him.

"Better a busted knee than a busted skull," Li'l Monk said.

"Very funny," Omega said moving to stand beside Li'l Monk. When he looked down at the corpse of the girl holding the shotgun his mouth suddenly became very dry. He had seen her before on one of his trips to try to negotiate with Petey for his territory. She worked the register at the restaurant he hung out in.

"You staring at that bitch like you know her," Li'l Monk said.

"Nah, I don't know her. Let's see what we got." Omega headed toward the driver's side of the wrecked car.

Li'l Monk spared one last glance at the corpse and moved around to the passenger side. Inside the car was a mess. The driver's airbag failed to deploy so the brunette caught the full impact of the dashboard in the crash. The bridge of her nose and part of her forehead were completely crushed. She never stood a chance. The blonde was still alive, but for how long was anyone's guess. One of the display racks that decorated the Dollar Store window had pierced her chest like a spear. At the rate she was bleeding, she wouldn't be long for this world.

"Who sent you?" Li'l Monk asked, trying to interrogate the girl for as much information as he could before she expired. She was trying to say something, a name, but her voice was faint. Li'l Monk was about to lean in closer to try to hear clearer what she was saying, when the blonde's head suddenly exploded. Li'l Monk jumped back, and saw Omega standing on the other side of the car holding a smoking gun. "What the fuck did you do that for? She was trying to tell me who sent them."

"Man, you can't put no stock in the ramblings of muthafuckas who know they're about to die.

They'll say anything just to live." Omega dumped another shot in her for good measure. "Don't matter who sent these bitches. They'll get the message that we ain't to be fucked with when they see their hitters on the morning news. Let's get out of here before the cops come. Your block is hot now, so we can go back to my pad and get cleaned up before we go see Ramses. We don't want to keep him waiting any longer than he already has been."

# CHAPTER 17

When Persia made the call to Asia, she felt awkward about it, almost desperate. She felt silly for being so hard up for a friend that she called a girl she hardly knew. As it turned out it was the best decision she had made in a while.

Asia invited Persia to a charity event that her mother was hosting in Manhattan. Persia was hesitant about going, but when she discovered that the event was in support of suicide prevention she changed her mind. After what happened to Marty the cause hit close to home for her.

Michelle was initially suspicious about Persia going out with Asia. The last time she let her daughter go out with her friends unattended the dynamics of their life had changed. It took quite a bit of begging on Persia's part, and some guarantees from Nya before Michelle finally agreed to let Persia attend the event. Nya also extended invitations to Michelle and Richard to attend the event, but they declined. This would be Persia's first social outing in a very long time and they didn't want to hover over her like they didn't trust her.

Persia had fever trying to find something to wear. Since her stint in recovery she had put on a bit of weight and couldn't really fit into any more of her good dresses. Thankfully Michelle was able to find something she had that Persia was able to fit in. It was a nice strapless black dress that hugged Persia's curves perfectly.

Richard and Michelle came outside with Persia while she waited for her ride. They were all surprised to see two long black Lincoln Town Cars pull up in front of her house. Nya got out of one and Asia the other. Both of them looked stunning in matching silver dresses and had their faces flawlessly made up. All dressed up, Asia looked far older than seventeen and a time or two Persia caught Richard looking at her. Nya made small talk with Richard and Michelle who stood off to the side, whispering and giggling. After a while, Nya announced that they had to be going and they headed toward their respective Town Cars. Nya rode in the lead car with two assistants while Asia and Persia got into the car that would follow.

Persia did a double take when she saw the hulking man behind the wheel of the car they'd be riding in. He was so big that the steering wheel was almost pressed against his chest while they were driving. Asia had introduced him as her cousin, Basil, but from the way he doted over her he felt more like a bodyguard. After waving good-bye to her parents, Persia was off.

Asia was way cooler than Persia had expected her to be. At school she seemed quiet and sometimes stuck-up, but when it was just she and Persia, Asia loosened up. She was smart and hilariously funny. She had Persia in tears as she made jokes and talked about the different chicks in school. In a lot of ways she reminded Persia of Marty and wished the two could've met. She knew they would've gotten along famously.

"You know, I wanna thank you for inviting me out tonight, Asia. It's been awhile since I've been anywhere except school and the library," Persia told her.

"It's okay, Persia. It's like I was telling you, I think you're a cool chick. Besides, we got off on the wrong foot and I kind of wanted to make it right between us. As a matter of fact, I have a peace offering." Asia reached into her purse and pulled out a rolled-up joint. "Do you burn?"

"No, not anymore," Persia said, looking away from the joint.

"It's cool. Will it bother you if I smoke?"

"No, not at all," Persia lied. In all truthfulness, she didn't know how she would react to being around the weed smoke. Since she was in recovery she hadn't touched a drug, or even a drop of alcohol. Her mother and Richard had even gotten rid of the bar they had at home just so she wouldn't be tempted.

Asia lit the joint and inhaled deeply, closing her eyes and letting the smoke fill her lungs. From the smell of it, Persia knew it was some high-quality weed. She felt her mouth watering, wanting to hit the blunt so bad, but knew she couldn't. Weed was a relatively harmless drug to most, but there was no such thing as a harmless drug to someone in recovery.

Halfway into the joint, Asia grabbed two glasses and some small bottles of Scotch from the mini bar. She offered one to Persia, but she declined. "Damn, you don't drink or smoke? What kind of teenager are you?"

"One who has been through a lot," Persia said.

"I totally understand. It's a lot like how I feel about sex," Asia said.

"How do you mean?" Persia asked.

"Well, in my old school in Germany I had sort of a reputation as being a lose *mädchen*," she said in perfect German.

"A what?" Persia didn't understand the word.

"A loose girl," Asia translated. "In America you'd call it being a ho." She laughed. "For me, it was like sex was my drug of choice. Didn't too much matter where or who I got it from, as long as I got it. I didn't set out to be like that, but it was like having sex was the only thing I could do to feel good about myself. In those few moments when a man was professing his love for me I felt important, even when they were lying. After a pregnancy scare, it made me reevaluate how I was living and the things I was doing and realize that even though the sex was feeling good it wasn't necessarily good for me, so I stayed away from it."

"So, you're celibate now?" Persia asked.

"Heavens no! As stressful as my life is, celibacy would probably drive me thoroughly insane. I still have sex when I feel like I need a release, but I don't feel like I need it anymore to make me whole. Let's just say I've decided to do my drug of choice in moderation."

"Wow, I'd have never figured it. You don't strike me as the type," Persia said.

"Just like you don't strike me as a recovering addict. Some of us hide our shame better than others," Asia said, surprising Persia. "Don't look at me like that, Persia. You know how women talk. I know all about your fall from grace."

"If you know all this why would you want to hang out with an ex-smoker?" Persia asked.

"Because I believe in judging people for who they are, not what they've done. If I moved solely based on gossip then I'd have disowned my mother years ago, because God knows that woman's name has been tied to more than a few scandals."

"That's crazy because your mother seems so straight laced," Persia said, thinking of how Nya had been the epitome of a lady from the moment she'd met her.

"Yes, she is now, but she had her time. During the time my father was killed my mother was really out there," Asia said as if it pained her even to mention her father.

"I'm sorry," Persia said.

"No need to be. You didn't kill him, that honor went to a one-eyed priest who my father had made an enemy of."

"Asia, if it's not too personal of a question, why was your father killed?" Persia wanted to know.

"Not a personal question at all. Quite frankly, my father was killed for the same reason most young men die far too soon, he wanted to be a gangster. I don't judge my father or speak ill of him for the things he's done. Even in death his deed provides my mother and me with a lavish life, but honestly, I'd trade it all just to have him back," Asia said emotionally.

"I feel you on that," Persia said, thinking of her own father who was rotting away in prison.

"Enough of this sad talk, we're supposed to be having a good time. Tell me, have you ever been to a fundraiser?" Asia asked, changing the subject.

"No, this will be my first one."

"Excellent." Asia clapped excitedly. "This should be fun for you, but I'm afraid not so much for me. I'll be working."

"Are you modeling tonight?" Persia asked.

"No, but I might as well be because I'm sure my mother will be parading me around while annoying men snap pictures and rude women ask me uncomfortable questions," Asia said in an irritated tone.

"I don't know why you sound so bitter about it, Asia. What little girl wouldn't want to be a famous model?"

"I'm more notorious than famous, and that's because of who my mother is and who my father was. In the beginning, I used to love it, but after doing it since I was four years old it's becoming so bland. Always the same thing, 'turn this way, walk that way, stand up straight.'" Asia made a dismissive gesture with her hands. "Sometimes

I just want to be a regular teenager and not the focal point of every eye in the room."

"We're here, cousin," Basil said over his shoulder. Persia and Asia had been so deep in conversation that they hadn't even realized they were in Manhattan already.

Persia looked out the window at all the people in front of the venue and the red carpet leading up to the door. Flash bulbs began popping before the Town Car had even come to a complete stop. There were athletes, entertainers all dressed to the nines, waving for the cameras or conducting interviews. All of the city's elite had come out for the event. Security lined either side of the red carpet, keeping journalists and onlookers at a safe distance from the stars. It was unreal.

"Are you ready?" Asia asked.

"As I'll ever be, I guess," Persia said nervously.

"Loosen up, Persia. This is a night of fun and no stress, try to enjoy it. Think of tonight as your coming-out party," Asia said, throwing on a pair of sunglasses. "Now let's go and greet our adoring public," Asia said and flung the door open.

To say that Persia was overwhelmed by the experience would've been an understatement. They had barely made it out of the Town Car before the media swooped in on them. There were flashes from so many different cameras that Persia was temporarily blinded and Asia had to lead her by the hand. Persia now understood why she was wearing sunglasses at night.

Basil bullied his way through the throng of media personnel and fans, clearing a path for the women. Persia was scared shitless, but Asia took it all in stride, smiling and waving to people like she was the first lady of the United States. She made it all look so effortless. As soon as they got inside, members of security came and whisked them away. Nya had to take her place on the main stage, as the hostess, while Asia was taken to the green room to conduct a few interviews and take some publicity pictures. Asia offered Persia to join her, but Persia declined. She didn't want to crowd her, so she just agreed to hook up with Asia when she was done.

Persia stood off to the side, sipping from a crystal glass filled with water, trying her best not to look like a star-stuck teenager, while she eye-balled some of her favorite celebrities. Never in a million years would Persia have thought she'd be partying with the stars of some of her favorite movies and television shows. She had been there less than an hour and it was already one of the best nights of her life, but little did she know things were about to get far more interesting.

"You know, if I didn't know better I'd say you were following me," a voice spoke up behind Persia. She turned, surprised to see Vaughn. He was immaculately dressed in a black tuxedo, with black shoes polished to a high shine.

"You're the last person I expected to see here," Persia said, looking him over. Vaughn looked good enough to eat.

"Is that a compliment or an insult?" Vaughn asked. His tone suggested that he was offended.

Persia covered her mouth to hide her embarrassment. "Oh, I didn't mean it like that. I'm sorry."

"I'm just teasing you, ma." Vaughn smiled. "You must have some pretty important friends if you were invited to this joint."

"I came with my homegirl." Persia pointed at Asia, who was doing an interview in front of the backdrop of one of the event's sponsors.

"Oh, you're with Asia?" Vaughn asked in surprise.

"Yeah, do you know her?" Persia asked, hoping to God Vaughn wasn't one of Asia's conquests.

"Who doesn't know Asia Sudan? She's kind of a big deal, ya know, but not as big a deal as you," Vaughn said with a wink.

"Here you go, running game again," Persia said.

"If you call me keeping it real running game then so be it. I just call it like I see it and the view from here is breathtaking." Vaughn openly ogled Persia, causing her to blush.

"Smile, guys." A photographer popped seemingly out of thin air. Vaughn pulled Persia into a lover's embrace, and posed for the picture. "Thanks." The photographer scurried off.

"What was that all about?" Persia asked, confused.

"I told you, you're a big deal. Hey listen, after this is over do you wanna go somewhere and get a real meal? The portions they serve at these things ain't fit for a kid and I'm sure you're gonna be hungry when it's over."

"I don't know, Vaughn, you're moving kinda fast," Persia said.

"Persia, it's just a meal. You're acting like I asked for your hand in marriage, that'll come later." Vaughn smirked devilishly. "But seriously, Persia, my intentions are nothing but pure. I ain't trying to crowd you. I just wanna get to know you a little bit. Scout's honor." He held three fingers up like the Boy Scouts salute.

"We'll see," Persia told him with a smile.

Vaughn rubbed his chin. "Not the answer I was looking for, but I'll take it because it beats you telling me flat out no. I'm making progress."

The white girl Persia had seen at the record store walked up. She cut her eyes at Persia as if she was wondering what she was doing there, before turning her attention back to Vaughn, but didn't bother to speak. She whispered something in Vaughn's ear, which made him frown. There was a brief exchange between them, before Vaughn finally relented to whatever she was asking.

"Persia, I hate to dip off but I gotta take care of something real quick," Vaughn told her. The white girl stood a few paces behind him, with her arms folded like she had an attitude about something.

"Handle your business. I'm good." Persia told him.

"Promise me that you won't leave until we've had a chance to finish our little discussion."

"I'm not making any promises, but I can't leave until Asia and Nya are ready to go anyhow, and from the looks of things they'll be awhile," Persia said, glancing over at Nya and Asia who were both on the stage by that point.

"Fair enough. I'll see you in a bit," Vaughn said before allowing the white girl to lead him through the crowd.

When Nya took the microphone everyone gathered around the stage to hear what she was saying. She went through a scripted speech about bringing awareness to teen suicide and some more stuff that Persia only half listened to. What made her really start paying attention was when Nya announced that they were about to start the celebrity auction. The bids to win a night with the celebrities ranged from as low as $1,000 to as high as $50,000. Persia shook her head at the display of thirst as men and women alike pledged ridiculous amounts of money to keep company with some of the celebrities who volunteered to be auctioned off. She was about to take a bathroom break, until Nya introduced the last celerity to be auctioned off. Her head almost spun around backward when Vaughn was brought onto the stage.

"Okay, ladies," Nya began. "I'm going to need you to reach deep in those purses for this fine piece of eye candy. Some of you may know him from breaking records and hearts as the starting quarterback at Virginia Tech, but come this fall he'll be giving women and defenses fits on prime-time television. So tell me, ladies, how much is it worth to you to spend a night with Philadelphia Eagles rookie quarterback, Vaughn Tate?" Persia was stunned. She couldn't move, nor speak. All this time she had been treating Vaughn like a pauper and he was really a prince. She felt like such a fool. Persia was so embarrassed that she wanted to crawl under a rock and die, but since a rock wasn't available she slipped out the back door. She felt bad about dipping out on Asia and Nya after they had shown her so much hospitality, but she would make it up to them at another time. All she was focused on at that moment was jumping in a cab and going home.

# CHAPTER 18

Roughly two hours after leaving three corpses on the Avenue, Li'l Monk was showered, changed, and back on the streets as if nothing had ever happened. He had traded his bloodied black hoodie for a fresh gray one and blue jeans. He and Omega made it a point to always keep a spare outfit or two at each other's houses. They were always in the mix so you never could tell when they would have to make a quick change, much like that night.

The whole time Li'l Monk was getting ready, he replayed the series of events over in his head trying to make sense of them. Being down with Pharaoh made them all targets to enemies both known and unknown, but the strip was their save haven. Within those few blocks of territory they had always felt safe. No one would dare come into the heart of Pharaoh's empire and try something stupid, or so he thought. The fact that they had almost been whacked on their own block said different.

The three Spanish chicks coming through and trying to take them out was no random occurrence. They were specifically targeting for members of Ramses's street crew, but the question remained, why? Li'l Monk was certain that the blonde had been about to reveal something important before Omega had killed her, sending whatever secrets she was keeping to the grave with her. This bothered Li'l Monk, not because he didn't think Omega was capable of killing, but because he was usually the one who tried to avoid bloodshed when necessary. It wasn't like him to just commit coldblooded murder.

In truth, Omega had been acting strange for the past couple of weeks. He wasn't his normal happy-go-lucky self. Lately he had been especially irritable and quick to anger. Li'l Monk initially attributed it to the extra responsibilities Ramses had placed upon him. With Benny dead and Chucky a fugitive, Ramses leaned more heavily on Omega to handle the day-to-day operations of their businesses in West Harlem. Since Li'l Monk also had to take on extra responsibilities he could definitely understand Omega being affected by the added job stress, but it felt like there was something deeper that was causing the changes in his friend. Maybe he was becoming power drunk with his new position or even possibly beginning to crack under the added pressure. Li'l Monk wasn't sure what it was, but something felt off and the way he had shot that girl added to Li'l Monk's suspicions.

The designated meeting area was a steak house on Fifty-seventh Street. Li'l Monk had been there several times, as it was one of Ramses's favorite places to eat as well as talk business. At that hour the restaurant was closed to the public, but not to Ramses.

When Li'l Monk and Omega arrived at the spot there was a small gathering of men in front of the joint. Some of them they recognized as a part of their organization, but the white dudes they didn't know. They wore jogging suits with gold chains and had heavily gelled hair. They were stereotypical Italians. This struck Li'l Monk as odd, because for as long as he had been working for Ramses he rarely saw him deal with white people at all, and here was a group of them congregating outside the restaurant.

Li'l Monk led the way toward the entrance of the restaurant. To his surprise and amusement, one of the Italians moved to cut him off. He was a bear of a man, whose jogging suit looked a half size too small.

"Something I can help you with?" Li'l Monk looked him up and down.

"Gotta check you for weapons before I let you pass," the Italian bear told him.

"Homeboy, if you put your hands on me I'm going to break them," Li'l Monk growled. He had been having a shitty day and didn't have time for foolishness. He had expected the warning to be enough to persuade the bear to step aside, but it wasn't. He held his ground, ready to challenge Li'l Monk. Before the situation could escalate, Huck appeared in the doorway.

"Nah, they're good," Huck told the bear. The bear gave Li'l Monk one last hard look before stepping aside to let him pass. "Sorry about that." Huck greeted Li'l Monk and Omega with handshakes.

"What the fuck was that all about?" Li'l Monk asked.

"Difficult times we're in so everybody is a little bit on edge," Huck explained.

"Tell me about it," Li'l Monk said, thinking of the attempt on his and Omega's lives earlier.

"Come on in the back. Ramses is waiting for you." Huck led them inside.

Li'l Monk and Omega made their way through the empty dining tables to the private booth that Ramses kept on reserve in the back of the restaurant. As they got closer they saw that Ramses wasn't alone. Standing next to him, just outside the booth was King Tut. When he and Li'l Monk locked eyes you could instantly feel the spark of hostility that passed between them.

Sitting across from Ramses was a handsome Italian with dark skin and wavy black hair. The salmon-colored suit he wore clung to his body perfectly as if it had been created just for him. When the Italian noticed Huck leading the two young black kids to the back, he abruptly ended whatever conversation he and Ramses had been having.

When Ramses spotted Li'l Monk and Omega he waved them over. "About time you two got here," he said in the way of a greeting.

"We got held up in traffic," Li'l Monk said sarcastically, which got him a serious look from Ramses. He was obviously in no mood for jokes.

"Boys, this is Frank Donatello," Ramses introduced them to the Italian.

The Italian didn't bother to try to shake hands, instead offering a simple nod in greeting. "My friends call me Frankie the Fish."

"You want me to pull up some extra chairs?" Huck asked Ramses.

"Nah, Frankie was just leaving," Ramses told him.

"Yeah, I've got a few more people to see before I can turn in for the night. Thanks for the meal and your time." Frankie shook hands with Ramses before standing to leave.

"Anytime, Frankie. I look forward to a prosperous working relationship between our two families," Ramses said.

"As do I. Maybe next time Pharaoh will see fit to sit down with us. I'm not used to doing business with people who I have not looked in the eyes," Frankie told him.

"My apologies for that, but Pharaoh has been extremely busy lately. I can assure you that I am authorized to speak for him in these matters though."

"I guess your word will be good enough, for now," Frankie said. He picked his salmon-colored fedora off the seat and placed it on his head, running his finger across the brim. "I guess I'll leave you boys to it. Nice meeting you fellas." Frankie tipped the brim of his hat to Omega and Li'l Monk and left the restaurant.

"Sit down you two," Ramses told Omega and Li'l Monk. They slid into the booth on the opposite side of Ramses and Tut. "Y'all been with me long enough to know how much I hate being kept waiting. What were you doing that was important that you couldn't come immediately when I called for you?"

"Sorry about that, but we were busy trying to keep our heads from getting blown off," Li'l Monk told him then went on to tell the story about the chicks who had rolled through the block. He didn't miss the look that passed between Omega and Tut when he got to the part of the story about them being a carful of Spanish broads.

"Any idea who sent them?" Ramses asked. He seemed genuinely concerned.

"No, we never got a chance to find out." Li'l Monk cut his eyes at Omega. He would never throw his partner under the bus, but he didn't try to hide his displeasure.

Ramses shook his head. "Wolves at our front and back doors. I'll get some people to look into it, but that'll have to wait. I got some other shit I need y'all to handle, but first, what's this business between you and Tut?"

Li'l Monk shrugged. "Ain't no business between me and Tut. One of his boys came through talking reckless so I had to discipline him."

"You call putting a man in intensive care because you broke a half dozen of his bones discipline?" Tut asked heatedly.

"At least I didn't kill him. Be thankful for the small blessings," Li'l Monk said sarcastically.

"I got a blessing for you." Tut shot to his feet and Li'l Monk was immediately on his.

"Do I have to have Huck put the both of you on timeout?" Ramses looked from Li'l Monk to Tut. Just a look from him was enough to get them to both wisely retake their seats. "It's bad enough that we're beefing with niggas in the streets. I don't need my lieutenants trying to off each other, too."

"I apologize, Ramses," Tut said, still glaring at Li'l Monk.

"Me too," Li'l Monk added, matching Tut's glare.

"Now, I need to know that this shit between y'all is dead and won't go any further," Ramses told the both of them.

"So long as respect is given, I got no problems with Tut or any of his people," Li'l Monk said.

"I'm cool, Ramses," Tut agreed.

"Now that we've settled that, let's get on to a more pressing piece of business. A friend of the family was recently murdered in the Bronx," Ramses revealed.

"Anybody we might know?" Li'l Monk asked.

"I don't think you two have ever met, but Omega knows him. His name was Petey Suarez."

Li'l Monk saw Tut's body tense at the mention of the name. It was a small tell that had probably gone unnoticed by everyone else on the table, but Li'l Monk caught it.

"Say word somebody capped Petey?" Omega asked in fake shock. "Damn, and that was a cool-ass little dude. Why did he get clipped?"

"It's hard to say at this point. Petey had a hot temper and was always into some shit so it could've come from anywhere. I know he had been having some troubles with the Jamaicans and the Dominicans recently, but I can't say for sure where the hit came from. Before it's all said and done I'll find out though. Petey came from a very well-respected family and his uncle Poppito was not happy to hear about his death," Ramses said.

"Why does that name sound so familiar?" Li'l Monk thought out loud.

"Probably because it's always in the news. Poppito is the head of a powerful cartel based out of Old San Juan, Puerto Rico. Until recently our relationship has always been good with his cartel, but that all changed when his nephew died on my watch. When Petey's father died, I promised his uncle Poppito that I would do what I could to keep him out of harm's way, though with Petey that proved easier said than done. Every time I turned around Petey was into some shit and obviously his chickens finally came home to roost. Honestly, I'm surprised that it took this long for somebody to split Petey's wig. It's been a long time coming, but it doesn't change the fact that it happened right in our back yard and his uncle is demanding answers."

"How can we help?" Omega asked.

"I need you to go to the Bronx and assist Poppito's people who are looking into the murder. Petey's whole crew was killed with him, but apparently there was a witness to the crime."

"A witness?" Omega asked, not able to hide his surprise or discomfort.

"Yeah, the owner of the restaurant. Whoever killed Petey locked all the restaurant employees inside and set the whole place on fire in an attempt to cover their tracks, but two people survived. One of the waitresses and the restaurant owner. There's no sign of the waitress, but the owner is in the hospital. She was burned so bad that the doctors say it's a miracle that she survived."

"A miracle indeed," Omega said, looking at Tut. "So you want me and Li'l Monk to take care of it?"

"No, I got something else I need Li'l Monk to handle for me, so I'm sending you and Tut," Ramses told him.

"Me?" Tut asked in surprise.

"Yes, you. The Bronx is your area so I figured you could be helpful in the investigation. Why, do you have a problem with what I'm asking you to do?"

"Not at all," Tut said, trying to hide his nervousness.

"Good, I need y'all to get on that as soon as possible," Ramses said.

"A'ight, we on it," Omega assured him, standing to leave.

"Omega, I'm sure I don't need to tell you that this has to be handled with kid gloves, right? Poppito is livid about what happened to his nephew and is looking at everybody as a suspect, including us. With all the other shit we got going on, the last thing we need is to make an enemy of Poppito's cartel. Do what you can to put this shit to bed as quickly and as cleanly as possible."

"I got you, Ramses. Let's make moves, Tut." Omega started for the door. Tut slid out of the booth and fell in step behind him.

Ramses waited until they were gone to address Li'l Monk. "What I need you to do is a bit less complicated, but equally important."

"Run it down to me." Li'l Monk gave Ramses his undivided attention.

"As you've probably already figured out, we're working on improving our foreign relations with our spaghetti-eating friends from downtown," Ramses said, speaking of the Italians.

"I wanted to ask you about that, but I didn't want to overstep my boundaries. I was always under the impression that you hated white folks."

Ramses laughed. "Hate is a strong word. Let's just say I'm no fan of the so-called master race. Still, during these trying times we'll take our allies where we can get them, which is what has us crawling into bed with the Italians."

"Ramses, what's going on? Are we about to go to war?" Li'l Monk asked.

"Son, we've been at war for years, but not in the traditional sense. It's like this, whenever you're in a position of power they'll always be people who want to remove you from that position. Me and Pharaoh been at this a long time, and we've fought hard to maintain our position as kings of the hill, but times are changing. This is no longer a game of gentleman, but a game of savages and snakes. Between this new breed of youngsters, who don't respect human life, and these spineless cowards that have made snitching an acceptable course of action, I fear we are approaching the end of an era."

The tone of Ramses's voice disturbed Li'l Monk. He was used to Ramses being quick-witted and confident, but he sounded tired. "What does that mean for us?" he asked, but wasn't sure if he was ready for the answer.

"It means we tighten up ranks and do what we gotta do to keep what's ours until somebody gets balls or guns big enough to take it from us!" Ramses said confidently. There was the fire Li'l Monk was used to. "Right now it ain't quite serious enough to go to the mattresses, but we're covering our asses just in case it does get there. This is why our partnership with the Italians is so important and the point of me picking you for this little task. I trust you to handle it accordingly."

Hearing that Ramses had such confidence in him made Li'l Monk's heart swell with pride. "I'm up for it. What's good?"

"I need you to go downtown to see a friend of ours. He's going to give you something which you are to bring directly to me and nobody else."

A look of disappointment crossed Li'l Monk's face. "Ramses, I'm a soldier, my place is on the battlefield, busting my gun. I know you're salty at me for beating Tut's boy up, but this is a fucked-up punishment. I'm not a delivery boy."

"You're whatever the hell I say you are for as long as you're on my payroll," Ramses shot back. "Listen, Li'l Monk, this ain't got nothing to do with you laying hands on Chief. I know if he pushed you that far, he had it coming. This isn't about punishment, it's about being able to handle whatever tasks you're called on to undertake. I need to know that I can depend on you. Can I depend on you?"

"Of course you can, Ramses. You know that," Li'l Monk assured him.

"Then show me, and handle this business."

"Okay, Ramses," Li'l Monk reluctantly agreed. "Can I go now?"

"Yeah, you can go," Ramses dismissed him. Li'l Monk rose to leave, but Ramses had some parting words for him. "Li'l Monk, it's important that this stays between you and me. Go by yourself and don't tell anyone, not even Omega. I need you to handle this on your own, do you understand?"

"You got it, Ramses," Li'l Monk said and left.

"I send you to handle a simple task and you managed to fuck it up. This is all bad," Omega was telling Tut once they were away from the restaurant.

"My nigga, are you really gonna stand here and act like this was all my fault?" Tut asked. "You're the one who said it would be an easy job and there would be no repercussions."

"And it would've gone exactly how I said it would've, had you not decided to play David

Koresh and burn everybody up, instead of just putting a bullet behind their ears and being done with it. Now we've gotta worry about the one person who might be able to finger you as the killer."

"Ramses said there were two survivors," Tut corrected him.

"There were, until a few hours ago. The other one won't be snitching on anyone, at least not in this lifetime." Omega went on to tell Tut about the shootout with the Spanish chicks and the girl he'd recognized.

"You think Li'l Monk is wise to what's going on?" Tut asked.

"Nah, he's suspicious but he doesn't know enough to put all the pieces together," Omega told him.

"Well, you better keep it that way. If your pet dog starts snooping around too much, I might have to put him to sleep along with the last witness," Tut said seriously.

Omega grabbed Tut by the shirt and pressed him against the store front they were standing next to. "Let's get something clear, I don't give a fuck what's going on between you and Li'l Monk and how you feel about him, that's my friend. If I even think you got ill intentions for him, I won't hesitate to bust your muthafucking brain."

Tut laughed. "First of all"—he slapped Omega's hands away—"keep your fucking paws off me, nigga. I'm getting a little tired of you throwing your weight around like I'm one of your workers, Omega. Ramses gave me rank, same as you. Second of all, this is your fucking mess. You sent me into a situation without all the facts. Had I known this kid was related to some heavy hitters, I'd have told you to go fuck yourself and find somebody else to get involved. You might as well get your head wrapped around the fact that we're married to this thing, for better or worse. If I burn, you burn too and don't forget it. But let's deal with the bigger problem we have here. Ramses ordered both of us to go and see Poppito's people to talk to the survivor, but I don't know how comfortable I am with that. All it will take is that broad recognizing me and pointing the finger and I'm a dead man. Hell you'll probably be too, since we're both a part of the same crew."

"Yeah, this is gonna be tricky to pull off, but I think I know a way we can get everybody to play nice," Omega said, running through a series of scenarios in his head. He was a man who liked to be prepared for all eventualities so as soon as Ramses told him what was going on, he started scheming.

"I sure hope so, Omega, because this shit looks like it can only get messier. Either way this plays out our destinies are connected to the outcome of this. I'm ready to die about mine, but I don't think you can say the same," Tut capped.

Omega hated to admit it, but Tut was right. In him bringing Tut in on his scheme he had created a monster and a huge problem. Tut was like a captive animal who had tasted blood for the first time and now anything short of live prey wouldn't do to feed his hunger. He had known about Petey's connection with Poppito, which was one of the reasons that he went to Tut instead of picking someone from his inner circle. He thought he was being cleaver by using Tut to solve his problems, but what he succeeded in doing was giving Tut a way to hurt him. For as long as he had the dirty deed to hang over Omega, he was stuck.

# CHAPTER 19

Li'l Monk was in a rank mood when he got back to the hood. He had been tested, shot at, and demoted all in under twenty-four hours. Most of the things that had occurred were chalked up to another day at the office, but Ramses sending him to make a delivery stung. No matter how Ramses dressed it up, Li'l Monk still felt like it was grunt work and he had put in too much work to still have to prove himself. Times like those he thought about his father's warning about the men he pledged his allegiance to and wondered if there had been some validity to it. Still, Ramses had given him an order and like it or not he would carry it out.

Before he handled the task Ramses assigned him he wanted to go back by his house and grab some extra clips for his gun. Simple delivery or not, with the way things had been going for Li'l Monk he reasoned it was better to be safe than sorry. As he approached his building he noticed someone standing outside, huddled in the shadows of the doorway. Erring on the side of caution, Li'l Monk pulled his gun and took measured steps. When he neared the building he realized that it was only Charlie.

"Fuck you doing out here creeping around like a crackhead?" Li'l Monk asked Charlie.

"Not too much, man. I'm just out here," Charlie said, sounding stressed out.

"Everything okay?" Li'l Monk asked him. For all Charlie's faults, Li'l Monk still had a soft spot for his old friend and it bothered him when he wasn't in good spirits.

Charlie shrugged. "It's a small thing to a giant man. I'll be cool." He sounded uncertain. "Yo, did you hear about the shootout earlier?"

"Nah," Li'l Monk lied. "What happened?" He listened to Charlie give him the rundown about what the streets were saying as if he were truly clueless. From what Li'l Monk gathered, nobody had fingered him and Omega as the shooters, which was a good thing.

"While I got your attention, I wanted to tell you my bad about earlier. I didn't mean to be talking business in front of Droopy like that," Charlie said sincerely.

"Don't sweat it. Droopy is a good soldier, but I just like to keep my business out of the streets," Li'l Monk told him.

"Nah, I completely feel what you're saying. I don't know what I was thinking about throwing it out there like that, but a nigga is getting a little desperate. Shit is getting tight for me."

"You need a few dollars?" Li'l Monk asked Charlie, ready to dip into his stash.

"I ain't on it like that, Li'l Monk. For as bad as I can use a few dollars, you know I'd rather work for mine then have anybody give me anything. That's why I was asking you about putting me on the money."

"Honestly, Charlie, with the way things are going out here lately, I don't know if that's the best idea, at least, not for right now," Li'l Monk said. Charlie nodded his head as if he understood, but Li'l Monk could see disappointment on his face. It made Li'l Monk feel bad that he couldn't help his friend at the moment, but he knew Ramses was tightening ranks and bringing someone new in would've been out of the question. Still, he didn't want to see Charlie in the streets going without. There had to be something he could do to help his friend. That's when it hit him.

"Dig, Charlie," Li'l Monk continued. "I might not be able to put you on the money right now, but I got something you can get down with and I'll put a few dollars in your pocket for it. You feel like taking a ride?"

***

It didn't take Li'l Monk and Charlie long to get downtown in the taxi. They had the driver let them off on Centre Street and walked the rest of the way to the apartment building on Mulberry Street. It was an older building with no elevator, so they had to hike the three flights of stairs to their desired floor. Li'l Monk tapped on the apartment door Ramses had sent him to and gave Charlie some last-minute instructions while he waited for someone to answer.

"Now remember, Charlie, you ain't even supposed to be here with me so don't go shooting your fucking mouth off about it, or you could get us both fucked up," Li'l Monk warned.

"I ain't gonna say anything, Li'l Monk. I'm just thankful you're looking out for me," Charlie said. "So what are we picking up again?"

"Ain't none of your business what we're picking up. Your job is to keep me company and I'm going to make sure you get paid for it," Li'l Monk said sharply. Charlie didn't particularly care for how Li'l Monk was speaking to him, so he kept his response to himself.

After a few seconds, Li'l Monk heard somebody move the peephole, trying to get a good look at who was in the hallway. Li'l Monk stepped into the light so that whoever was behind the door could clearly see his face. One by one the locks came free and the door opened. Standing on the other side was the man Ramses had sent Li'l Monk to see, Mr. D.

Mr. D was an older Italian man with silver hair that had started thinning in the front. He adjusted the glasses sitting on the end of his nose and examined Li'l Monk and Charlie as if he was trying to gauge what they were about. "Can I help you?"

"I'm Li'l Monk," he introduced himself to Mr. D.

At the mention of the name a light of recognition went off in Mr. D's head. "Right, you're Ramses's boy. Come on in." He opened the door wider so that Li'l Monk and Charlie could enter. Mr. D led them down a long hallway and into a cluttered living room. "You boys can have a seat. I'll only be a second." He headed toward the bedroom. Mr. D pushed the door closed behind him, but didn't put enough behind the push, so it was left partially ajar.

Charlie pretended he was looking around the apartment curiously, but he was really peeking inside the bedroom where Mr. D had gone. Through the crack in the door Charlie could see a large safe sitting in the corner. Mr. D only had the safe open for a few seconds, but it was long enough for Charlie to see it was fat with cash. When Mr. D came back out, Charlie busied himself looking over the different trophies on the bookshelf, pretending that he hadn't been watching.

Mr. D walked over to Li'l Monk and handed him a thick envelope. "Give this to Ramses with my thanks."

"Will do." Li'l Monk stuffed the envelope into his pants for safekeeping. "Nice meeting you, Mr. D." He shook the old man's hand.

"You also, Li'l Monk. Hope to see more of you," Mr. D told him.

"Let's boogie," Li'l Monk told Charlie before heading for the door.

Charlie shook Mr. D's hand also, before following Li'l Monk. As he exited the apartment, he gave one last look over his shoulder at the bedroom with the safe in it.

It was late when Li'l Monk got back to the hood. He was tired and still needed to go check Sophie. He started to hold on to the envelope of cash until the following day before dropping it off to Ramses, but thought better of it. He had already gone against what Ramses told him by taking Charlie with him to Mr. D's, when Ramses specifically told him to go alone. It was best that he dropped it off to Ramses that night to get it out of the way.

"Thanks for taking that ride with me, Charlie." Li'l Monk handed him some folded bills.

Charlie took a minute to count through the bills before happily stuffing them in his pocket. "No problem. That was the easiest money I've ever made. This shit felt like old times, me and you out here getting this money."

"There's way more where that came from if you play your cards right, Charlie. Just give things a few days to die down over here and I'll talk to Ramses about putting you in position."

Charlie smiled. "That's why you'll always be my man fifty grand. You stay looking out for your people."

"It's only right."

"So what you 'bout to get into?" Charlie asked.

"About to go holla at Ramses then take it down. I been neglecting my lady and so I'm gonna go spend some time with her tonight," Li'l Monk told him.

"You should. Not for nothing, Sophie is good people. Don't fuck up a good thing, real talk," Charlie said seriously.

"You ain't gotta tell me, I already know," Li'l Monk replied. "Get with me tomorrow." He gave Charlie dap and went to make his last rounds.

Charlie waited until Li'l Monk was out of sight before heading for the nearest payphone. He dropped a quarter in and dialed one of the few numbers he knew by heart. After a few rings someone picked up on the other end. "Chucky, it's me. I got a business opportunity you might be interested in."

# CHAPTER 20

When Sophie snatched her front door open, her mood was clearly etched across her face. She was pissed. Standing on the other side was Li'l Monk. He had come bearing gifts of flowers, candy, and a bottle of Hennessy, but she was unmoved. When he leaned in to kiss her, she turned on her heels and started back down the hall.

"Well, hello to you too," Li'l Monk said sarcastically. He followed her down the hallway into the living room. Sophie flopped on the couch and started flipping through the channels with the remote as if he wasn't even there. "What the fuck is your problem?"

Sophie paused her channel surfing and cut her eyes at him. "Are you really gonna stand there and ask me that?"

"Sophie, I know you're salty at me for beating dude up earlier, but he had it coming," Li'l Monk said.

Sophie shook her head. "Is that what you think this is about? You getting into a fight? You just don't get it do you?"

"Then tell me what it is that I'm missing."

"What you're missing is that I really don't appreciate how you played me to the left when all I was trying to do was look out for you. Do you know how embarrassing that was for you to walk off and leave me standing there like I'm some side bitch? Save that for your other hoes, but don't do it to me, Li'l Monk."

"Sophie, I ain't got no other hoes. You know you the only ho I got eyes for." Li'l Monk laughed. Sophie did not. "I'm just playing, babe." He leaned in to kiss her.

"Get out of here, I'm not playing with you." Sophie tried to push him off, but he was too heavy.

"Stop acting like that, boo. Let me make it up to you." Li'l Monk planted soft kisses on Sophie, starting at her forehead and working his way down to her lips. She was still resisting, but not very hard. Li'l Monk kissed her passionately on the lips while fondling her breasts in his strong hands. He could feel her nipples getting hard through her tank top.

"You think coming in here and playing with a little tittie is gonna make up for your bullshit?" Sophie asked between kisses.

"Nah, but I know something that might." Li'l Monk slid down between her legs. Gently, he pulled her sweatpants off and found that she wasn't wearing any panties, which worked for him considering what he was about to do. Li'l Monk spread Sophie's legs and dipped his head into her midsection. Like a kitten on a bowl of milk, he started lapping at her clit gently. When she was moist, he dripped the tip of his tongue inside her and started exploring her insides. When he heard a low hiss escape her, he knew he had found her spot and focused on it.

Li'l Monk came up, with his lips and face moist with her juices. There was an animalistic look in his eyes. "Can I feel you, baby?" he asked softly, while undoing his belt, and pushing his pants down over his hips.

"No, I'm not giving you none, Li'l Monk," Sophie said while spreading her legs wider.

"Just a little bit," he breathed in her neck. "All I need is a little bit." Using his thumb as a guide, Li'l Monk slipped his massive cock inside her. He had barely gotten the head in when her body tensed.

"Be gentle," she warned.

"I got you," he said, taking his time sliding the rest of him inside her. Sophie's womb was as warm as fresh baked bread, and super tight.

It took him a minute of working himself back and forth before he was able to get all the way inside her. After a few strokes they were able to establish a rhythm. Li'l Monk grabbed the back of the couch, balancing himself on his toes and began dipping in and out of Sophie. "I love you so much," he panted.

"I love you too, baby," she whispered. Li'l Monk's dick felt like it was going to split her wide open, but it was such a good hurt. She dug her nails into his ass and forced him deeper.

Li'l Monk hooked her legs in his arms and started thrusting into her harder and faster. His face twisted into an evil mask as it started getting good to him. Sophie's face said that she was in pain, but he was too far gone to notice. Li'l Monk flipped her over on her stomach and entered her from behind. He forced Sophie's head into the couch cushion with one hand and hooked her around the waist with the other, holding her in place. Li'l Monk stroked her feverishly: slow, fast, fast, slow. He was pounding her like a man fresh home from prison who hadn't seen a woman in years and to her credit, Sophie took it like a champ. When he felt the telltale buildup in his hips, spreading to his dick, he grabbed her by the back of her hair and pulled it like a jockey holding the reins of a horse. Li'l Monk came so hard, and so much that it spilled from Sophie's womb and dripped down both their legs. When he was spent, Li'l Monk climbed on the couch, spooned Sophie from behind, tenderly. Just like that, he went from a beast back to his gentle self. That's how it always was with Li'l Monk.

As they lay there, holding each other, listening to their respective heartbeats, Sophie said. "I hope you know you're gonna get my hair done over."

All Li'l Monk could do was laugh as he drifted off to sleep.

# CHAPTER 21

Omega and Tut stepped off the hospital elevator on the floor that served as the burn unit. They stopped at the desk and gave the name of the person who they had come to visit. The nurse at the desk told them which room to go to, but first they had to slip on two gowns and scrub caps. It was important that they kept the floor as sterile as they could to lessen the chances of any of the victims catching random infections. Omega's dreads couldn't all fit into the scrub cap, so they gave him what looked like a shower cap. As he was stuffing his hair inside, Tut noticed a purple and gray ribbon tied around one of his dreads.

"What the fuck is that?" Tut asked.

"A good luck charm," Omega told him and started down the hall.

It didn't take long to find the room they were looking for. Standing outside the door was a hard-faced Hispanic man with a pork chop

mustache and a bad haircut. Hanging from his
shoulder was an automatic weapon. The fact that
he was armed in the hospital, like it was legal,
gave them an idea of what kind of people they
were dealing with and just how far Poppito's
reach went.

As the man with the mustache searched them,
Omega looked over at Tut. He looked nervous,
which was a good thing. The fact that he still had
the good sense to be afraid was a good sign. Men
who knew no fear were dangerous, and prone
to do stupid shit. After making sure neither of
them was carrying a weapon, they were allowed
inside.

There were two beds in the room, but only one
of them had a patient in it, the one closest to the
window on the far side. The other was empty,
except for a guitar case. What a guitar case was
doing in a hospital room was anyone's guess, but
Omega reasoned he didn't want to find out if he
could avoid it.

In the next bed there was a woman, sitting
propped up on some pillows. Her arms and half
her face were heavily bandaged, but the little
skin that was exposed was raw and blistered.
It looked like even the most subtle moves were
painful. Omega gave Tut a dirty look.

Sitting on the edge of the bed, rubbing ice chips on her lips, was the man Omega assumed was Felix, Poppito's mouthpiece in the States. He was an average-sized man, whose hairline was starting to recede, with big ears. Dressed in a simple white shirt and black pants, he didn't look much like what Omega had expected from the stories he'd heard. Felix was supposed to be a real piece of work who they spoke about in the streets like the bogeyman, but he didn't look like much. It wasn't until he turned around that Omega saw it: the unmistakable look of death in his eyes.

Felix whispered something to the woman in the bed before standing to greet Omega and Tut. "Which one of you is Omega?" His voice was sharp and to the point.

"That would be me." Omega stepped forward, extending his hand. When Felix shook it, Omega could feel the extra squeeze. "First let me say that I am sorry for your loss. Petey was a good guy."

Felix gave Omega a look. "No, he wasn't. Petey was a fucking asshole and we both know it. That still doesn't change the fact that he was Poppito's family. Let's not mince words between us, Omega. I have not the time nor the patience."

"Fair enough," Omega agreed.

Tut stepped forward. "Nice to meet you, Felix. I'm—"

"Not important right now," Felix cut him off. "Let's make this quick. She needs her rest." He led Omega to the bed where the woman was propped up.

Tut stood there with a confused expression on his face, not sure whether to follow. Omega motioned for him to stay put, so he lingered near the door.

Felix led Omega to the woman's bedside and pulled the curtain so they would have a little privacy. "Maria, this is Omega. He's one of Ramses's people who have come to help us find the monsters who have done this."

"I remember you," she said weakly.

Felix gave Omega a suspicious look.

"I came to the restaurant with Petey a few times," Omega clarified. "Maria, I'm sorry that this has happened to you and you have my word I'm going to have my people do all that they can to make sure justice is served for this. Now, is there anything you can tell me about the men who attacked you?"

Maria went on to recount the events that had occurred the day Petey had gotten killed and her restaurant was burned to the ground with her in it. He listened intently as she gave descriptions of the man she had seen, who bore a striking resemblance to King Tut. Omega glanced nervously over his shoulder to make sure Tut was still out of sight.

While Maria was talking, Omega noticed that Felix kept giving him funny looks. It made him nervous, but he didn't show it. At some point he heard Felix say to Maria, "*¿Es uno de ellos?*" asking if he was one of them. Few people knew Omega was fluent in Spanish, and he kept it that way. He watched Maria closely to see how she answered. He stared at her closely, waiting to see how she would respond. Maria studied his face for a few seconds then shook her head no.

Tut felt like a sucker, just standing off by the door doing nothing. He knew that it was best that he stay off the radar because of his involvement in the crime, but not knowing what was being said behind that curtain was killing him. He looked back at the door and saw that the Hispanic with the pork chop mustache was more interested in one of the duty nurses than he was with watching Tut. Moving stealthily, Tut crept closer to the curtain to see if he could hear better.

"Thank you, Maria. You've been very helpful," he could hear Omega saying. Tut cursed himself for having missed the meat of the conversation. Unexpectedly the curtain was flung back and Tut was busted eavesdropping.

"What the fuck are you doing, bro?" Felix asked angrily. Hearing his raised voice brought in the Hispanic with the mustache, gun in hand and ready to kill at his boss's word.

Tut found himself at a loss for words. As if catching him listening in on a private conversation wasn't bad enough, things took a turn for the worse when Maria saw Tut. Her eyes went wide and her body seized with fear. She started gasping as if she was having trouble breathing, which momentarily took the attention off Tut and brought it back to her.

"What's the matter, Maria?" Felix rushed to her side.

"No, no, no," she said over and over, looking at Tut. She was clearly spooked by his presence.

Felix followed her line of vision and it only took a split second for him to leap to his feet, and draw his gun on Tut. "You piece of shit, did you have something to do with this?"

"Wait a minute, Felix." Omega stepped forward, but was backed up to the wall by the man with the pork chop mustache jamming his gun into Omega's chest. Things were getting real ugly, real quick.

Felix pressed his gun into Tut's forehead. "I'm gonna ask you one time and if I think you're lying, I'm going to blow you and your friend's fucking brains out. Did you touch my family?"

"Bro, I ain't never seen this lady a day in my life," Tut lied with conviction. It sounded convincing enough, but the look on Felix's face said he wasn't buying it.

"I don't believe you," Felix said, cocking the hammer.

Omega saw the situation getting away from him and had to do something. He snatched the shower cap off, letting his dreads spill freely, and held the cap in his hands humbly. "Felix, I don't know what's going on, but why don't we just talk about it."

"Ain't shit to talk about. If this pussy was involved with what happened in Maria's restaurant, both of you are going to sleep and then we're gonna wipe Pharaoh, Ramses, and anybody loyal to them off the map." Felix looked to Maria. "*¿Es uno de ellos?*" He repeated the question from earlier. The lives of Omega and Tut depended on how she answered.

Maria looked from Tut, to Omega. When Omega made eye contact with her, he tugged at the loose dread that had the purple and gray ribbon tied around it. From the look on her face she had gotten his signal loud and clear.

"*¿Es uno de ellos?*" Felix asked for the final time. Omega held his breath and prayed to every God he could think of for them to make it out of that hospital room alive.

"No," Maria said looking down at her hands.

"Are you sure?" Felix pressed. It looked like he would've liked nothing more than to shoot Tut and Omega.

"I'm sure. He wasn't there. Please, I'm tired. I just want to rest," Maria said wearily.

Felix kept his gun aimed at Tut for a few seconds longer before finally tucking it and giving his bodyguard the signal to release Omega. "Wait outside," he said, not bothering to look at either one of them. Wisely, Omega and Tut got their asses out of the hospital room. The Hispanic with the automatic weapon kept them company, and in sight, while Felix tended to Maria.

When Felix emerged in the hallway the anger was apparent on his face. He looked at Tut as if he wanted to continue his inquisition, but thought better of it. He started toward the elevator and motioned for Omega and Tut to follow. When they got to the elevator doors he turned around to address the two youngsters. His face was hard and his eyes cold. "Let me just go on record as saying that this all sounds like some nigger bullshit either orchestrated by Ramses or two of his stooges with big ideas."

"Yo, Felix—" Omega began, but Felix waved him silent.

"Don't talk, just listen. This whole situation stinks like shit to me. For as much as I would like nothing more than to publically execute you and your little friend I still have enough respect for Ramses not to go about it like that, which is more than I can say for the respect my family has been shown. Regardless of my personal feelings, I'm not going to open the faucet of blood . . . yet. You take a message back to your bosses for me. You tell Ramses that I will have the head of the person who has done this or I'm going to hold all of you accountable."

Omega had never been so happy to taste stale New York air as when he stepped outside. For a minute things looked like they were about to go way south. Thankfully they were able to walk out with their lives, but it was only a temporary reprieve.

"Man, you hear them wetbacks talking that gangster shit?" Tut was asking him. "They lucky I didn't have my gun or else it would've been some shit in there. Bitch-ass niggas."

"Tut, do me a favor and shut the fuck up," Omega told him and started toward the Avenue to get a taxi. He knew when he broke the news to Ramses he was going to be pissed. Heads would surely have to roll for this and he just prayed that his wasn't one of them.

"O, I know we had a little scare but we both walked out in one piece." Tut tried to make it seem as if it wasn't that serious.

"But for how long?" Omega snapped. "Do you realize that you almost got us killed?"

"But we ain't dead!"

Omega shook his head. "You just don't get it. If I hadn't been able to change her mind we would've died in there."

"Speaking of which, how did you get the chick to change her story midsentence?"

"With my good luck charm." Omega pulled the purple and gray ribbon from his hair. Upon closer inspection you could tell that it wasn't a ribbon at all, but the necktie from a child's school uniform. "It's the same uniform colors that her daughter's school wears."

"You kidnapped her daughter? Damn, you a cold muthafucka, O!" Tut said proudly.

"No, I didn't kidnap her daughter, you dumb fuck. They're giving out double digits for kidnapping grown people, so ain't no way I'd have kidnapped a kid. I found out what school her kid goes to and picked this up at the uniform store just to let her know we knew how to hurt her."

"Genius, man, pure genius."

"Which is more than I can say for you," Omega capped.

"So what now? Do we go and tell Ramses we might be going to war with these Spanish niggas?" Tut asked.

"Not yet." Omega ran his hands through his hair as he often did when he was contemplating doing wrong. "If we can find somebody to pin the murders on, Ramses will never have to know."

# CHAPTER 22

Li'l Monk felt like he had only been asleep for a few minutes, but when he opened his eyes again the first rays of dawn were peeking through Sophie's curtains. He reached for Sophie only to find she was gone and he was alone on the couch. Li'l Monk rolled off the couch, damn near tripping over his jeans, which were still around his ankles. He pulled them up and then went to find Sophie.

Sophie was in the kitchen, leaning against the refrigerator, smoking a blunt to the face. She was staring off into space, deciphering the signs in the smoke rings she blew out. When she noticed Li'l Monk standing there, she smiled.

"Morning, love." Li'l Monk kissed her on the cheek before plucking the blunt from her hand and hitting it. "Why'd you let me sleep so long?"

"Because you looked like you needed the rest. You spend so much time in the streets that you neglect the body's basic needs, like sleep."

"Shit, I ain't never seen a nigga make a million dollars by lying around and sleeping all day. I got shit going on in the street that needs handling," Li'l Monk replied.

"What about the shit you got going on here that needs handling?" Sophie tapped her finger on the counter for emphasis.

Li'l Monk grabbed her by the waist and pulled her close. He took a long pull of the blunt then leaned in to blow the smoke in Sophie's mouth. "You must be ready for me to knock that out again."

Sophie pushed him away. "I'm not talking about sex, thirsty-ass. You been in the streets real heavy lately, Li'l Monk. Why don't you take a minute to stop and smell the roses while they're still in bloom?"

Li'l Monk sucked his teeth. "Here we go with this shit."

"What shit, Li'l Monk?" Sophie asked.

"You thinking that you're my mother and trying to tell me what to do."

Sophie gave him a look. "Li'l Monk, you know better than that. How am I trying to be your mother by just trying to make sure you're good? That's what a good woman is supposed to do, take care of her man."

"A good woman also knows when to let her man be so he can do what he gotta do," Li'l Monk shot back.

Sophie's face said she was about to go in on him, but she caught herself and softened her tone. "See, that's your problem, you're too damn stubborn to take good advice when it's given to you. You question everything I say, but you never second-guess your friends. If this had been you and Omega having this same conversation I'll bet you'd be open to listening to him."

"What are you trying to say, that I'm a follower or some shit?" Li'l Monk's tone was hostile.

"No, I didn't say anything like that, why you tripping? Li'l Monk, I don't know what's been going on with you lately, but those demons of yours have been working overtime."

"My demons I have under control. It's my girl I'm having the issue with," Li'l Monk snapped. "Man, I got some shit I gotta do for Ramses. I'll check up on you later."

"Once again I'm put on the backburner for Ramses. I don't know why I'm not used to it by now."

"Sophie, what do you want from me? If I'm out grinding then I'm neglecting you, if I'm not grinding then I'm a lazy nigga who ain't bringing nothing to the table. I can't win for losing."

"That shit you just came at me with is what I mean by you getting me confused with your other bitches. Let's not forget that I loved your black ass long before you had two nickels together." She checked him.

"Yeah, you rode out with me when I was down, baby, but you're also reaping the benefits while I'm up, so let's not pull out the scales and start weighing deeds."

Sophie shook her head sadly. "Sometimes talking to you is like talking to a brick wall. Why do you have to be so angry all the time?"

Li'l Monk thought about it before responding. "Because sometimes anger is all I have to keep me going." Li'l Monk kissed her on the lips. "I'm about to go handle business. I'll call you later, ma."

Sophie wanted to stop him and make him finish the conversation, but it was pointless. Lately it had been like the closer she tried to get to Li'l Monk the more distant he became. Her heart went out to Li'l Monk. Her man was like a walking mystery and every time she thought she had figured him out, things just got more complicated. She knew better than most how he had come up and the things that made him the way he was, but it didn't make it hurt any less. She and Li'l Monk didn't always get along, but Sophie had his best interests at heart. All she wanted to do was love Li'l Monk, but in order for her to give love he had to be ready to receive it.

The moment Li'l Monk stepped out of Sophie's building he felt it. There was something in the air that he couldn't put his finger on, but it made him feel uneasy. Butterflies fluttered around in his stomach and the chill of the grave settled into his bones. Li'l Monk had always been slightly more paranoid than most and it was this trait that had kept him alive during his run in the streets, but what he felt that day was different than his normal paranoia. It was as if someone somewhere was watching him, stalking him, and Li'l Monk didn't like it.

He made hurried steps down the Avenue toward his building, hands tucked snuggly in his hoodie, wrapped around the handle of his gun. His eyes constantly swept back and forth, looking for signs of some hidden danger. Li'l Monk slipped inside his building and bounded up the stairs to his floor. When he came out of the stairwell he was surprised to find Huck and two of Ramses's shooters standing in front of his apartment door, waiting for him. The minute he saw the worried expression on Huck's face he knew something was off. Huck was one of the coolest cats he knew and nothing ever rattled him, but he seemed deeply disturbed.

"What's all this?" Li'l Monk stopped short. He let one hand dangle at his side, while he kept the other one in his pocket on his gun. He didn't like the way the shooters were sizing him up.

"Relax, Li'l Monk. If we meant you ill you'd have never seen us coming," Huck assured him. "Why don't you let me see that other hand, just to put an old man at ease?"

Li'l Monk was hesitant. He and Huck shared a bond that was a bit deeper than anyone else's on the team and he had come to trust and admire the old head, but at the end of the day he knew that Huck was loyal to Ramses above all others. Still, it was like Huck said: if they meant him harm, Li'l Monk would've never seen them coming. After some internal debate, he let them see both his hands.

"Thank you." Huck nodded.

"Huck, you wanna tell me what's going on?" Li'l Monk asked.

"Where're you just coming from, kid?"

Li'l Monk thought it was an odd question. "I'm coming from Sophie's, why?"

"Can she or anyone else verify this?" Huck asked as if he was conducting a police investigation.

"Since when do I have to verify my where-abouts?" Li'l Monk asked angrily.

"Since there's a trail of blood leading to Ramses's doorstep," Huck replied.

This shocked Li'l Monk. He wondered who had been killed this time and what it had to do with him. "What's this all about?"

"I think that's for Ramses to tell you himself. He wants to see you."

Li'l Monk was tired and irritated. The last thing he wanted to do was sit through another meeting with Ramses, especially after he had just seen him a few hours prior, but the meeting wasn't a request; it was an order.

The ride to the steak house where Ramses took his meetings was one of the longest of Li'l Monk's life. The car was deathly silent, except for the soft sounds of the radio playing. He tried to engage Huck in small talk to see if he could get a feel for what was going on, but the older man wasn't receptive, which bothered Li'l Monk. There had been times he and Huck would talk for hours on end about this or that, but the old head was eerily silent. The only positive thing Li'l Monk had to hold on to was the fact that they had let him keep his gun with him.

The first thing he noticed when he got out of the car in front of the steak house was that Ramses had doubled up on his security. It wasn't unusual for him to keep a couple of his soldiers lingering around for protection when he was doing business, but from the double-parked cars and the men loitering on the curb, it looked like Ramses was gathering a small army.

Li'l Monk followed Huck inside the steak house, still unsure what to make of all of it. He greeted a few of the men he knew from the block, but they too seemed distant. Dudes who Li'l Monk hung around with all the time now wouldn't even look at him. It was as if there was some running joke being told that he hadn't yet been let in on.

Sitting in his regular booth in the back was Ramses. He was smoking a cigar, and talking on the phone to someone. Worry lines were etched all across his face, and his eyes were red as if he had been up all night. Ramses looked haggard and stressed more so than Li'l Monk had ever seen him. When he spotted Huck walk in with Li'l Monk he ended the phone call. Li'l Monk extended his hand to shake Ramses's and to his surprise, Ramses didn't return the gesture. Instead, he motioned for him to sit down opposite him.

"You wanted to see me, Ramses?"

"Yes, I did. Look, you know I don't beat around the bush about shit so let's get straight to it. What happened last night?" Ramses asked.

Li'l Monk looked confused. "What do you mean?"

"Li'l Monk, now ain't time to play the big dummy role. I need you to answer my questions, and I need you to tell me the truth. What happened last night when I sent you to see Mr. D?"

Li'l Monk shrugged. "Nothing, I picked up the package like you told me to and came straight back."

"Was there anyone else in the apartment with you two, or did you notice any suspicious-looking cats anywhere around?"

Li'l Monk hesitated. He wasn't sure if he liked where the conversation was headed or the way Ramses was looking at him. He started to tell him that he had taken Charlie with him, but until he was sure what was going on, he decided not to tip his hand. "Nah, I went alone," he lied.

Ramses studied his face. "You sure?"

"Yes." Li'l Monk tried to hide the nervousness in his voice. "What's going on?"

Ramses sighed deeply. "Mr. D was found dead in his apartment this morning. Somebody robbed the old man then off'd him."

Ramses's revelation hit Li'l Monk like a blow to the chest. When he'd left the old man, he was still very much alive so to hear that someone had killed him came as a shock. "Wow, I'm sorry to hear it."

"Not as sorry as you're going to be if we don't get this sorted out. Do you know who Mr. D was?" Ramses asked.

"No, can't say that I do."

"Mr. D, Mr. Donatello, was Frankie the Fish's uncle. More importantly, he was a Capo in the Parizzi crime family, which means he was a made man. Do you know the penalty for touching a made man?"

"Death," Li'l Monk said in a shaky voice. His mouth had suddenly become very dry and he found it hard to swallow.

"Yes, slow and painful death, for the offender and anyone close to you. Li'l Monk, I'm gonna ask you something and it's important that you be truthful with me. You shoot straight and I can help you, but if you lie then there's nothing I can do. Did you kill Mr. Donatello?"

"Absolutely not," Li'l Monk said with conviction.

There was a tense silence between Li'l Monk and Ramses, with Ramses just staring as if he could read Li'l Monk's mind. When he was satisfied with Li'l Monk's answer, he nodded in approval. "This is bad, all bad. Mr. D getting hit not only tanks our deal with the Italians, it also puts us in a very, very delicate situation. Heads will roll behind this and I don't plan on mine being one of them."

"Ramses, if you need me to do something, all you have to do is give the word and I'm on it. What do you need me to do?"

"For now, do nothing. Our people as well as Frankie's people are looking into it. In the meantime, I need you to go about everything as if it's business as usual. They're going to be watching all of us and I don't want any of my people doing anything suspicious that would give the Parizzis a reason to ride down on us until we're clear on everything that's going on."

"You got it, Ramses." Li'l Monk stood to leave.

"And Li'l Monk."

"Yeah?"

"Don't make any unexpected trips."

"You got it," Li'l Monk agreed and left.

Li'l Monk's steps were slow and measured as he left the restaurant. He was scared almost to the point of losing control of his bowels and didn't trust his legs to support him if he tried to move any faster.

Ramses had just dropped a bomb on him. Li'l
Monk knew the Parizzi crime family by reputation. They were an especially ruthless lot and one
of the strongest of the remaining mafia families
in New York. Someone killing one of their inner
circle meant that there was surely a shit storm on
the horizon.

Li'l Monk knew he didn't kill Mr. D, but Ramses didn't seem so sure, which was what bothered him. When dealing with criminal politics
it wasn't the same as dealing with the law where
you would be granted a fair trial before sentenc-
ing was passed. In the underworld, being suspected of something was enough to get you killed
and him being a suspect in the slaying of a made
man did not sit well with him at all.

Li'l Monk replayed the events of the prior
night over and over in his head to see if he
had missed anything, but kept coming up with
blanks. He had done everything Ramses had told
him to do, with the one deviation being bringing
Charlie with him. Charlie was the X factor. Could
it be possible that Charlie could've doubled back
and killed Mr. D after he and Li'l Monk had
parted company? Anything was possible, but
the theory didn't sit right with him. Charlie was
a slime ball, but he wasn't a killer. He couldn't
see Charlie taking on a heist like that, let alone

committing murder; but what if he'd had an accomplice? Li'l Monk and Charlie knew all of the same people and there wasn't one of them who Li'l Monk could say was built like that to take on such a caper, but then again you never knew. His best course of action was to track Charlie down and question him. He would give his friend the benefit of the doubt, but if he suspected he had crossed him, Charlie wouldn't have to worry about Ramses catching up with him because Li'l Monk planned to kill him personally.

After Li'l Monk had gone, Ramses gave a signal to one of his men who disappeared into the kitchen area and came back out escorting a woman. She was an attractive older woman who was slightly underdressed for the weather and wearing a cheap-looking wig. Ramses motioned for her to take the seat Li'l Monk had just vacated. She looked nervous and couldn't seem to sit still.

"Relax, sis. I gave you my word you would be safe here," Ramses told her.

"I know, but I feel kind of funny about all this. You know we don't snitch in the hood," she told him.

"Don't look at it as snitching, look at it as doing a public service for your Pharaoh," Ramses tried to ease her mind. "The kid who just left, is that the man you saw leaving the apartment building?"

The woman thought about it. "It was dark and he was moving fast, but I think that was him."

"I don't need you to think. I need you to be sure," Ramses said sternly. "Was that him?"

"Yes, that was him."

Ramses heart sank. He looked at Huck, who just shook his head sadly. They both knew what needed to be done, but neither of them was looking forward to it. Ramses slid an envelope full of cash over to the woman. "Thanks for your time. You can go now."

The woman took the envelope and made hurried steps from the restaurant.

Ramses took a few minutes to collect his thoughts before wearily rising to his feet.

"Ramses," Huck began, but Ramses waved him silent.

"Not now," Ramses told his friend and walked out of the restaurant. He had so much on his mind that he had no idea where to begin as far as sorting it out. His heart was heavy. He had grown quite fond of Li'l Monk and saw great potential in him, but like so many of the others who had come before him, Li'l Monk was getting overly ambitious, just like Chucky and Benny had. Ramses felt like a failed father.

Outside the restaurant, a white Rolls-Royce sat idling. Ramses moved through the throngs of soldiers, and climbed into the back seat of the car where Pharaoh was waiting.

"I take it by the look on your face things didn't go well," Pharaoh said, using his pocket knife to carve off slices of a fresh peach.

"Not well at all. The broad fingered Li'l Monk as the one she saw leaving the apartment," Ramses told him.

"And do you believe her?"

Ramses hesitated before answering. "No, I believe Li'l Monk. I know that kid and he's loyal."

"That was the same thing you said about Benny and look how that turned out," Pharaoh reminded him. "This isn't good, Ramses."

"I know," Ramses said. "This isn't sitting right with me. Give me a little time and I'll get to the bottom of this."

"Time is a luxury we don't have, old friend. Between the Clarks, the Puerto Ricans, and now this, we have wolves scratching at our walls on all fronts. We've worked too hard to build this organization to sit back and watch it be picked over by vultures."

"I know," Ramses said sadly. "But I'm telling you, Pharaoh, there's something we're overlooking. I don't think Li'l Monk would go out like that."

"Maybe you're right and maybe you're wrong, but why even take the chance?" Pharaoh asked. "When you leave a sore untreated it's likely to fester and infect the rest of the body. I can't have that. Are you going to take care of this or should I?"

"No, I'll take care of it."

Pharaoh nodded. "So it is said, so it shall be done."

"It's done," Maggie said once she was back in the car.

"Do you think he believed you?" Chucky asked from behind the wheel.

"This envelope says he does." Maggie held up the reward money Ramses had given her.

It had been Chucky's idea to send Maggie into the restaurant and feed Ramses the false information. When he had gotten wind of who the old man was that he had killed, he knew he would have to cover his ass. The best way to do it was to feed Ramses someone else to blame for the murder. It was a risky plan, but thankfully it had worked.

"Let me help you with that." Chucky plucked it greedily from her hand. Chucky eyeballed the contents and guesstimated it to be at least three grand. That coupled with what they had ripped off in the wee hours of that morning would hold them over while they went underground for a little while. "Good job everybody, especially you, Charlie," he said over his shoulder.

Charlie was sitting in the back seat, next to Rissa, with a nauseated expression on his face. For the millionth time he wondered how he had let Chucky suck him into such a mess. As soon as Charlie laid eyes on the safe at Mr. D's house he immediately saw it as an opportunity in waiting. Mr. D was an old man who should've been an easy enough mark to take off, but he brought Chucky in for added insurance. It should've been a simple job, in and out, but nothing could ever be simple with Chucky.

The first sign of trouble was the fact that Chucky had showed up as high as a kite. His eyes were wild and the edges of his nose were red and irritated. Charlie wanted to put it off until another time, but Chucky wouldn't hear it. He wanted what Mr. D had and wouldn't be swayed. Charlie knocked on the door in the same rhythm he had heard Li'l Monk knock. Mr. D recognized Charlie as the young man who had been with

Li'l Monk so he opened the door for him. Almost immediately Chucky was on him, hitting the old man in the head with his gun. They dragged Mr. D into the bedroom where he kept the safe.

Charlie waited in anticipation as Mr. D opened up the safe. He had expected it to be stacked with cash, as it had been when he and Li'l Monk had visited earlier, but there was only about twenty grand in it at that point. Chucky was livid. He had come expecting a king's ransom so to find only a few thousand dollars pushed him over the edge. He began slapping Mr. D around, demanding that he tell them where the rest of the money was. Mr. D kept trying to tell Chucky that the bulk of the money had been picked up not long after Charlie and Li'l Monk had left, but Chucky accused him of lying and was determined to beat the truth out of him.

Charlie tried to stop Chucky, but he was so high out of his mind that he was unreasonable. At one point he had even turned his gun on Charlie, threatening to shoot him if Charlie didn't help him find the stash of hidden money. They tore up every inch of Mr. D's apartment and found nothing, which infuriated Chucky. Things went from bad to worse when Chucky caught Mr. D reaching for something on his dresser drawer. Without even thinking about it, Chucky shot Mr. D in the back and killed him. Chucky had assumed that Mr. D had been reaching for a gun, but as it turned out he was trying to get to his heart medicine. Just like that, Chucky had turned a robbery into a homicide and Charlie was caught smack in the middle.

Just when Charlie thought that things couldn't get any worse, they did. Charlie had been all for the robbery, but Chucky's plan to blame it on Li'l Monk was an unexpected twist. For whatever Charlie's differences with Li'l Monk might've been, he didn't want to see harm come to him. He understood that Li'l Monk was standing in the way of progress, but that wasn't enough for him to want to see him hurt; too bad the same couldn't be said for Chucky. It had started to become abundantly clear that Chucky didn't want Li'l Monk out of the way; he wanted him dead. Charlie had fucked up royally by trusting Chucky and found himself on a speeding train straight to hell. He knew he didn't have the heart to go on, but he had come too far to turn back. The only choice left to him was to see it through to the end, no matter how it might play out.

Chucky turned to Rissa, who was sitting next to Charlie reading a newspaper, and was about to say something to her, but the words died in his throat when a picture on the lower half of the page caught his attention. He snatched the paper from Rissa and zeroed in on the picture and the accompanying article. He had to read it twice to make sure he was processing the information correctly.

"Rotten bitch." Chucky crumbled the newspaper.

"What's wrong, baby?" Maggie asked, picking up on Chucky's sudden anger.

"Nothing I can't fix," Chucky told her. He popped open the glove box and began tossing papers around, as he searched for something. After a few minutes, he finally found it. It was a small CD that was marked TRUMP CARD. "Somebody tell me where the closest library is. I need to use a computer."

# CHAPTER 23

Persia was awakened by the sound of her bedroom phone ringing. Without taking her head from under the pillow she'd fallen asleep hiding beneath, she reached blindly for the phone, knocking over a cupful of pens trying to find the phone. She snatched it off the cradle and put it to her ear. "Yeah," she answered groggily.

"Are you still sleeping?" Asia's voice came over the line.

"Something like that. What's up?"

"I wanted to find out what happened to you. You vanished last night."

"I'm sorry, Asia. I wasn't feeling well, which is why I left," Persia lied. "I left you a message, didn't you get it?"

"Yeah, I got it. Hope you're feeling better."

"I will be after I get some rest," Persia told her.

"Well, rest is going to have to wait. Have you seen the newspaper today?" Asia asked.

This got Persia's attention and she sat up. "The newspaper? No, why?"

"Oh my God. I'm going to need you to get a copy of the *Daily News*, ASAP. As a matter of fact, do you have a computer?"

"Yeah, I have one."

"Okay, go on the *Daily News* Web site and look in the society section. I'll hold."

Persia slid from the bed and sat at her computer desk. It took a few minutes for the computer to boot up. She typed in the Web address for the *Daily News* and clicked on the link that took her to the society section. There were several articles, one of which covered the event she had attended. She wasn't sure what Asia wanted her to see at first, but when she eventually found it, she almost fell out of the chair. It was the picture she and Vaughn and Persia had posed for. The caption under the picture read: PHILADELPHIA EAGLES ROOKIE SENSATION VAUGHN TATE AND MYSTERY WOMAN.

"Oh my fucking God!" Persia blurted out.

"You sneaky little heifer. You know I'm going to need all the dirty details about this," Asia said.

"Asia, I'll call you back." Persia hung up the phone. Persia was too stunned to speak. She went on to read through the article that detailed the Teen Suicide Awareness fundraiser. There was a whole paragraph of the article dedicated to Vaughn Price, one of the Philadelphia area's most eligible bachelors, and the mysterious woman who he was reported to be seeing. Persia smiled from ear to ear as she read the article twice more.

The phone rang again. Persia picked it up without looking at the caller ID thinking it was Asia again. "Asia, I told you I'd call you back."

"Hey, baby girl." Chucky's voice, and not Asia's, came over the line.

Just like that Persia's mood darkened. "Oh my goodness. Dude, are you not getting the hint that I don't want to be bothered? Why the fuck do you keep calling me?"

"Just wanted to congratulate you on your good fortune. I saw the paper with you and that football nigga you fucking. I see you've raised your standards."

"First of all, it's none of your business who I am or am not fucking, and second of all, if I slept with a homeless nigga on the streets it'd be an upgrade from you!"

"Is that any way to talk to the man you love?"

Persia looked at the phone as if she had misheard him. "Look, you psycho fuck, I don't know how many languages I have to say it in for you to finally get a clue and step the fuck off. You're a piece of shit, Chucky, and I ain't fucking with you."

Chucky laughed. "I had a feeling you'd say that, so I decided to give you a little incentive to change your mind. Check your e-mail, Persia."

Persia opened her e-mail inbox and saw that she had received an attachment from an unknown sender. Curiously she clicked it and her media player popped open. When the video came onto her screen, Persia felt like she wanted to die. In the video was she and Chucky having one of their marathon fuck sessions. She didn't even remember the night, let alone him videotaping it. She watched in horror, seeing her strung out and shaking cocaine on Chucky's dick and sucking it off.

"What is this?" Persia asked with a trembling voice.

"Your wakeup call, bitch," Chucky spat. "Now I've tried to play nice with your junky-ass, but you done made me get nasty."

"Why are you doing this to me, Chucky?" Persia asked, fighting back the tears.

"You did it to yourself when you tried to shit on me, Persia. Now you're gonna get your ass off that high horse and fall the fuck in line or I'm gonna make sure this tape goes to every newspaper from here to Philadelphia. I wonder how damaging this would be to your new boyfriend's career if they found out his bitch is a reformed junkie whore?"

"What do you want from me, Chucky?"

"That should be obvious by now, revenge."

## ORDER FORM
## URBAN BOOKS, LLC
97 N18th Street
Wyandanch, NY 11798

Name  (please print):_____

Address:_____

City/State:_____

Zip:_____

| QTY | TITLES | PRICE |
|---|---|---|
|  | 16 On The Block | $14.95 |
|  | A Girl From Flint | $14.95 |
|  | A Pimp's Life | $14.95 |
|  | Baltimore Chronicles | $14.95 |
|  | Baltimore Chronicles 2 | $14.95 |
|  | Betrayal | $14.95 |
|  | Black Diamond | $14.95 |

Shipping and handling-add $3.50 for 1ˢᵗ book, then $1.75 for each additional book.
Please send a check payable to:
   **Urban Books, LLC**
Please allow 4-6 weeks for delivery

ORDER FORM
URBAN BOOKS, LLC
97 N18th Street
Wyandanch, NY 11798

Name (please print):_____

Address:_____

City/State:_____

Zip:_____

| QTY | TITLES | PRICE |
|-----|--------|-------|
| | Black Diamond 2 | $14.95 |
| | Black Friday | $14.95 |
| | Both Sides Of The Fence | $14.95 |
| | Both Sides Of The Fence 2 | $14.95 |
| | California Connection | $14.95 |
| | California Connection 2 | $14.95 |

Shipping and handling-add $3.50 for 1st book, then $1.75 for each additional book. Please send a check payable to:

**Urban Books, LLC**

Please allow 4-6 weeks for delivery

## ORDER FORM
## URBAN BOOKS, LLC
97 N18th Street
Wyandanch, NY 11798

Name  (please print):_____

Address:_____

City/State:_____

Zip:_____

| QTY | TITLES | PRICE |
|---|---|---|
| | Cheesecake And Teardrops | $14.95 |
| | Congratulations | $14.95 |
| | Crazy In Love | $14.95 |
| | Cyber Case | $14.95 |
| | Denim Diaries | $14.95 |
| | Diary Of A Mad First Lady | $14.95 |
| | Diary Of A Stalker | $14.95 |

Shipping  and  handling-add  $3.50  for  1st book, then $1.75 for each additional book. Please send a check payable to:

**Urban Books, LLC**

Please allow 4-6 weeks for delivery